A Bitter Taste

ANNIE HAUXWELL

arrow books

Published by Arrow Books 2014

2 4 6 8 10 9 7 5 3 1

First published in Great Britain in 2013 by William Heinemann

Arrow Books
Random House, 20 Vauxhall Bridge Road,
London SW1V 2SA

www.randomhouse.co.uk

Addresses for companies within The Random House Group Limited can be found at:
www.randomhouse.co.uk/offices.htm

The Random House Group Limited Reg. No. 954009

A CIP catalogue record for this book is available from the British Library

ISBN 9780099571391

The Random House Group Limited supports The Forest Stewardship
Council® (FSC®), the leading international forest-certification organisation.
Our books carrying the FSC label are printed on FSC®-certified paper.
FSC is the only forest-certification scheme supported by the leading
environmental organisations, including Greenpeace.
Our paper procurement policy can be found at:
www.randomhouse.co.uk/environment

Text design by Samantha Jayaweera © Penguin Group (Australia)
Typeset in Adobe Garamond Pro by Samantha Jayaweera © Penguin Group (Australia)
Printed and bound by Clays Ltd, St Ives plc

For Julie,
who left too soon

The past is never dead. It's not even past.

William Faulkner

She was ten years old, but knew enough to wipe clean the handle of the bloody kitchen knife. The night was stifling. The windows were closed, sealing in the chaos: a table upturned, shattered crockery.

Her distraught mother, bare shoulders raw with welts, knelt beside her motionless father. A taint seeped through his faded black T-shirt, staining the worn boards beneath him. A leather strap lay at his side.

The child dropped the knife as the sobbing woman rose and reached for her. She slipped through the grasping hands, snatched up her backpack, and ran.

28˚C

I

It was early but the dust was already rising from the concrete, suspended in shimmering thermals. Curtains of diesel fumes hung in the fetid air. Cars boiled, tempers frayed, ice-cream vans were mobbed and robbed. There were reports of pigeons dropping from the sky, stone dead. It was the hottest spell on record, with no end in sight.

London was parched.

Catherine Berlin's scars didn't sweat. The red-raw tissue banding her throat felt like a tourniquet, sealing in her agitation. She wanted to scream. She sipped her tea.

She sat in the café and watched the procession of women flowing into the mosque for morning prayers. Some wore simple headscarves, some a veil, others were swathed in black burqas. The woman she was waiting for entered the mosque in her nurse's uniform with only her hair covered. She would emerge an hour and a half later. In that time she could come and go fully veiled and no observer would be any the wiser.

Berlin paid for her tea and left. She was scraping the bottom of the investigative barrel with this job: matrimonial. And there was only a drink in it for her.

The bell rang as she walked into the shop, still referred to locally as 'the Indian' although it had been run by a Turkish family for the past eighteen months. The proprietor, Mr Demir, sat on a high stool behind the counter, his eyes dulled by sleepless nights. His inhaler always in his hand.

Mr Demir shifted his belt, which was buried in the rolls of fat around his middle, and turned to a young man flicking through the magazines. 'Murat, please attend to the crates at the back,' he said, each word punctuated by a wheeze.

Murat stared at Berlin, but didn't move.

'Please, son,' repeated his father.

Murat took his time. He ducked under the counter and emerged, still scowling, on the other side, then slunk through a beaded curtain and disappeared into the back of the shop. Mr Demir waited until the curtain was still, then greeted Berlin in the same way he had done for almost a month.

'Any developments, Miss Berlin?'

Berlin could see a shadow falling across the plastic beads. Murat was lurking within earshot. She shook her head in response to Mr Demir's query. 'She kept to the usual routine.'

'It's very *un*usual, very worrying. She was never religious,' said Mr Demir, bemused. He took a hit from his inhaler and held it deep in his chest. 'We have never been strict. About anything.' He cast a rueful glance at the back of the shop; this had clearly been a mistake with respect to their son's upbringing.

Sighing, Mr Demir handed Berlin a bag containing bread, milk and a cheap bottle of Scotch. It wasn't Talisker but it would do in an emergency. Which occurred at five o'clock most days.

'Perhaps she'll get over it,' offered Berlin, aware how weak this sounded.

Mr Demir gazed into the middle distance, perhaps seeking an answer to his own prayers. There wasn't one that held any joy. Mrs Demir's religiosity began and ended at a nearby apartment in a smart new conversion. Discreet enquiries had yielded the name of the occupant: a doctor who worked at the hospital. A burqa protected the nurse's, and no doubt the doctor's, reputation.

It seemed Mrs Demir, working in the shop during the day and caring for twenty psycho-geriatrics by night, knew paradise each morning. Berlin couldn't bring herself to tell poor Mr Demir. Besides, she needed the groceries. And the Scotch. It was unethical and unprofessional. How low could she go?

'Thank you so very much, Miss Berlin,' said Mr Demir. 'You will continue with the, er . . . enquiries until you reach a conclusion about these events?'

Berlin nodded. There was her answer. Pretty low.

In the storeroom Murat watched the street on the CCTV monitor. The camera, branded L-S-S, was state of the art. Using the joystick he could swivel it in any direction, switch to wide-angle, or zoom and focus. He could even print out an image of his target. He watched Berlin leave the shop and limp away. He pressed print.

His father had decried the expense for such a modest business. His father was an old fool. London Superior Systems offered the best after-sales service money could buy.

Berlin limped slowly to her next appointment with her tawdry payment in kind, wondering whose betrayal was worse, hers or Mrs Demir's. She was stringing Mr Demir along too, postponing the inevitable. It was sleazy duplicity; the type that involved self-deception.

The pavement was crowded, but she had the impression quick footsteps were approaching. Before she could turn someone swerved in front of her. She came to an abrupt halt.

'Stay away from my family,' said Murat.

He was breathless, but she couldn't tell if this was from exertion in the heat or the drama of the situation.

She wanted to take a step back but knew this would send the wrong signal.

'I don't know what you're talking about,' she said.

Sweat plastered his dark curls to his temples. He shoved her in the chest with the flat of his hand. She staggered slightly but stood her ground.

'Stay away,' he growled. 'I'm warning you.'

Commuters surged around them, taking not a blind bit of notice of the well-built young man threatening a woman in her fifties.

Against all reason Berlin suddenly regarded Mr Demir as a valued client and one to whom she owed a professional obligation.

'Get fucked,' she said.

She pushed Murat out of her way and walked on, crossing her fingers and hoping he wouldn't follow and take the opportunity to smack her one. Turning your back was always risky.

When Berlin finally reached the clinic, behind the Royal London Hospital, the queue was snaking down the narrow street. Arms in slings and wrists encased in plaster were over-represented.

She shuffled up the hot concrete ramp. The small, pointed-arch windows set into the plain brick façade were sealed with thick wire grilles. The door, constructed of heavy steel around a panel of reinforced glass, was propped open with an old lump of cast iron, no doubt because of the stultifying heat.

The queue inched forwards and at last she made it into the waiting room, where she could gaze at the supposedly calming prints: the azure Mediterranean, a yacht at sunset and dolphins. She found the dolphins particularly irritating.

The clinic used the same ticket system as the deli counter at the supermarket. Berlin watched the red digital counter high on the wall tick over.

Finally, her number came up.

Berlin took one of the hard chairs, although armchairs were on offer. Opposite her, in an armchair, sat Dr Terrence Rolfe, known to his clients as 'Rolfey'. He must have been in his late forties, but he retained a boyish look. His cowlick of fair hair was thinning, but it still perfectly complemented his gentle manner. You couldn't help but like him.

Rolfey was always tired, slightly dishevelled and just a little distracted, but Berlin knew he was no fool. He seemed to care, and she'd heard this led to clashes with his management committee, who had a different agenda. He sat in front of his desk, not behind it, making it clear that he wanted to remove all barriers between himself and his clients. Which couldn't be easy. They wanted so much and his mandate was to offer as little as possible.

He flipped open a file and scanned it.

'Berlin, we've been meeting for nearly three months. The clinic protocols require a quarterly review, which is due next week. Are we making any progress?'

Berlin knew he had a difficult job. Substance abusers with chronic pain unrelated to their addiction were Rolfey's speciality; in addition to pain management, she and Rolfey were supposed to agree on a regime that would address her heroin addiction. In other words, break the habit of a lifetime.

The clinic was the only place in London that offered this holistic approach. Addicts got cancer, were injured and suffered as many diseases as the next person. Research indicated that opiate dependents were more sensitive to pain. What analgesia do you give them and how do you get them off it again?

Berlin understood Rolfey's problem: he had no way of knowing if the agony she endured had actually diminished; she could mislead him and claim there was no improvement, so he would keep prescribing the morphine capsules. Pain is very subjective.

She felt a detached sympathy for him, but not much. It wasn't any easier for her. She couldn't tell, any more than he could, where the pain from her injuries ended and her aching addiction began.

Morphine is morphine sulphate. Heroin is diacetylmorphine. Just morphine with an acetyl molecule attached. But what a molecule.

Heroin moves across the blood-brain barrier faster, and is three times stronger, dose for dose. Rolfey prescribed morphine because of its acceptable cultural profile as analgesia. Heroin was recreational.

Berlin wanted to believe she could be weaned off morphine just like anyone else, and to ignore the fact that before she acquired these scars she had spent twenty years on pharmaceutical heroin as a so-called 'registered addict'. But she wasn't very good at pretending.

Uncertainty hovered, wings beating a tattoo of doubt. She sat mute, inscrutable.

'We need to talk,' said Rolfey.

He closed her file and tossed it on his desk.

It wasn't a good sign.

2

It should only have been a twenty-minute stroll from the clinic to her flat, but limping in the heat took considerably longer. Her severed Achilles tendon had healed badly, despite surgery. There were buses, but she had to be careful with her money now that she was on sickness benefit.

The gig with Mr Demir had arisen out of desperation on both their parts. The local paper had covered her last case, when she was still employed by the Financial Services Agency. It was a job that had nearly killed her. Mr Demir had seen the publicity, of course, and one day when she called in for bread and milk he had sheepishly asked her to do him a favour.

Her foot jarred on cracked concrete and she winced. The sweet smell of putrefaction drifted from the sewers. Without rain, the detritus of the city was forming rotten seams of decay in the sewers beneath the pavement. It would take more than rain to flush away the rot above.

Berlin limped on. She needed the exercise and it gave her time to contemplate her session with Rolfey.

She had seen him nearly every day since being discharged from the hospital. After her consultation she would pick up the caps from the chemist, counting herself lucky as she watched others undergo the humiliation of consuming their drugs on the premises. She belonged to an elite with a take-away morphine prescription. But for how much longer?

The capsules that the pharmacist had handed her today were much weaker than usual. Rolfey had changed her prescription. It made her nervous.

For more than two decades she had lived the life of a regular citizen, apart from her daily ampoule of diacetylmorphine. Legal, injectable heroin from her GP. Those days were over. Rolfey's 'managed reduction' strategy confronted her with a new temptation: to break open the sustained-release caps, crush the pellets and cook them until they dissolved.

Once it was in a form she could shoot up, the drug would act more quickly and the effect would be more profound. It was called 'bio-availability' and she knew it would deliver her to that golden place.

The only thing stopping her was her dignity. Ironic. She had spent years distancing herself from stereotypical junkie behaviour and she wasn't about to dissolve her standards, such as they were, along with the caps.

Rolfey had said, 'You can't make rational choices when you're in the grip of an addiction.'

She had always thought of it as an embrace.

Berlin had barely closed her front door when someone knocked on it. Impatient to take her medication, she considered ignoring them. But whoever was out there had seen her come home. She put the caps back in her pocket and glanced through the spy-hole. Someone with her back to the door. Berlin opened it and the woman turned to face her.

'Hello, Cathy,' said the gaunt creature on her doorstep, who was shivering despite the heat. 'Remember me?'

Berlin frowned. It took a long moment, but when she looked beyond the cracked lips and dank hair, the milk-blue eyes held a faint echo of the past.

Berlin stepped aside and Sonja Kvist walked back into her life.

'How did you find me?' asked Berlin.

'I followed you from the clinic,' said Sonja. 'You never noticed me. I suppose I've aged.' Her cheekbones were so high and her skin so taut that her attempt at a smile was almost grotesque. Berlin knew Sonja wasn't fashionably thin. She was wasted. 'Rolfey's managing your pain?' Berlin asked.

Sonja didn't seem to notice her sardonic tone. She touched her left arm and Berlin noticed it hung at an awkward angle. 'He was,' said Sonja. 'I had a bad break.'

'You're not alone there,' said Berlin.

She watched Sonja take in the piles of books, the sleek computer on the table, the comfortable sofa, the rugs and curtains in soft blue and yellow tones. The contrast with Berlin's head-to-toe black.

'Do you see Rolfey because of . . .' Sonja touched her own face and neck, mirroring the places where Berlin was scarred.

'Yeah,' she said.

Berlin wore a thin black scarf when she went out. But she couldn't hide the crimson pattern that flushed one side of her face and jaw. It gave her a Janus-like quality.

Unable to bear being pitied, she turned and crossed the room to the tiny kitchen in one corner. She picked up the kettle, filled it, then lit the gas underneath it and fussed with cups and saucers. Tea. The ritual would give her a moment to recover.

Seeing Sonja was disconcerting. She could have been Berlin's portrait in the attic: a picture of the life she could have led. Not that the life she *had* led was any big deal, but at least she'd managed to put the worst of her behaviour behind her. Now here was someone who could dredge it all up again. She turned off the kettle.

This wasn't a social call. Sonja was probably going to ask for money. Berlin could see she was struggling to keep her agitation under control. From the look of her, Rolfey's approach had failed. No doubt she'd burnt all her bridges and when she saw Berlin she saw an untapped source. They weren't going to drink tea and chat like old friends.

Berlin faced her unwelcome visitor, leant back against the sink and folded her arms, resisting any further niceties.

'So what do you want, Sonja?'

Sonja picked up on the attitude.

Berlin watched her vacillate, unable to decide whether to plead or demand.

In the end she went for despair. Her voice broke.

'I want you to find my daughter,' she said.

Berlin went to the bathroom and swallowed a cap. She was about to put the pack in the cabinet above the basin, but hesitated. She put it back in her pocket, just in case Sonja wanted to use the loo. There wasn't a junkie born who could resist a peek into a bathroom cabinet.

She sat on the toilet lid and took a moment to consider Sonja's pitch. Her performance had been very convincing, but there was nothing Berlin liked about her story.

Sonja's ten-year-old had run off last night. School was closed for the summer holidays, they had no relatives in the country to speak of, and from the sound of it the kid didn't relate well to her peers. She was a loner.

Sonja wouldn't go to the police because she was afraid they would take the girl into care when they found her. At the very least they would put her, and Sonja, under the supervision of a social worker: an intervention by the state to which Sonja was ideologically opposed.

When Berlin emerged from the bathroom Sonja was sitting at the table, writing on something.

'I couldn't find a bit of paper, so I used —'

Berlin cut her off.

'Don't settle in, Sonja, this isn't going to happen,' she said.

'Why not?' asked Sonja, apparently bewildered by Berlin's attitude. 'I don't know where to start, but you know how these things work. You've got contacts. It's what you do, isn't it? You're an investigator. Rolfey said you'd worked for the government.'

So much for patient confidentiality, Berlin thought.

'Did you tell him your kid was missing?' Berlin asked.

'No,' said Sonja. 'I noticed you leaving the clinic a while ago, when I was still seeing him. I was sure it was you, but you've changed so much . . . I told him we were old friends. He said you'd busted some East End villain and we just talked a bit and . . .'

'I don't do missing persons or matrimonial,' snapped Berlin, bitterly aware it wasn't true any more. 'Anyway, you can't afford me.' Unless you've got the price of a loaf of bread and a pint of milk. She was really top-drawer these days. 'Your kid'll turn up, tired and hungry,' she said, making an effort to appear sympathetic.

Sonja stood, nearly upending the chair. 'She won't. I know her. She's not coming back.'

Berlin noted Sonja had lost the struggle to contain her agitation. 'Then go to the police,' she retorted. 'What kind of mother are you, leaving a ten-year-old kid out there on her own?'

'I've looked everywhere. All day and night,' shouted Sonja. 'I ran after her, but it was dark and she just seemed to disappear. I thought she would come back after a couple of hours. I just don't know what to do!'

She began to cry, her hands fluttering, birds with nowhere to rest.

'For god's sake, Sonja, turn off the waterworks,' said Berlin. 'Are you using?'

'There's a drought on,' said Sonja, sniffing.

Berlin knew she wasn't referring to the lack of rain. Heroin had dried up throughout western Europe. Various theories circulated: a fungus had blighted the Afghani crop or the war was to blame or kingpin traffickers were trying to force up the price. Or it was that old favourite: a CIA conspiracy.

Sonja laid her head down on the table as if she could no longer support its weight.

'My baby's gone, Cathy,' she sobbed.

'No one calls me Cathy any more.'

'Okay then, Berlin. I'm begging you,' said Sonja.

'What about her dad? Maybe she's with him,' said Berlin.

Sonja mumbled something.

'What?' asked Berlin.

Sonja raised her head and wiped her face on the corner of the tablecloth. 'I said he's out of the picture. We haven't seen him for ages.'

There was something about the way she said it.

'Who is he?' asked Berlin.

Sonja hesitated.

'Well?' demanded Berlin.

'Cole,' said Sonja.

'Cole? Cole Mortimer?' said Berlin, incredulous.

Sonja nodded.

Berlin walked to the front door and opened it.

'Get out,' she said.

Sonja didn't move.

'Now.'

Sonja stood slowly, then flew at Berlin. She had one more card and she played it. From the bottom of the deck. She got in Berlin's face.

'All right, I'm going. You were always a hard bitch. But don't forget, it was you who put me here. It was you who gave me my first taste.'

Berlin shoved her out onto the landing. 'You were so fucked up you wouldn't remember,' she said.

'And neither would you. Cathy!' screamed Sonja.

Berlin slammed the door.

A seventeen-hour midsummer day was too much for Berlin. She drew the curtains against the light and cursed Sonja for lifting the veil on the past.

When they had met, Berlin was already using, a seasoned party animal. Sonja was the British-born daughter of a Scandinavian consul. She had only just left school and was gagging to get on the scene. The age difference between them had seemed huge then; now Berlin was fifty-six and Sonja was fifty-one and it was insignificant.

The fresh-faced blonde had eyes of a blue so pale they were milky. She'd recently moved into the tiny attic, the only space left in the decrepit west London Georgian terrace squat. It had been the parlourmaid's room once. Berlin dubbed Sonja 'the Nordic fairy'.

When the Nordic Fairy had first wandered into the kitchen, she had stood wide-eyed watching Berlin and her tight band of 'serious' users cooking brown tar on small squares of aluminium foil.

They loved smoking heroin then because of the ritual. It was easier to do with a partner too, which gave it a vaguely communal feel. They even decorated the toilet-roll tubes they used to inhale the fumes. They joked it was very *Blue Peter*: hello, children, in your favourite television programme today we're going to have fun turning an old toilet roll into drug paraphernalia. Ask Mummy to explain 'paraphernalia'.

Later, when the squat was busted, some believed the Nordic Fairy's old man had set it up. Sonja, Berlin and a couple of others had crawled through a skylight and made it across the roof to safety. Some weren't so lucky, including Cole Mortimer.

After that close call Berlin had 'done a geographical', the term addicts use for someone who tries to get clean by moving away from old haunts and associates. It had been a nice idea. She returned to her roots in East London and lost touch with her friends. But not her lover. Heroin.

She'd heard later that Cole Mortimer did three years for possession and intent to supply.

During long, stoned evenings in the squat, Cole had enjoyed recounting tales of his childhood to his fascinated public-school clients. He'd been dragged up in South London and his daddy wasn't a diplomat or a Right Honourable, but a 'knocker' in an abattoir. Mortimer Senior was a Nat King Cole fan, hence his son's name.

One foggy, bitter morning he had taken his five-year-old son to work with him, to teach him where the food on his plate came from and the hard graft that put it there. Cole watched as his father crooned 'Unforgettable' while stunning the frantic beasts with a bolt gun before slitting their throats. With the hot, steaming breath of slaughter on his face the lesson Cole learnt was that where there was blood, there was money.

He was a smart dealer with dark, pouty good looks and working-class cred, who kept his sadism under control in front of his upper middle-class mates. His history became infected with myth: it was said that when Cole was a kid a neighbour had pissed him off, so he dug a hole, put the neighbour's cat in it with its head protruding, then ran the lawnmower over it.

Berlin knew it was actually a pet rabbit.

Proximity to evil gave the bourgeois crew Cole Mortimer ran with a sense of authenticity. It was just so cool to sit at your rustic hand-hewn table in the sixteenth-century gamekeeper's cottage that had been in the family forever and smoke joints with handsome, unpredictable violence. Cole frightened them, and they adored it, especially when he strummed his guitar and quoted Bukowski.

But when a fifteen-year-old girl nearly haemorrhaged to death after Cole raped her with a bottle, the judge hadn't been swayed by his charms. He did a ten stretch. Berlin knew what hard time could do to someone like Mortimer. His spite would plumb new depths of depravity. She shuddered.

The morphine caps were burning a hole in her pocket. She wasn't supposed to take another for eight hours. But that would be about seven hours and fifty-five minutes too long.

There are two kinds of pain: the kind that racks your body and the kind that wrecks your mind. She popped a cap and took care of the latter. It would be a quiet day.

3

Detective Sergeant Grant Xavier Kennedy was preoccupied. He wasn't really taking in the murmured exchanges between the prosecution and the defence at the case conference. He had a pocketful of prescriptions for his wife and son that he had forgotten to drop in to the chemist and he had to remember to pick up something for tea on the way home. Even his kids would baulk at fish fingers again. Plus he'd been up half the night with his mum and he was knackered.

When he heard the words 'we have agreed on a recommendation to the judge', he realised too late what had transpired. The lawyers shook hands and began to pack up their papers. Kennedy was suddenly seized with the urge to leap the table, take the prosecuting counsel by the throat and choke the life out of him.

The word had gone out from the Crown Prosecution Service that where a trial would take more than two days, a guilty plea to a lesser offence would be accepted. The CPS, known to coppers, amongst other things, as the Criminal Protection Society, had almost run out of money for the fiscal year. It was a good time to commit murder.

Kennedy would dearly have liked to make the most of this window of opportunity. Instead he slammed his brief of evidence down on the table. The gesture was lost on the lawyers; they'd already gone.

Kennedy went straight from the courthouse to the boozer across the road. The pub was heaving with happy crooks and miserable coppers, partners in the barn dance known as the criminal justice system. Kennedy ordered a double Scotch and a pint of Stella and immediately felt guilty because it was money he needed for the prescriptions.

He weaved his way through the throng to a small, sticky table, where he sat down opposite Detective Chief Inspector Burlington.

Burlington was known as Bertie, after the old music-hall song. It suited him, and not just because he was from Bow; it was also well known that these days he resented rising before ten-thirty. Once he had been a serious thief-taker with a fearsome reputation. Now he just had a fearsome temper.

Bertie was a big man in every way. Big body. Big mouth. Big head. Impervious to criticism. Untouchable.

Kennedy knew he would always be in Bertie's shadow; he was just 'that skinny bloke with glasses'. It had its advantages, but sometimes it rankled. They were the Laurel and Hardy of the constabulary, but it wasn't much of a laugh if you were always the fall guy.

Bertie pushed away his plate, streaked with the remnants of a burger and fries, and glanced at his watch.

'You were quick,' he said. 'Don't tell me. They dropped it down to common assault and he went for it.'

Kennedy knocked back his Scotch and nodded.

'He was cautioned,' he said. 'Now he's at the bar celebrating. How am I going to tell his ninety-three-year-old victim?'

'Don't worry, you won't have to,' said Bertie. 'I just got a call from the station. She died an hour ago. But it's taken so long to get to court they can't say for sure it's because of the attack.'

They both knew it was. They drank up in silence.

The tremor that infected Kennedy's right knee grew worse as he thought about the old lady. He was a man in perpetual motion. He suffered not just from restless leg syndrome, but from restless mind and body as well.

He saw Bertie glance at his juddering leg with contempt: a man who couldn't even control his own limbs. Too fucking sensitive by half. That's what his boss thought of him.

'Move on,' recommended Bertie. 'We've got bigger fish to fry.'

Kennedy fumbled with a packet of crisps to disguise his wretchedness. 'What's the latest then?' he asked, affecting the callous indifference of a hard man. He doubted he was fooling anyone, let alone himself.

'The intel is the logistics chain has been disrupted, but it's not clear if that's due to internal or external factors,' said Bertie. His fingers plunged into Kennedy's crisps and grabbed a handful.

'Someone else might have their hands on the goods?' asked Kennedy.

'Yeah,' grunted Bertie, crisps spraying from his full mouth.

'So what's the plan?'

'High-level target interface and maximum leverage of all covert sources,' said Bertie.

'A good kicking then,' said Kennedy, without relish.

Bertie nodded. 'First thing tomorrow,' he said. 'It'll mean an early start, but needs must. A man's work is never done.'

They drank to that.

4

DS Kennedy didn't go back to work after he left the pub. He went home to a three-bedroom terrace in Walthamstow, which barely accommodated his three kids, a mother with Alzheimer's and a wife who was bipolar. His youngest boy had cystic fibrosis.

Kennedy stayed positive.

His mum had always described him as 'a streak of nothing'.

Which was exactly what he felt like. If he stood sideways you would miss him. His pallid complexion, mousey hair and frameless glasses completed the nondescript picture. Then there was the relentless jigging about, a tic he couldn't control. But he was a good detective.

When he was assigned to Serious Crime he was happy because he knew the overtime was good. Without that money the creaking edifice he called a family would collapse.

The house was never quiet. Even in the middle of the night his mum would wander about in her nightie, turning on all the electrical appliances. He went into the kitchen to dig about in the freezer for tea. His wife appeared and gave him a wan smile.

'How about beefburgers and oven chips tonight?' he asked.

He gave her a quick kiss, ignoring the fact that she was still in her dressing-gown. She handed him the day's post. A pile of bills.

The economy was in the crapper and no overtime was being authorised, although crime was on the rise. Kennedy had given up trying to understand the rationale of the government that employed him. It was the same everywhere.

His mate at the Border Agency had told him he'd been ordered not to bring in any illegals rounded up in raids unless they'd been caught before and were already on the books. That way, the numbers didn't rise. The Home Office was worried about how the stats would look.

Kennedy had a lot of time for illegals. They worked long hours for little money, contributed to the economy and didn't put a strain on the social security budget. *We should all be illegal*, he thought. *The country would be a lot better off.*

He had followed this logic to its conclusion and discovered that illegality was not synonymous with immorality. It had made it that much easier to throw in his lot with Bertie. Not that he'd had much choice.

Once the beefburgers and chips were in the oven he went into the sitting room where his boy was asleep, the machines that helped him breathe sentinel at his bedside.

Kennedy put his hand gently on his son's chest, just to feel the tiny ribs rise and fall. He wondered again at the mentality that would do violence to such small, fragile beings. He'd seen some terrible cases. He never smacked his kids; it just didn't seem right, a fully grown adult using force against a child. He rarely lost his temper, even when the little devils tried to wind him up.

But he had lost it once at work, and once was enough. A smarmy paedophile had told him he wasn't bothered about being locked up because his teeth needed attention and Her Majesty's prison would be obliged to pay for his dental work.

Detective Constable Kennedy had relieved the taxpayer of this burden by removing said teeth.

Bertie had been the senior officer on duty at the station and had covered for Kennedy in the ensuing inquiry. After that there was no going back. Bertie sorted his promotion, and Kennedy joined Burlington's crew as a detective sergeant.

He belonged to Bertie.

The rake-off from their joint ventures had been good. A man was supposed to take care of his family, and that's what he had been doing. No one had got hurt. Yet.

5

Rolfey switched off the lights and illuminated the glowing neon sign that announced to the world NO DRUGS KEPT ON PREMISES. It had been a long day; too many walk-ins and new clients to whom he just couldn't say 'no'.

He tried not to think about the letter from the General Medical Council stuffed in his pocket, requesting an interview at 'his earliest convenience' to discuss reports of apparent anomalies in his prescribing practices.

The CDAO, the Controlled Drug Accountable Officer, which was him, hadn't filed the correct reports with the CDLINS, the Controlled Drugs Local Intelligence Network. Some nosy bureaucrat at the CQC, the Care Quality Commission, had grassed him up. He was drowning in acronyms and paperwork. Patient care was a long way down the list of priorities for these bods.

He set the clinic's alarm and stepped outside. The warm, stale air of Whitechapel was ripe with the aroma of curry. He hadn't eaten all day, but he had no appetite. He was tired; exhaustion had seeped into his bones and he could never imagine being free of it. It wasn't just work, it was everything.

A gaggle of noisy medical students passed him on the way to the pub, their energy a reminder of his diminished state. He followed in their wake, emptying his pockets of change as he walked up the street, a soft touch for every polystyrene cup thrust at him and every grubby hand that tugged at his sleeve.

The young students ignored the beggars. Their sights were set high, well above street level. They couldn't wait to take the Hippocratic oath: first do no harm. They had no idea how difficult that could be.

Even at their age he had lacked the ability to distance himself from his patients; his instructors had reproached him for his empathy. How could he expect to practise medicine with the necessary degree of objectivity if he identified with every patient?

He had been a young fool then, which was bad enough. Now he was the worst kind, an old fool. A fool for love. It was a folly that could deliver or damn him. The current prognosis wasn't promising. He followed the students into the pub.

6

Night was brief at this time of year, darkness stretched too thin. Berlin limped through the City of London, the so-called Square Mile. The nickname was misleading; the size was approximate and the bankers and financiers who populated it during the day were not known for being on the square.

She hadn't taken this route during her nocturnal wanderings since she nearly lost her life six months earlier. A routine job had become a nightmare of treachery after she ignored a directive from her erstwhile boss to shut down an investigation.

Driven by her addiction to heroin and a stubborn attachment to the truth, she had led others into traps far worse than that which had finally ensnared her. She touched her ravaged throat. The physical scars bequeathed to her were the least of it.

The heat of the day was still trapped in the airless lanes. Gargoyles squatted on ledges high above her, ready to spring. She knew they were there but didn't look up.

Sonja was wrong. Berlin did remember.

It was 1 April. She recalled the date but not the year. It was nineteen eighty-something. For some bizarre reason the household decided to commemorate the day Marvin Gaye had been shot by his father, and the squat was grooving to 'Sexual Healing'.

On that day of fools Sonja had asked and Berlin had answered. She remembered she told her to sit, in case she fell, and set up the foil for her. They all laughed as the novice struggled to inhale the vapour given off by the boiling tar. The acrid smell hung in the air with the smoke they exhaled.

The sour taste rose in Berlin's throat.

Turning to enter Catherine Wheel Alley, a twisting, narrow passage between Middlesex and Liverpool streets, Berlin was brought to an abrupt halt by two twig-like legs stretched across her path. They belonged to a thin, stoned youth leaning against one wall with his feet braced against the other.

'It's private, innit,' he said.

Berlin stepped over him and kept walking.

'Oi!' he said.

A few yards down the alley, a shadow detached itself and resolved into a pale child, a slight girl of about fourteen. Berlin stopped, expecting the boy to come up behind her, the pair executing a half-baked mugger's pincer strategy. The alley had once been the haunt of highwaymen. The tradition lived on.

Then a larger figure loomed out of the darkness behind the girl, a man in his forties, zipping his fly. A creep.

The girl spat and wiped her mouth on her T-shirt.

Berlin felt rage explode in her guts, a swift, hard force as shattering as a blow to her sternum. She reached behind her and withdrew the tactical baton that was tucked into her jeans: the Asp. She flicked her wrist to release the friction lock, extending the telescopic steel to its full, venomous length.

'Go,' she said to the girl.

'What about my money?' wailed the girl, but took off anyway.

The creep frowned at Berlin, confused and fearful.

'Look, I . . . it's not what you think.'

She took a step closer. The smell of alcohol rolled off him in putrid waves. He looked beyond her to the end of the alley. No pulsing blue lights, no uniforms. He probably thought it was a shakedown.

'Fuck off,' he snarled.

The Asp cut through the stagnant air and struck. The creep howled and fell to the ground, clutching his elbow.

Berlin stood over him and with the tip of the baton flipped opened his suit jacket. The lining was silk. She reached inside and took his wallet.

The thin boy and the slight girl were hanging about on Liverpool Street when Berlin emerged from the alley. They backed up beneath the grand arch of the Bishopsgate Institute as she approached, beyond the reach of the CCTV cameras and well out of the way of the drunks and the clubbers waiting for the night bus.

She went straight to the girl, opened the wallet and withdrew the fat wad of notes.

'Here,' she said, and thrust the cash into the girl's hand, then turned to the boy.

'Listen to me, Twig,' she said.

He looked around, unsure if she was talking to him. He pointed to himself, a question.

'Yes, you,' said Berlin. 'That money is hers, understand? If you touch it, or hurt her, I'll find you and snap you in half.'

Twig nodded. Message received.

The girl gazed up at Berlin, awestruck.

'He's all right, miss,' said the girl. 'He's my brother.'

Imbued with newfound authority, the girl addressed her dopey sibling, trying out a line dredged up from some shared memory of a maternal lexicon.

'What do you say to the nice lady?'

'Thank you,' said Twig.

The gloomy interstices of London had always provided boltholes for orphans and urchins; good citizens avoided alleys, lanes and passageways, impenetrable by even the brightest sun. The chill air and murk were a curtain for depravity. It was a natural habitat for small, darting figures that went unremarked. Until there was a spate of housebreaking or one was found dead.

Berlin flicked through the wallet. The creep's driving licence named him as Mr Derek Parr. She took out a photo and held it under the streetlight. Three happy, healthy young faces beamed out at her. Cute. She wondered if Daddy took his vice to the streets to spare them.

The yellow light shimmered, the night fractured and all she could see was the pale girl, her thin T-shirt glistening with semen, and her pitiful brother. Had they been abandoned by feckless parents or were they fleeing routine violence and degradation at home? Either way, they had run into the arms of evil.

She thought of Sonja's daughter. Too many backs were turned on these kids. It made her uneasy to think Sonja's would be one of them. Why visit the sins of the mother on the child?

She kept Mr Parr's family photo and driver's licence, and consigned the rest to the sewer.

29.5°C

7

It was early, too early for a junkie anyway, and Berlin knew there was a very good chance she would find Sonja at home. Sonja had scribbled her address and mobile number on the jacket of a book lying on Berlin's table. Berlin had found the place easily enough; it was east of the East End, between Canning Town and the City Airport. Silvertown.

Silvertown had always been on the outer. Home to nineteenth-century manufactories that rendered carcasses, burnt sugar, boiled chemicals and smelted rubber. In the heat, the earth seemed to sweat the poison of the past.

The land, and its residents, had long been regarded as expendable. During the First World War officialdom decreed that a munitions factory should be built in the midst of the community. In 1917 fifty tons of TNT went up and with it seventy-three people. Four hundred were injured and seventy thousand houses damaged. The blast rattled the windows of the Savoy Hotel and even Westminster felt a slight tremor. The government issued an expression of regret.

Sonja lived on Silvertown Way in a dilapidated edifice, a Victorian remnant that might have once been doctors' rooms or a home for unwed mothers. The developers had not yet arrived on this side of the road. They stuck to the riverbank, which was only half a mile away in a straight line. Over there, scrapyards and warehouses were gradually giving way to smart apartments.

Over here, a few truncated sections of fence were no longer able to hold the line against an encroaching wilderness of thistle, scorched by the sun, and rusty car bodies.

Sonja's building had a pockmarked façade and cracked windows. The portico was adorned with local gang tags. The 'grounds' around the building were carpeted with gravel.

Pontoon Dock, the Docklands Light Rail station, was about a quarter of a mile away and there was a twenty-four-hour petrol station on a roundabout a few hundred yards in the other direction.

Berlin sat in the shadow of one of the towering concrete pylons that supported the light rail. The line ran fifty feet above Silvertown Way on the other side of the road from Sonja's. The road traffic was commercial, mostly lorries, and no doubt it was pretty dead at night. She imagined it would be difficult to set up surveillance here.

Two beaten-up cars were parked on one side of the premises, and a pizza company's scooter was propped near the old-fashioned front door, which was open to let in any breeze there might be. But everything was still.

Berlin wanted to pay Sonja a visit unannounced. If her kid had been befriended by some creep who was now hiding her, it might easily be someone in the immediate vicinity. Someone who thought they had more chance of getting away with it given Sonja's chaotic lifestyle. Or Sonja might have a new boyfriend.

She stood, flexed her stiff leg and was about to cross the road when a blue van drove up, turned sharply onto the gravel and fishtailed to a halt near the scooter.

Two blokes in jeans and trainers got out, strode across the gravel and disappeared inside. One was fat and the other was thin with glasses.

During a brief lull in the traffic Berlin heard a scream coming from the building. She ran across the road to the door, kept close to the wall and peered in.

A staircase and two corridors branched off a wide entrance hall, its floor just bare boards. A green felt noticeboard dotted with drawing pins hung on one wall. An ancient rack of numbered pigeonholes indicated the place had long ago been converted into a rooming house.

Just inside the hall another door, on the right, also stood wide open. The sound of canned laughter drifted through it. Inching forwards, Berlin could see a raddled woman in a grubby dressing gown watching breakfast TV. Her grey curls tumbled from beneath a gaudy scarf. Gold chains and religious medallions hung from her neck. One bony hand, its wrist festooned with bangles and charm bracelets, clutched a tumbler of clear liquid.

Berlin doubted it was mineral water.

There was no way to cross the hall without being seen and it was apparent from the angle of her armchair that this was exactly what the old girl intended. Berlin didn't want to have to deal with some nosy crone.

Raised voices came from somewhere on the ground floor, followed by a thud and another sharp scream.

Berlin watched the crone wave the remote at the TV.

The volume went up.

Bertie's fat fingers gripped Sonja's throat and forced her to look him in the eye.

'I'm going to ask you one more time,' he said. 'Where is Cole?' He said it slowly, enunciating each word.

Sonja gurgled, unable to speak because of the pressure on her larynx. He relaxed his fingers a fraction.

'I don't know,' she gasped. 'It's the truth.'

Bertie released her throat, transferring his grip to her arm.

Kennedy was tossing the room. There wasn't much to toss. He turned over the mattress. There were balls of dust beneath the old-fashioned spring bedstead.

'Slut's wool, Sonja,' said Kennedy.

'Yeah, I'm not competing for the Good Housekeeping Award this year,' she said, rubbing her throat.

Bertie gave her a slap and she bounced off the wall.

Kennedy winced. 'You'd think Cole could afford somewhere decent,' he said.

'These people don't put anything by for a rainy day,' said Bertie. He watched Kennedy searching the cupboards. 'Anything?' he asked.

Kennedy shook his head, then turned to Sonja and tried a more reasonable tone.

'Give yourself a break, Sonja. We know he was here the other night. Then he disappears. Doesn't answer our calls, nothing. Where is he?'

'I don't know. He just walked out. He does it all the fucking time,' said Sonja, rubbing her jaw, tears welling up.

Bertie was unmoved. He grabbed hold of her and flung her to the floor.

'Give him a message,' he growled. 'Don't be a stranger.'

He took a step back to give himself more leg room.

Kennedy turned away.

Berlin heard a door slam and heavy footsteps approach down the corridor. She ducked behind a portico pillar and watched as the two men got back in the van and drove off.

The TV volume went down.

Now Berlin was even more cautious. She circled the building, taking care to make as little noise as possible on the gravel. A sad-looking dog tied to a skip stood up, but didn't bark. Most of the windows were boarded up or hung with blankets. But through one, obscured by grime, she could make out the blurred figure of Sonja bent over the sink, being sick.

She tapped on the glass. Sonja snapped upright and spun around, staring at the shadowy figure peering in at her.

'It's me,' hissed Berlin.

The heavy double casement window slid up with surprising ease.

It struck Berlin that neither of them thought it odd she chose this method of entry.

Sonja slumped onto a double bed and groped on the bedside table for her cigarettes.

The rest of the tatty furniture consisted of a single bed, a wardrobe, a scored oak dining table, and two kitchen chairs. There didn't appear to be a fridge. The doors of the cupboards were all open. There was no sign of food in them. A porcelain sink with a cold-water tap and an ancient gas burner completed the set-up.

The single concession to modernity was a plasma TV. Berlin imagined that someone had recently listed it on an insurance claim form. A curtain hung across a doorway into what she supposed was the bathroom.

Berlin sat on the edge of one of the chairs.

'Who were they?' she asked.

Sonja lit a cigarette and leant back against the wall. The wallpaper had been worn bare by the dozens of heads that had rested there.

'I don't know. They were looking for Cole,' she replied, her voice flat with resignation.

'I thought he was out of the picture.'

'He is,' said Sonja. She inhaled and coughed, wincing.

'So why did they come here?'

'Just doing the rounds, I suppose. He turns up sometimes. Christmas, her birthday, that sort of thing.'

'What did they want from you?' asked Berlin.

'To give him a message.'

Berlin could see it: the imprint of a trainer on the side of Sonja's face.

8

There was a hole in the sheet of purple plastic that was her make-shift doorway. If she stood on tiptoe she could see through it.

She took stock of her hideout, assessing her defences. She'd strung old Coke cans above the plastic and now caught sight of herself, distorted in crushed aluminium. The plastic tinged her face a mauvey colour. It was like war paint.

Outside, the ogre was having a good look around. She knew what he was after.

A noise drew her attention back to the spy-hole. He was watching. Her fist tightened around the spike she'd sharpened on concrete. She'd found a bunch of them among stuff spilling out of one of the abandoned containers. He would get it right in the eye if he came near her.

Her dad had always told her never bring out your big guns too early.

She hoisted her backpack over her shoulders and brandished her new weapon, ready for anything. But after a few minutes her arm got tired and she had to change hands.

She'd hardly slept and she was tired all over. It was different here at night. When she'd come during the day it was great, there were a lot of places to explore. The containers went on forever, and lots of them were full of stuff.

But at night there were weird noises, dogs howling and fights. She'd picked a quiet corner, which might have been a mistake. There was no one at this end of the yard except him. The thing was, she had to hide. They would be looking for her.

Her sweaty palm was stained red. She dropped the spike.

Rubbing her hand on her jeans, she told herself it was just rust. But the smears wouldn't budge. Frantic, she spat on her palm and rubbed harder, and harder, and harder, until her skin was raw.

She looked outside again. He'd gone.

Relieved, she flopped down, took off her bag, opened it and found her felt-tip pens. She found the blue one and began to tattoo the back of her hand. It would make her look tough.

Suddenly the plastic wobbled and fell. The shape of the ogre loomed in the gap. The light dazzled her for a moment. He said something, but she was screaming and couldn't hear anything except her own cry.

She scrabbled for the spike, but her hand came to rest on a lump of concrete. She flung it with all her might and caught him on the side of the head. She heard him swear as he scuttled away.

She dragged the plastic back into place. Her knees went weak and she had to lie down on the piece of foam she had found. Her heart was beating so hard she shook with every thud.

But she didn't cry.

9

Berlin waited for Sonja to focus. She'd disappeared into the bathroom and when she emerged, she had stretched out on the bed.

Berlin watched as a blanket of tranquillity settled over her. Given the drought, what was it? There was a cocktail containing a potentially lethal sedative, ketamine, doing the rounds: Special K. But it was difficult to come by and expensive. She imagined that Sonja would go on the game when things got really bad.

'Okay Sonja, let's get real here, shall we?'

Sonja opened her eyes. Her gaze was frank, disarming.

'Tell me exactly what happened before your daughter took off,' said Berlin.

'She's a special child,' mused Sonja. 'We had an argument, just a stupid mother-daughter thing. She ran off before I could stop her.'

'And that's it?' said Berlin. She looked around the room, which was devoid of anything of value, sentimental or otherwise, apart from the TV. 'Have you got a photo?'

Sonja hesitated. Berlin watched as she slowly put it together: Berlin was going to look for her daughter.

'What brought this on?' Sonja asked.

'I'm not responsible for your shitty life, Sonja. But if I made a mistake a long time ago perhaps this will square it. After this, we're done.'

'Karma,' said Sonja.

'Call it what you like,' said Berlin.

The realisation that Berlin was on the case galvanised Sonja. She flung open a drawer in the bedside table and tossed aside unpaid bills, letters from the dole office and a collection of credit cards. No doubt stolen. Finally she produced a picture, a school photo, and handed it to Berlin. The child in the picture was about seven years old.

'When was this taken?' Berlin asked.

Sonja looked blank.

'At one of her schools. We've moved around a lot, so maybe . . . a while ago,' she said.

'God, Sonja, haven't you even got a recent photo of your own daughter?' said Berlin.

Sonja was unperturbed. 'I don't really subscribe to bourgeois values, making a fetish of the child,' she remarked airily.

Berlin wanted to give her a good shake. Instead she tried to glean something useful from the conversation.

'How does she spend her time? What's she into? Has she got a mobile or a Facebook page? Any mates?'

'Oh, you know, she just hangs around. She's always found it difficult to make friends. The kids at school would tease her and say she was . . . ' Sonja raised her hand to her temple: touched in the head. 'She stopped going. Maybe it was because I had her so late. At forty-one she was a surprise.' She stared into space, seeking inspiration. 'She makes things up,' she added, and lapsed into silence.

Berlin could see her drifting away. That was the end of the exhaustive description of Sonja's daughter. She asked herself again what she was getting into and why.

But the photo of the child in her hand left her with no choice. No one had bothered to say 'smile'. The dark eyes held Berlin's; the soft, unformed face was perplexed, the slight frown defiant. A picture of innocence was always compelling.

'I'll be in touch,' said Berlin. 'Call me if she turns up, okay? You've got my mobile number.'

No reply.

'Sonja?'

She looked up.

'What's she called?' asked Berlin.

Sonja looked stricken, as if for a moment she'd forgotten her daughter was missing and Berlin had just reminded her of this unpleasant fact. 'You will find her, won't you? She means everything to me,' she said. Desperation shone through the dope haze.

'What's her name?' said Berlin.

'Princess.'

Berlin didn't even try to catch up on her sleep when she finally got home. At least during the heatwave she didn't endure sleeplessness alone; nobody could rest. She rubbed her shoulder, which she had wrenched using the Asp. It had been a long time and she was out of condition. No doubt the creep was suffering a lot more. She hoped so.

She made a pot of strong Arabica, fired up the computer and journeyed to Google Earth, where she could think strategically about the task at hand.

She had to start somewhere and she was working alone, so she would limit the field of operations. Sonja's place was ground zero and she would fan out from there, superimposing a grid on the map to prevent doubling up.

She swept across the cyber-landscape to get a feel for the terrain and identify abandoned buildings, houses with sheds and old workmen's huts. Classic hiding places for runaways. The satellite images might be out of date, but the pace of change had slowed considerably since the financial crisis.

She would log the CCTV cameras when she got out there. If there were any, she might be able to get the operator to review their tapes. Although without a court order it would cost.

She would inspect abandoned cars, refrigerators, culverts, tunnels and stormwater pipes. Anywhere a kid could crawl inside and sleep. Presumably Princess had little or no money, unless she'd been thieving, and she'd be unlikely to travel far from what she knew. If she'd been left to her own devices most of the time she would have a much better grasp of the area's topography than her mother.

Printing out the results of her research Berlin slipped them into a plastic envelope. Opening a file, preparing logs, mapping the intel. As if it were a proper job.

Was she really doing this to assuage some absurd sense of guilt she felt about Sonja? After all, Sonja had made her own bad choices. Perhaps it was more about keeping herself sane, working, or pretending to work, at something that was a step up from errant wives.

Perhaps she wanted to take her mind off heroin and the impending nightmare of detox and methadone or subutex. Maybe she was just keeping busy, as her mother would say.

II

His ear was throbbing, probably infected. It would go septic quickly in the heat. But he couldn't go to the hospital. It was too risky. He couldn't afford to leave her alone.

He hadn't meant to frighten her, quite the opposite. He just wanted to talk to her, to explain that he wasn't going to hurt her. But he couldn't get near her without a scene, which would attract the attention of the other residents. That could complicate things and his patient vigil would be wasted.

His scalp was itchy under the cap. He kept his coat collar up and a thick scarf wrapped around his face, defying the heat, so there was very little chance anyone would recognise him. He didn't want to bump into any old acquaintances. And he didn't want anyone remembering his face.

She had been here two nights and she hadn't gone unnoticed. He would watch and wait a little longer, but he couldn't afford to let it drag on. If he got it wrong, things could turn nasty. Very nasty. It would be better done under cover of darkness, so he would have to endure another long, trying day. Then he would make his move.

Sooner rather than later.

There were times when Berlin didn't recognise her city. It had become a dazed and petulant beast, slithering into a pit, lashing out in confusion as it sank. Its descent was observed by mechanical eyes, which at three in the morning tracked her progress from Trafalgar Square to Temple Bar.

She tramped from shelter to hostel to soup kitchen, leaving photos of the kid with agencies that could be relied on not to contact the police. She felt as if someone was watching her. Of course, they were. She just had to keep reminding herself that it was nothing personal.

Small, vicious acts of vandalism, and ideologically motivated attacks on a grander scale, had combined in an overwhelming discourse of threat. Surveillance had been the response. She gazed at the skyline. The reassuring icons that marked out English liberality – Parliament, St Paul's, the Old Bailey – were cowering beneath the weight of the state.

Everything was political these days.

The theatres on the Strand were dark and the tourists safely ensconced in their hotels in air-conditioned comfort. Charles Dickens had lived right here. Berlin had no doubt he would be unsurprised to see charities feeding these dwellers at the margin, who crept from doorways and beneath bushes to feed on supermarket discards.

Her mobile rang. It was Sonja. 'It's me,' she said. 'I wondered if there was any news, you know, if anyone's seen her, or —'

Berlin broke in. 'It's early days, Sonja,' she said, although it wasn't. The kid had been gone for forty-eight hours, which statistically was about twenty-four too long. 'I'm doing the rounds, letting people know to look out for her.'

'People?' Sonja sounded nervous.

'People we can trust. I'll call you if there's any news.'

She hung up.

What she couldn't tell Sonja was that her search was doomed to fail: one pair of boots on the ground was ridiculously inadequate. Working alone also meant there was no one to test her approach or challenge her assumptions. She could be overlooking something. What did she know about kids?

At ten years old she was helping her dad, Lenny, in the shop on Saturdays, polishing the rings. It was a different world then.

There was no point approaching hospitals or morgues. If an unidentified child of that age turned up she would have seen it on the news. Missing children were found quickly or never.

'Never' meant sold or dead.

Princess was not strictly missing; she had run away. This put her in the category of not wanting to be found.

It made no difference.

Chances were she would still be sold or dead.

13

He crouched deep in the shadow of his container, rubbing at his painful ear. It was beginning to smell. He had struggled to keep his eyes open until the night was absolutely still. But now he was wide awake: two figures were approaching down one of the long, narrow passages between the rows of containers.

It was a pair of hoodies, stumbling through the darkness, half-pissed or stoned, and all the more dangerous for that. Their voices grew louder, bouncing off the sheer steel walls.

'Where is she?' whispered the smaller one.

'If I knew that I wouldn't be fuckin' looking for her, would I?' said the taller, thickset one. He was trying to keep his voice low, but failing.

'Wassa plan then?' said the smaller one.

'We don't need a fuckin' plan,' came the reply. 'Just grab her.'

By now the girl must have heard them.

He swore. He had run out of time, and patience. The last thing he wanted was a showdown with this pair of toe-rags. It was dangerous and he could lose the initiative.

Something rattled. It sounded like a chain being dragged through the dust. He crept away from his container, crawled over to her lair and tapped on the plastic.

'They're coming,' he whispered. 'I won't let anything happen, promise.' He had to win her over somehow.

There was no response.

'Come out,' he said. 'You're not safe in there.'

The stumblers were getting very close.

He had a torch, but didn't dare use it.It was now or never. He slid back the plastic.

The container was empty. The kid was one step ahead of all of them. Fuck it.

When she reappeared – *if* she reappeared – it was over. No more Mr Nice Guy.

14

Trudging up Bethnal Green Road towards home at the end of a long and fruitless night, Berlin made a call. It was answered on the second ring.

'Hello, Del,' she said.

'It lives,' said Del. She hadn't been in touch for a while. Delroy Jacobs had been her partner when she worked for the government chasing illegal moneylenders. Loan sharks.

'How are you, mate?' he said. Genuine concern. No complaints about the fact that she'd woken him before dawn, just a mild reproach that he hadn't heard from her, but now he had and it was okay. He just wanted to know how she was doing.

'I've been better,' she confessed. 'What about you?'

'I'm a dad now,' he said.

'That was quick,' she said.

'Not really. The standard nine months.'

Berlin remembered.

Linda had come with Del to the hospital once, when she was pregnant. It had been a mistake. When she saw the state Berlin was in she put even more pressure on Del to get out of the operational side. Their outfit was disbanded soon after, so he'd gone to work for a prestigious private intelligence company as a manager. Safe and sound behind a desk. Berlin knew he must hate it.

'What's that like?' asked Berlin. 'Parenthood?'

'It changes everything,' said Del.

'What do you know about ten-year-olds?' asked Berlin.

Del laughed. 'It's a bit soon to be worrying,' he said. 'I know they grow up fast these days, but . . . ' He paused. 'Why do you ask?'

'I'm working on a missing kid,' said Berlin.

'That's heavy,' said Del. 'How long?'

'Getting on for sixty hours.'

She listened to Del breathing and knew what he was thinking.

'Is there anything I can do?' he asked.

Berlin heard the thin wail of an infant's cry in the background. 'Look after your kid,' she said. *And just be there for me*, she thought, *that's enough*.

15

The canal was a grey ribbon of sludge. The broad road under which it ran took a bend, so there was no light at the end of the tunnel.

Low and dark, the arch dripped a ceaseless tattoo on the oily surface of the water, melding with the soft coo of pigeons and faint rodent squeaks in a subdued soundtrack of menace.

A thin child, a girl, had been stuffed into a crevice that some thoughtful Victorian engineer had provided for strangers who must pass on the narrow towpath.

The small broken body lay undisturbed by the clamour.

31°C

16

Berlin woke to another torpid morning, feeling as if she had slept for about five minutes. She stumbled out of bed to find she had run out of bread and milk. And Scotch.

She'd been neglecting her surveillance of Mrs Demir. It was a waste of time anyway, and she was just putting off delivering the bad news to the husband. She'd have to pay Mr Demir a visit before she went any further with the search for the missing kid.

On the way out she pulled her usual trick of dumping her empties into a neighbour's dustbin. She didn't want to get a reputation.

Murat was occupying the stool behind the counter. Commuters about to brave the malodorous furnace that was the Underground were cranky as they bought their newspapers and bottles of tepid water. The temperature had risen to 47 degrees on some lines; posters advised travellers to stay hydrated.

Berlin suspected a conspiracy between the bottled-water companies and Transport for London. The mayor had once offered a substantial cash prize to anyone who could come up with a solution to the problem of the overheated tunnels, but the competition ended without a winner.

Mr Demir wasn't getting any prizes either. She was going to give him the heads-up on his wife's early morning activities, take her last bag of groceries and draw a line under this job that wasn't even a job. It was barter. No invoice. No tax. No comeback. Now he wasn't even here.

'I'd like to speak to your father,' she said to Murat.

'What do you want with him?' he said.

His demeanour was cool, and there was no hint of the aggression he had displayed the other morning. This smug confidence was somehow more unnerving.

'Just tell him Berlin would like a word,' she said.

He continued to serve his customers until there was a brief lull, then disappeared out the back. A moment later he returned with Mrs Demir.

Berlin had never seen her this close. Her deep brown eyes were puffy, ringed with dark, ingrained circles. Years of insufficient sleep. Her hair was flecked with grey.

'May I help you?' she asked Berlin.

Berlin didn't miss a beat.

'Hello. My name's Catherine. Mr Demir was kind enough to complete a brief consumer survey for me the other day. I'm just following up on that.'

Mrs Demir glanced at Murat. Anxious.

'I'm afraid my husband is unwell,' she said.

'Oh. Nothing serious, I hope?' said Berlin.

There was no response. Murat watched her, his gaze hard and steady.

Berlin picked up the *East London Advertiser* and put sixty pence on the counter.

'I'll call another time then,' she said.

After Berlin had gone, Murat left his mother to run the shop and went out the back to stack cartons of canned lager. He threw each one higher and faster than the last. The taller the pile, the more his arms ached, the greater the justification for his fury. The stack of cartons swayed. He could see the whole tower come tumbling down in a heartbeat.

He leant against it, resting his forehead on the cardboard and wrapping his arms around the quivering pile. He had worked so hard, he couldn't give up now. Failure was not an option. He had to do something.

Rolfey was taciturn, not his usual cheery self. Berlin wondered if he had personal problems, or if he was just running out of patience with her. He scribbled her perscription, then handed it over.

She checked: he had prescribed fewer caps. First the reduced dose, now this. She stared at it for a moment, assessing its implications.

'An old acquaintance of mine has turned up. A patient of yours. Sonja Kvist,' she said quietly.

'Former patient,' said Rolfey.

'One of your success stories,' she said.

She saw him struggle to meet her gaze and affect ignorance of the sarcastic slur.

'How is Sonja?' he asked.

'Her kid's run away,' said Berlin.

'Oh?' said Rolfey.

'Do you know the kid?' asked Berlin.

Rolfey stood up. 'I've got patients waiting,' he said.

She sighed. He was such a terrible liar.

Rolfey glanced with longing at a painting of a yacht on the wall.

'She's ten. This is the third day,' said Berlin. 'Do you know what that means?'

'Of course I do,' he snapped. 'What do you take me for?' He pulled himself together and continued in a more measured tone. 'Sonja brought the girl with her a couple of times. I asked her not to. This is no environment for a child.'

'Sonja said she'd seen me here. Did you ever talk about me?' said Berlin.

'She may have asked about your scars. I mentioned what you did for a living, you know, what happened last winter.'

Berlin raised an eyebrow. 'And what else, Rolfey?'

He obviously didn't have the energy or the temperament.

'Okay. You got me. She called in a distressed state and said she needed to get in touch with you. She wanted you to help her find Princess. I urged her to go to the police, but she wouldn't hear of it.'

So that was Sonja's first lie. She had told Rolfey about the missing kid. It would have tugged at his heartstrings.

'You told her where I lived,' said Berlin.

'No,' exclaimed Rolfey. There was a pause before he muttered, 'I told her when you had your next appointment.'

Berlin shook her head and tut-tutted, as if he were a naughty little boy.

'The General Medical Council are on your case, aren't they?' she said. 'A breach of patient privacy may be a minor infraction. But on top of everything else.'

'Like what?' said Rolfey, defensive.

She brought out her big guns.

'Like junkies using a vice to break their arms so they can get a referral to your clinic during the drought.'

All those plaster casts on the arms and wrists of Rolfey's patients were no coincidence. The method of ensuring a clean break was hot gossip and Berlin even had the name of one local mechanic said to be doing a brisk trade.

The look on Rolfey's face was enough. He couldn't deny it. Any clinician would have picked up the pattern among new clients. Rolfey had plenty of experience and constant contact with addicts. He couldn't plead ignorance. By prescribing for them it was arguable that he was encouraging an epidemic of self-harm. If it became public, the scandal would destroy him. The CQC would close the place in a flash.

Rolfey sank into his chair and put his head in his hands.

'I just can't stand to see them suffer,' he said, defeated.

She watched carefully for any hint of manipulation or deceit. It wasn't there. She believed him. He had to deal constantly with the misery the law caused and she was unsurprised that he could be driven to break it.

But she was unmoved.

She stared at the prescription in her hand. Now she had something on him that she could leverage to her advantage. More caps. The temptation made her palms sweat.

'What are you going to do?' he asked.

'Nothing,' she said. 'For now.'

She would bank it.

Rolfey grimaced.

'What was your impression of the kid?' asked Berlin.

He seemed surprised by the question.

'As smart as a whip,' he said. 'But a bit . . . ' he hesitated.

Berlin pointed to her temple. 'Touched?' she said.

Rolfey shook his head, no. 'Unpredictable,' he said.

On her way home Berlin contemplated the often-fraught relationships between mothers and daughters, of which she had firsthand experience. Sonja had practically said Princess was mental; Rolfey's more objective assessment was simply that she behaved erratically. It seemed that Rolfey had a higher opinion of the kid than her mother. And he was a shrink, after all.

Mothers and sons were different. Mrs Demir seemed in thrall to Murat, who had no doubt been brought up as a little prince. Berlin had to tell Mr Demir the truth. But his asthma had apparently taken a turn for the worse, probably stress, and her news wasn't going to help.

There was something going on in the Demir household; perhaps the son was aware of his mum's infidelity and was using it against her, or he knew and felt disgust or shame. Or all of the above. Whatever it was, she reminded herself, it was outside the scope of her instructions, if she could dignify them with that term.

As she made her way slowly up the worn, stone stairs to her flat, her limp reminded her to leave it alone this time. It was none of her business.

She unlocked her front door, went inside and dropped the local paper on the table. The headline screamed 'Girl Found Dead Under Bridge'. Her heart juddered. She was too late.

It was thought that the girl had been in the tunnel crevice for at least twenty-four hours. She had been found by a dog that had run off during an early morning walk on the towpath. Its owner, an elderly man, was receiving treatment for shock. Police were appealing to the public for assistance in identifying the girl.

Berlin grabbed the old photo of Princess and walked out again, slamming the door behind her.

17

Getting into a police station these days was harder than getting out. Berlin had to state her business into an intercom, wait while a camera focused on her, and then step through an airport-style scanner. Luckily she didn't have the Asp on her. It was legal to own it, but it was an offensive weapon on the street.

The vestibule, which acted like an airlock before you actually made it to the counter, was lined with plastic seats attached to the wall. Only one was vacant. Access to justice was carefully controlled.

Someone had forgotten to install air conditioning and the atmosphere was heavy with the scent of the street: fear, anger and defiance. A couple clutched each other and sobbed. Five youths sat in a row, knees bobbing, faces blank. Meeting their bail conditions. A young woman with a black eye flicked the top of her cigarette packet in an incessant, desperate rhythm.

Berlin took a number from the electronic dispenser and sat on the spare chair. She touched the photo of Princess in her pocket.

Beyond the Plexiglas wall that separated them from the guardians of law and order, she could see harassed officers bent over computers, tightly packed desks piled high with documents, walls and floors littered with cables, boxes of kit shoved against peeling walls.

The hi-tech secure waiting room had been bolted on to a crumbling structure that couldn't accommodate twenty-first-century wiring, let alone twenty-first-century policing.

Berlin watched as two plainclothes officers, a man and a woman, led a boy through the warren of desks. The boy's face was buried in his hands and his shoulders trembled. The male officer went ahead, clearing a path. The female officer gently put her arm around the youth as his knees buckled. The man held a door at the back of the office open and the woman helped the youth through. It was Twig.

Berlin stood up slowly. Girl dead under bridge. She crossed the space with calm, deliberate steps. She stood in front of the automatic exit and waited for the motion detector to register her presence and release the door. A lifetime passed as she waited for it to open.

The movement of the train was comforting. Berlin needed time to process what she'd seen at the police station, to make sense of it.

The dead girl wasn't Princess. It was Twig's sister. Strangled and dumped the same night that Berlin had done her Dirty Harriet act. From the way the police were treating him it was clear the brother wasn't a suspect.

What were the chances that, with an arm that was probably broken, the creep had gone after the girl and killed her, for revenge or to get his money back? Almost nil. He was more likely to have spent the rest of the night in hospital.

A random robbery didn't fit the facts either. Too much of a co-incidence after her intervention. Those kids were smart enough not to go flashing cash about on the street late at night.

The other option was a random punter. But that explanation didn't really withstand scrutiny either. With that much cash in her pocket, the girl would have been more likely to take the rest of the night off.

Berlin couldn't avoid the conclusion that her own actions and the girl's murder were linked. She had handed the girl five hundred quid and a death sentence.

If she went to the police and gave them Derek Parr's ID all she was doing was presenting evidence that she'd assaulted him. If Parr was smart he'd have reported a mugging by someone who looked nothing like Berlin. He wouldn't want his mugger found.

Twig would be shit-scared, as well as grief-stricken. If he said too much, he would think he was going to land himself in it. He wouldn't realise that in pursuit of a murderer the police would over-look his relatively minor offences. Would he mention 'the nice lady'?

If Twig and his sister had gone to buy drugs that night, he wouldn't burn a connection, someone he might need in the future. That same someone could do to him what they did to his sister. He wouldn't trust the police. But he might trust her. She was a civilian and she understood how his world worked.

A robotic voice announced they had arrived at Pontoon Dock. Berlin stood up. Her sense of guilt might be irrational, but it would be inescapable unless she did something to help catch the girl's kill-er. She would find Twig and have a quiet word. If she came up with something, she'd hand it on to the police.

She stepped out onto the deserted platform and realised she had got here on autopilot. The girl's murder had put Princess's situation into sharp relief. Sonja had to go to the police.

If she refused, Berlin would report it herself.

18

Kennedy ruminated on the fact that Bertie had him sitting in the back of a stinking hotbox of a van in Silvertown when he should have been off-duty.

It was funny how it was always him doing this sort of thing. Bertie saved himself for the high-end stuff, like belting people. Kennedy didn't have the stomach for it. Occasions when his own buttons were pushed were rare, but when they were it could get ugly.

He raised the telephoto lens and peered through the tinted back window at the building down the road. It was quiet, apart from a lone figure limping across the gravel towards the portico. There was no sign of a vehicle or a departing mini-cab, so she must have walked from the DLR station. Kennedy tightened the focus.

It was the woman he'd noticed the other day crouching against the wall, watching the place. He took a few shots just before she disappeared around the back of the building. Probably another junkie looking for a connection. *Good luck, love*, he thought, *that's what we're all waiting for*. He was bored half to death. Maybe he would take a closer look.

The dog tied to the skip didn't even bother to stand up this time. Berlin knew the feeling: it had lost heart.

Any child with Sonja for a mother must be a survivor, but however tough she was, a kid could only avoid the predators for so long. That fact was now abundantly clear. Berlin was acutely aware of institutional failures when it came to child protection, which was why so many kids chanced it on the street. But if Princess were murdered, maimed, or raped, could Berlin say, hand on heart, it had nothing to do with her? She had been a fool to go along with Sonja.

The dog was stretched out on the gravel, tongue lolling. An old bucket lay on its side nearby. She walked over. The dog managed a listless wag of its tail. It was thin and dehydrated. She picked up the bucket, then went and tapped on Sonja's window.

'Any news?' asked Sonja, looking past Berlin as she slid the window up. As if she expected the kid to be standing there.

Berlin thrust the bucket at her.

'Fill it,' she said.

Sonja's room stank of despair. She sat on the edge of the bed, head bowed. Berlin stood over her.

'You have to go the police,' said Berlin, for the third time. 'She's just too young to leave it any longer.'

Sonja still didn't respond.

'Sonja, are you listening to me?' Berlin said softly, and sat down beside her. She didn't want to bring up the fate of Twig's sister; it would freak Sonja out too much. But she had to make her see sense.

'I'm listening,' said Sonja.

Berlin saw snot dribble from Sonja's nose. She reached out to the weeping woman, her hand coming to rest lightly on Sonja's trembling shoulder. She gave it a squeeze. It was the best she could do. Then she stood abruptly and walked to the window, which she'd left open in order to get some air circulating in the rank room.

The dog was on its feet now, lapping at the water in the bucket.

'Whose dog?' she asked.

Sonja sniffed and wiped her face on her T-shirt. 'It's just some bloody stray Princess brought home. I told her to get rid of it but she never took any notice of me. Rita won't have animals in the place.'

'Rita? The crone who does sentry duty at the front?'

'Yeah. She's the landlady. She doesn't own the place. She works for the owner. I think she gets her flat for free. Calls herself the "conserger". Stupid old bat.'

Berlin watched the dog.

'Who feeds it?'

'She did. Princess. It followed her everywhere. But now, well. since she's been gone, to tell you the truth . . .'

The mongrel must be starving, thought Berlin.

19

Silvertown was built on a limb of reclaimed marshland beside the Thames. Three royal docks came later: the Victoria, the Albert and the King George V.

The docks had been silent for years, unruffled rectangular fingers of water that protruded into a landscape of abandoned warehouses, towering edifices that once housed industrial plant.

Brick ramparts were punctuated by grids of blank, broken windows. Warrens of rusted gantry sheltered pigeons and the occasional heron. These ghosts of industry were skirted by acres of cracked concrete, exposing its skeleton of twisted iron rebar. It was a Special Enterprise Zone.

Britannia Village, a social housing complex, had been built at one end of the limb and the City Airport at the other. Between them was Pontoon Dock, which boasted the Thames Barrier, Lyle Park and luxury apartments on the riverside. The other side of the road boasted waste-disposal facilities, a chemical works and an animal by-products factory.

Rita Braverman sat staring at the TV screen. She had lived in Silvertown all her life. A fan of *Law and Order* – it was one of her favourite shows – Rita's own relationship with the police had had its ups and downs over the years. The down part had involved three years for receiving in the sixties.

The rest of the gang, including her dear departed hubby, had done five to ten for armed robbery. He was never the same after he came out. She'd brought her boys up alone. But that was all in the past, along with victories in the World Cup, milkmen and proper telephone boxes. She especially missed the milkmen.

She was retired now, although she had been left to drag up her grandson Terry, a boy who wasn't the full quid really. He had his uses – he had grown into a strong lad – but he was a lazy little blighter and she had to keep an eye on him.

She was semi-retired in point of actual fact, because she had her various duties. The extras made a big difference. Information was what the modern economy was all about. She'd seen it on the telly. There was a market for it and no mistake. Her client list was growing.

The party in the back room had been very quiet of late. Rita made a note in her diary, which she kept in her voluminous dressing-gown pocket. The actual time of comings and goings wasn't her strong suit, particularly after lunch, so she had taken to writing things down straightaway. She liked to employ proper language in her records, to make it seem more official-like. No names, no pack drill was the rule.

She had watched that gimp in black take the dog and now she made a note. She was using the initials LW, Limping Woman, for her. The party of the first part was up to something, no doubt, and Limping Woman was involved. She would find out, she had her ways and means. It was just a matter of time.

One day, and it could be soon, the planets would line up and she would make that special phone call. Then her ship would finally come in.

Berlin let the dog lead her down a path through an industrial estate to a stretch of bare, dusty earth and rampant thistles beside the river, well demarcated from the landscaped gardens around the new estates.

The dog was thin but lively, clearly glad to be out and racing towards bins it knew would contain the desiccated remnants of burgers and fried chicken. Berlin let it have a good scavenge, then gave it a tug – they were moving on. The dog took off and she tramped across the wasteland behind it.

In the distance she could see a dark shape, a profile of sharp lines etched against the pale yellow murk of the sky. The effect was of broken battlements but, as the clouds moved and the light changed, the image resolved into stacks of shipping containers. The dog was heading that way.

As they got closer she saw three figures coming from the opposite direction, ambling towards the yard. She watched, shading her eyes not from the sun, but against the opaque glare of dust and heat. The figures moved towards a fence and then seemed to melt into it.

Berlin blinked and scanned for a gate, or a sign of one – a veil of dust kicked up by a gate opening and closing. But there was nothing. The people had just disappeared.

By the time she and the dog were close enough to actually touch the fence the sweat was stinging her eyes and her clothes were thick with dust.

The fence was heavy-duty chain link, at least eight feet high, solidly attached to concrete posts at regular intervals. It enclosed acres of abandoned shipping containers, rusted and broken, some stacks three and four containers high.

She stood very still. The dog collapsed into a heap at her feet and rolled onto its back. Playtime. Berlin ignored it. She couldn't hear any sound coming from beyond the fence. There was no sign of the people she had watched walk through it. She walked on, forcing the dog to its feet.

They followed the fence to a dirt track where double gates topped with barbed wire were secured by thick, padlocked chains. A faded sign forbade entry.

There seemed to be no way in except through the gate. But the people she'd seen hadn't had time to unlock and then re-secure all those chains and padlocks. She looked at the dog, which was obviously familiar with the place.

'Go on then,' she said. 'How do we get in?'

But if the dog knew it wasn't saying. It gazed up at her, tongue lolling, eyes bright and ready to continue the game. Useless.

There was only a foot of space between the fence and the first row of containers, which formed a solid wall across the gate and around the entire perimeter. It took her and the dog forty minutes to walk all the way around.

There didn't seem to be an inch of space left in the yard. The lorries that delivered the containers must have stopped coming a long time ago. But she was certain she'd seen people go in.

She'd just have to wait for them to come out.

20

Before his official shift began at three, Kennedy had to meet Bertie in the canteen for a quick cuppa and a heads-up on the day's events.

Once upon a time the canteen had been a bustling place with proper hot food prepared by a cook who knew everyone's favourites. When you came off a long night she would cook your bacon crispy and your scrambled eggs soft, with hot, sweet tea in a thick, white china mug.

Now there were just bloody machines dispensing weak espresso and soggy salads, in plastic containers that tasted better than their contents. Bertie never stopped moaning about it: the good old days when there was respect and decent, subsidised grub.

Kennedy missed the warm, supportive environment of the canteen as much as the food, but he was more adaptable. He had to be, given his domestic situation. Bertie never mentioned his home life and Kennedy doubted he had one.

'Mate, there's the bad news and the very bad news,' said Bertie.

Kennedy sipped his tea, which tasted like boiled cabbage water. He'd already done a day's work and now he was about to start another. He was so over it.

'You've been reassigned,' said Bertie. 'To Hurley's crew.' Bertie grimaced.

Kennedy struggled to contain his delight. This might be his opportunity to extricate himself from Bertie without pissing him off and unleashing all sorts of unintended consequences.

'Oh, shit,' he said, feigning dismay.

'Oh, shit is right,' said Bertie. 'And the very bad news is that it's a murder.'

A murder inquiry was a round-the-clock operation with a lot of scrutiny from the command structure. The logs had to be kept up to date, every move had to be accounted for and there wasn't much opportunity to pursue other interests. Kennedy's cup flowed over. There would even be overtime to make up for his losses.

'Of course, this means we'll have to sort out our mutual interests,' said Bertie, who was watching him closely.

'Of course,' said Kennedy, maintaining an air of disappointment. 'But how?'

'We're going to bring it to a swift, and if necessary bloody, conclusion quick smart,' said Bertie.

Kennedy wasn't sure what Bertie had in mind, but knew it wasn't going to be pretty. He tried to ignore a frisson of anxiety.

'What about this morning?' asked Bertie. 'Don't suppose there was any sign?'

Kennedy shook his head. 'Some junkie hanging around down there again. She paid Sonja a visit apparently, then took off towards the river with that dog from out the back. Going nowhere, from the look of it. Chasing, I suppose.'

'We better up the ante with the CHIS,' said Bertie, using the term loosely. The snout wasn't registered, so strictly speaking couldn't be referred to as a Confidential Human Intelligence Source. Bertie had long ignored such formalities. 'We're going to need more input from that quarter now that our surveillance will be reduced,' he added.

Kennedy noted the way Bertie referred to it as 'our' surveillance, though it wasn't him who had sweated out the hours in the van.

'Right. I'd better go and get briefed on this new job,' Kennedy said, and stood up, exercising his new-found freedom to turn his back on his erstwhile boss.

'Don't be a stranger,' said Bertie.

A gang of hoodies were hanging out in the lea of a derelict factory, drinking from two-litre bottles of cider. Berlin took no notice of them, but they watched in silence as she and the dog passed on their way back to Sonja's.

One of the boys detached himself from the group.

'Oi!' he shouted.

Berlin turned around. The dog kept going, but jerked to a halt when it ran out of rope.

'Where'd you get that fuckin' dog?' demanded the boy as he stomped towards her, shrouded in his voluminous hood.

When he got close, the dog sat down in the dirt. It tucked in its tail, bowed its head and watched the boy with a sideways look. It could smell something bad.

The boy, who was about sixteen, brandished a fist at it. Berlin noticed he had 'Diamond' tattooed on the back of his hand.

'What's it to you?' said Berlin.

'That's my fuckin' dog, innit,' said Diamond. 'I lost it.'

'Oh, yeah? How?' asked Berlin.

'How what?' said Diamond.

His mates had moved closer, in order to enjoy the event.

'How did you lose the dog?' said Berlin.

Diamond seemed incapable of normal speech. He could only shout. 'It got off the chain, down here near the river, we were just mucking about.'

'And?' said Berlin.

Diamond frowned, apparently trying to think.

'And . . . some chick took it,' he said.

The mates had formed a tight circle around her.

Diamond reached for the rope. 'Give me the fucking dog!' he demanded.

'Had you seen her down here before? This chick?' she said.

'What's it to you?' he sneered, mocking her. He waggled his fingers, indicating he wanted the rope.

Berlin gave it to him, but slid her hand along so she still had a grip on it.

'When she took the dog, where did she go?' she asked.

Diamond blinked. Berlin could see him reaching for something. The lights were on, but no one was home.

'Get fucked,' he said.

The mates pawed the stony ground with their Doc Martins, a herd ready to stampede.

Berlin released her grip on the rope.

Diamond screamed like a banshee. His hood flipped back as he broke through the circle of his mates, dragging the dog behind him. 'You fuck!' he yelled at the cowering animal. 'Man's fucking best friend. You fucking ran out on me!'

His face was flushed, his ruby lips twisted in a sneer, flecked with drool. *He's smashed out of his tiny mind*, thought Berlin.

Dragging the rope from the dog's neck, he scooped the animal off the ground and held it high above his head, a trophy. His mates roared with laughter and whooped in unison, hopping from one foot to the other in a circle, a crude imitation of a Native American war dance.

Diamond ran screaming to the embankment wall and with a bloodcurdling cry threw the dog into the river. The splash and frantic yelps soon evaporated into silence. It was high tide. The current was fierce and the riverbank was a steep wall of stone.

Diamond turned to face Berlin, defiant.

The sullen faces of his mates watched her, a spark of interest in their otherwise dull eyes. What would she do?

Nothing.

21

Berlin's flat trapped the heat. At night it was an oven, and she'd be glad to be out of it for a while. She dragged a sleeping bag from under the bed. It was stained and worn, all the better for her purpose.

Instead of going back to Sonja's she had come straight home. Sonja might not ask about the dog, but if she did Berlin had no answer.

She swallowed a morphine cap with a shot of cheap whisky. The caps kept her pain under control, but they weren't strong enough to take her to that special place. It was the difference between a nice cup of tea and a large single malt.

She felt momentarily guilty at her failure to follow up on the Demir situation: the confrontation with the son, and then the encounter in the shop with him and the mother had been a bloody nuisance. There was something perturbing about that situation which she couldn't articulate. But it was a family issue and by definition beyond the power of an outsider to resolve, or even comprehend half the time.

Now she had her hands full looking for Princess and Twig. The police would know where the boy was, but she couldn't exactly ask them. And she had one lead on Princess. If it didn't work out, she was calling the cops, despite Sonja's vehement protestations.

On top of everything else there was the nagging problem of Rolfey weaning her off the caps. She couldn't imagine abandoning a relationship that had sustained her for most of her adult life. Leaving was always tough, even to save yourself.

She stashed her cash, credit card and front-door key in her boots, drew on a black woolly hat and slipped a Ziploc bag containing her morphine underneath it. She checked in the mirror. With her current Hammer Horror looks and the limp she would have no trouble blending in.

That afternoon she had sat in the tall weeds watching the fence for over an hour, enduring the stinking heat while the dog slept. When finally someone approached the yard, she'd moved a bit closer and watched carefully. It was ingenious.

The fence was constructed of heavy-duty mesh, connected by thick concrete posts about every twenty feet. The mesh was intact, but one of the concrete posts had been severed from it, except at the very top. The dirt around the base was loose. The post hung neatly in place, but if you gave it a shove it shifted about a foot, leaving an ample gap.

The people who came and went were young and old, fat and thin, black and white. They all had one thing in common. They were sleeping rough. Berlin was going to join them.

Anxious to leave the flat, she took another quick shot of Scotch, then put the bottle in her overcoat pocket. For authenticity.

But before she set off for Silvertown, she had to sort the Demir job, such as it was. Loose ends had a habit of tripping you up.

A telephone call wasn't her preferred method of reporting to a client, but she had to tell Mr Demir about the doctor and where his wife went in the mornings.

She didn't want to confront Murat again, let alone his mother. She picked up her phone and dialled Mr Demir's mobile. When he answered, she adopted her professional voice. The one she used for delivering bad news.

On the DLR out to Silvertown she thought about Mr Demir's dignified reaction.

'I'm not a well man, Miss Berlin. Perhaps my wife is right to seek . . . companionship elsewhere.'

God, human relationships were so messy. What was the bloody point? She took a surreptitious pull on the Scotch, careful to turn away from the CCTV, lest the British Transport Police board at the next station and drag her off.

The other passengers averted their gaze from the alcoholic tramp.

She was just getting into character.

The concrete post swung aside silently. Berlin tossed her sleeping bag ahead of her and stepped through. Once inside, she was faced with a blank wall of steel. She eased along the gap between the fence and the shipping containers, searching for a way through the apparently impervious barrier.

A dog barked. She turned around, her heart skipping a beat. The head of a mongrel protruded from the bottom of one of the containers. But of course it wasn't Princess's dog. *For Christ's sake.* She was losing her grip, expecting a happy ending.

This dog stood apparently half in and half out of one of the containers. It barked again. *It wants to be let out*, she thought. She hesitated, but then went back and shifted the concrete post. The dog ran off into the night.

When she got down on her hands and knees she could see the hole in the container where the dog had appeared. She crawled inside.

22

Kennedy stifled a yawn as he scrolled through the witness statements and logs on the computer. He should be at home, giving his wife a break from the routine of back rubs and inhalations that his son needed just to be able to breathe. But he was working late to try to get up to speed on this murder.

It was a privilege to be assigned to a homicide, a vote of confidence from the bosses and one that he knew he didn't deserve. Perhaps it was more a reflection of how few bodies they had available to redeploy.

All the money and resources had gone into counter-terrorism, although Kennedy was of the view that neither he nor his family were any safer as a result. They were now more at risk from muggers and online creeps. He kept that opinion to himself.

The murder of Kylie Steyne was a case in point. The uniforms who had done the door-to-door had done a good job but there wasn't much to go on. They could have used a lot more forensic support on the ground.

None of the residents who overlooked the canal were peering out of their back windows in the middle of the night, although all commented that the path under the bridge was often busy after dark. The accumulation of rubbish collected by the Scene of Crime officers bore testimony to that.

Kennedy came to the garbled statement made by the deceased's brother, William Fitzgerald Steyne, known as Billy. Dad was in the nick, Mum was an invalid. The kids and their mum had been cared for by her mother, their gran, but when Gran passed away it all went pear-shaped.

Mum went into a government nursing home, the council took back the flat and the kids were put up by a variety of relatives and friends until they outstayed their welcome, swearing, thieving and fighting.

The children's home where they had been placed had shut down: the private-equity firm that owned it had subcontracted the operational side of the business, the operators defaulted on their loan and then the bank, which was a major shareholder in the private-equity firm, had repossessed it.

So by the ages of fourteen and fifteen and a half they were sleeping rough. Their local authority was obliged to house them, but the various authorities involved couldn't agree where the kids belonged: in bureaucratic parlance this was known as a stand-off. The kids wanted to stay together, but faced separation as part of a deal that would be done by agencies with different statutory responsibilities. Buck-passing.

A social worker who'd had some involvement with the family had written that the children had 'slipped through the net'. Kennedy snorted. That was probably because it was more holes than net.

Billy's statement was almost incoherent, whether from drugs or grief or both, but one thing caught Kennedy's eye. Earlier during the night that his sister Kylie was killed, 'something happened'. It wasn't clear what, but it involved 'a lady'. The description of the lady made Kennedy sit up straight. Particularly the part about her black clothes, her scarred face and her limp.

Billy had been placed in an emergency shelter until the case was either closed or, if there was no quick result, put on the back burner: that is, until he conveniently 'slipped through the net' again. Kennedy had to speak to him before that happened, or before Billy decided that life on the street beat staying straight.

Kennedy rang the shelter's night bell. When the light finally came on and the camera swivelled, he held up his ID. The solid steel door clicked open.

The worn sofa, threadbare carpet and bookshelves littered with battered toys and board games reminded Kennedy of home. He felt a surge of resentment that he couldn't do better for his kids than this charity could do for its waifs and strays.

As the worker steered Billy Steyne into the room it was clear the boy had been woken from a heavily medicated sleep. The worker put a chipped mug of hot tea into Billy's hand and glared at Kennedy.

'He's a minor, detective,' she said.

'Just one question,' promised Kennedy. He thrust his smartphone at Billy, who was nodding off. The screen displayed a photo that Kennedy had downloaded from the surveillance camera.

Billy was holding the tea at a dangerous angle. The worker took it from him and put it on the table.

'Billy, is this the lady? The lady who was there that night with you and Kylie?'

Billy peered at the photo, blinked and peered again.

'Nice phone,' he mumbled.

'Concentrate, mate,' said Kennedy. 'Is that her?'

Billy looked harder.

He pointed at the photo.

'The nice lady. Say thank you,' he slurred.

The Lord works in mysterious ways, thought Kennedy, as the worker steered Billy back to bed, *but what fucking wonders will He perform?*

He picked up Billy's mug.

The tea was hot and sweet. Just how he liked it.

23

Berlin took in the spectacle. She had crawled through the empty blackness of the shipping container and emerged into a long yard lit by fires burning in forty-four-gallon drums. The shadows of the inhabitants fell in monstrous relief across the tiers of steel boxes that enclosed the space on all sides. The labyrinth extended into the gloom.

Many of the containers were buckled and torn, the sides ripped away as if by a giant hand. Crude domestic arrangements were apparent, the spaces occupied by lone figures, couples, families. There might have been dozens of people living there, or hundreds, it was impossible to tell. The place was a maze.

The yard was littered with mounds of trash, each pile composed of identical items: a pyramid of warped plastic trikes; a leaning tower of cracked purple PVC sheeting; a heap of tarnished Christmas baubles. Thousands of discarded articles spilled from rotten cardboard boxes, or protruded from splintered timber cases.

A drunk's mournful song drifted along with the smoke. Rancid oil sizzled on barbecues made from manhole covers. A couple danced to a tune only they could hear. The mangy dogs, the smell of rotten meat frying and the drunk's dirge created a grotesque parody of a medieval peasants' banquet. It was more Bosch than Bruegel.

A message sprayed on one side of a container declared 'Welcome to Love Motel'.

Sleeping bag deployed, Scotch in hand, Berlin sat at the entrance to her new living quarters and watched and waited. She had never felt more at home.

For a child, the concentration of desperate, chaotic adults in one place would be terrifying.

No one had spoken to her, but she was aware that she had been observed and that the more alert citizens had evaluated the level of risk she posed.

Her position gave her a good view of what had obviously been designated as communal space: anywhere within the circles of dim firelight. Beyond that, she would have to wait for daylight. The kid could be hiding out in any one of the hundreds of containers, concealed in a dark corner.

There appeared to be a couple of families who were well dug in with camping stoves, large water containers and mattresses: whatever was left from homes they had lost or abandoned for the usual myriad banal causes that brought people to their knees. It was nearly impossible to get back up again in the current economic climate.

A tall woman, swathed in layers of fabric and wool despite the humid night approached Berlin.

'We have a rule here. We don't shit in our own nest,' she said.

Berlin nodded.

'There's a container there, three rows over, marked with an X.' She pointed beyond the fire. 'The bottom's gone out of it. Inside there's a pit.'

She held out her hand and Berlin passed her the Scotch. She took a long drink, then handed it back.

'Watch your step,' she said, and drifted off into the darkness.

It wasn't just a friendly warning about treading in shit.

24

Sonja lay in the dark, fretting. She found it difficult to stay still, but could only pace up and down as she couldn't leave the room for long. She daren't go further than the petrol station down the road. Empty Pot Noodle packets and chocolate wrappers littered the table. She couldn't keep anything else down, anyway. She touched a sore at the corner of her cracked lips.

If Princess wasn't found soon, she didn't know what she would do.

So much for her Honours degree in classics and modern languages from Oxford. Daddy had given her a generous allowance and paid the bills while she was a student, so she never really noticed the steadily rising cost of her dope.

She came from a good family. Whatever that meant. Her life had been mapped out: an easy path to a fulfilling career, marriage, a pied-à-terre in Sloane Square and a nice house in the country.

But Daddy finally declared her 'useless' and cut her off.

Cole looked after her. For a while. Then when times were tough he would 'turn her out'; she found herself servicing businessmen with a taste for well-bred women who could talk dirty in three languages. She left Cole more than once, but he always found her.

Then Princess came along.

This was the end of the road: tossing and turning on a dirty sheet, alone and desperate for a fix. It wasn't heroin – it was love that had brought her down.

When someone tapped on the window she didn't hesitate. She jumped up. By the time she realised who it was, he was already climbing over the sill.

Kennedy left the window open. He could see Sonja was disconcerted. He had always come with Bertie before. They stood with the kitchen table between them.

'What do you want?' she said. 'If you thought you'd find Cole here you can see you're out of luck. He's not been in touch either, before you ask.'

'I'm not interested in Cole for the moment,' he said.

Sonja grabbed a fork from the table and backed away from him. Kennedy sighed. Why did people always think the worst?

'Put it down, Sonja, you've got nothing to fear from me. Why do you think I've come on my own?'

'I've got a fair idea,' she said.

'Don't flatter yourself,' he said. Although she must have been a looker once. Those blue eyes. He pulled out a chair and sat down. 'Take a look at these,' he commanded, and put his phone on the table.

Sonja approached near enough to see the photo of Berlin on the screen.

'What?' she asked.

'Who is she?' asked Kennedy.

'No idea,' said Sonja.

Kennedy was tired.

'Come on, Sonja. Don't dick me about. I know she's been here.'

'I'm hungry,' she said, defiant.

Kennedy took a tenner from his pocket and put it on the table. It was an investment. When Sonja reached for it he slapped his hand down over hers.

'She's just an old friend,' exclaimed Sonja. 'What do you want to know for?'

'Look, this is nothing to do with Cole,' said Kennedy. 'It's about a kid, it's important, a murder inquiry, so you've no reason to . . .'

He was brought up short by Sonja's reaction. He didn't think she could get any paler, but he saw the blood drain from her face. Her hands twitched.

'What? What is it, Sonja? What do you know about her?'

'The kid. Is it a girl?' asked Sonja, her voice breaking.

Kennedy nodded.

Sonja's sharp intake of breath was a revelation. He remembered that Cole and Sonja had a kid. He hadn't seen her around for a while. He pointed at the photo of Berlin.

'Who is she and where can I find her?'

'Please,' said Sonja. 'The girl. Has she been identified?' Instead of taking her hand away, she gripped his. She was terrified. 'I'm begging you, Kennedy.'

Kennedy knew an opportunity when he saw one. Leverage. Better than cash. *I've picked up a lot of bad habits from Bertie*, he thought, rueful. But if he could get ahead of the game, he might escape those sweaty paws permanently.

'Let's hear it, Sonja,' he said. 'The whole story.'

Rita was paid to see some things, and ignore others. This particular matter left her in a right two and eight.

Anyone who thought they could evade her eagle eye by coming in the back in the middle of the night had seriously underestimated her. She wasn't so green as she was cabbage-looking. Or something like that.

She took another swig of vodka and ruminated.

Damned if she did, damned if she didn't.

The story of her fucking life.

After Kennedy left, Sonja was exhausted. She lay down and fell into a deep, dreamless sleep until she woke suddenly, unable to breathe. The room was pitch-black. She clawed at the hand that sealed her mouth and nose.

'Stay still,' came the command.

Sonja froze.

'What did he want?' he growled, easing his grip so she could answer. His other hand caressed her throat.

'Nothing. Just checking up,' she gasped.

'Did he say why he was on his own?'

'No.'

'What did he want then?'

'Nothing,' she said.

He exhaled, impatient, and his hot, sour breath assaulted her. Her kneejerk responses were those of a habitual liar or a fearful child: I don't know, it wasn't me, I didn't see nothing.

'Did he come for a fuck, was that it?' he demanded.

Sonja hesitated.

'Yes,' she said, struggling under his weight.

Thick fingers gripped her face and squeezed it.

'Well, you better not fuck with me, Sonja,' he hissed. 'Go back to sleep.'

The blow came from out of the darkness.

32°C

25

Berlin woke at first light with a stiff neck and a cramped leg. Her sleeping bag was damp with dew, but she hadn't had such a good night's sleep in years. The great outdoors. She lay there for a moment and considered the attraction of a rootless existence based on scavenging. No mortgage, no bills, no obligations.

A nomadic existence looked good during a warm summer. But could she do without a hot bath, good coffee and dope? How long before she was rolled by a desperate junkie?

She crawled out of the sleeping bag, dismissing her romantic delusions, and shuffled into the yard, contemplating her less than romantic future. If Rolfey cut her off, how long before she resorted to violence to get what she needed?

She had learnt to live with the difference between heroin and morphine. But could she live with the complete loss of that special ease coursing through her veins?

The fires in the drums had been extinguished and it was quiet in the yard, apart from the dogs rolling in the dust, snarling at imaginary foes. There was a hell of a lot of ground to cover in here, but now was a good time to get started, while everyone was still asleep. But first things first.

She found the pit, and beside it a mound of earth and a shovel. The hum of the flies reached a crescendo as she squatted and swatted, extinguishing the siren call of the open road.

26

Kennedy loped down the corridor towards the office, intent on getting to his desk and running some queries on the Police National Computer system before any bugger started taking an interest in what he was doing.

He had a muffin in one hand and a plastic cup of tepid tea in the other, and as he rounded a corner he ran straight into Bertie. He couldn't believe his eyes. He'd never seen him at the station so early. Bertie looked just as surprised to see him.

'Mate, where are you off to in such a hurry?' asked Bertie, taking hold of Kennedy's muffin and stuffing half of it in his mouth.

'Just going to catch up on some paperwork, you know,' said Kennedy.

'Oh? You're a busy boy,' said Bertie.

'Yeah. Domestic responsibilities and a murder investigation,' said Kennedy, watching his breakfast disappear. 'I've got a full plate. Or did have.'

'You've been making a few inquiries, I know that,' said Bertie.

The way he said it made Kennedy very nervous.

'That's my job, isn't it?' he said.

Bertie regarded him for a long moment.

Kennedy could see he was waiting for some kind of explanation. He felt more confident now that he wasn't officially reporting to the fat fuck. It was time to explore, in a small way, the limits of his new-found independence.

'What's up your bum, Bertie?' demanded Kennedy.

'Me, mate?' said Bertie. He looked offended as he brushed the crumbs off his girth. 'Nothing. Just making conversation. We're always straight with each other, aren't we? What you do in your own time is your business.'

He winked, which Kennedy found disconcerting.

'It's just that you don't start until three,' said Bertie. He glanced at his watch. 'You could forget the paperwork; you've got hours. I've booked the van. It's out the front.'

Kennedy didn't move.

'Come on. You can take that with you,' said Bertie, pointing at Kennedy's tea. Bertie's jaw was working with the effort of keeping his temper.

Kennedy could feel his own resolve weakening, but he still didn't make a move.

Bertie frowned, apparently puzzled by Kennedy's sudden recalcitrance. He leant closer and spoke softly into Kennedy's ear. 'You've got a lot to lose, mate. All those bleeding cripples you call a family, for a start.'

He stuffed the rest of the muffin into Kennedy's jacket pocket and squeezed.

Kennedy knew striking a senior officer could finish him. He felt Bertie's heavy hand gripping his arm.

'No offence, mate. But you've got a job to do,' Bertie said. 'I'll give you a call later to see what's what.'

He turned Kennedy around and pointed him back the way he'd come.

Kennedy slunk down the corridor. *One day, mate*, he thought. *One day.*

27

Berlin watched a derelict as he watched her. She had been trooping up and down the rows of containers for hours, peering inside and frequently copping a mouthful of abuse or, worse, a brick, for her trouble.

But this bloke was taking a particular interest in her as she inspected the containers at the far end of the yard. He sat at the entrance to his own rusty cave, his face and neck swathed in grubby scarves and rags, hunched in an old army greatcoat, defying the heat. He had a solid build under the coat, although it could have just been layers of clothing.

His eyes seemed weird somehow, but she wasn't close enough to see why. A makeshift bandage was wrapped around his head, covering one ear. He wasn't missing much. She kept going, working her way up the line; dragging open the doors, scrambling over the heaped contents to get to the back of each container, then retreating again.

As she got closer to the end of the row, the tramp stood up.

Sitting in the back of the van in Silvertown, Kennedy considered his dilemma. He had a good lead in the murder of Kylie Steyne, but he couldn't use it officially without a lot of questions about where he'd got a photo of Billy's mystery woman, 'the nice lady'. He had rehearsed a dozen scenarios but it always came out the same: badly.

He could hear himself saying to DCI Hurley, 'Well, sir, I was undertaking unauthorised surveillance on a junkie whose drug-dealer husband DCI Burlington and I are shaking down. I photographed this woman visiting the said junkie.'

Even more questions would be asked about who had put a name to the mystery woman. 'Oh that? Old-fashioned police work, sir. I blackmailed the junkie into identifying the woman by implying it was her missing daughter who had been found murdered down by the canal.'

A lorry roared past. The van shuddered in the turbulence, reflecting Kennedy's own tremor. Watching Sonja's place was a waste of time.

He started the van and wound down the tinted windows to let in some air. His foot hovered over the accelerator. He would have to take his chances that Bertie's threats were just bluff. After all, if he went down he would take Bertie with him.

The problem was that Bertie was so unpredictable lately. It was like he had nothing to lose; his behaviour had always been erratic but his attitude had deteriorated, along with his personal hygiene. But there wasn't much Kennedy could do about that.

Fuck Bertie.

He was going to go back to the station to pursue the lead on the woman Billy had described as intervening between his sister and the punter. An intervention that Kennedy held in high regard, despite it being vigilantism.

He put his foot down and took off in a cloud of dust. It was very satisfying.

Sweating and caked with dust, Berlin reached a buckled container; a gash in its side was protected by a sheet of cracked purple plastic. She took a few steps towards it. A movement at her back told her the tramp was on the move. She reached for the plastic.

From beyond it came a cry: 'Look out!'

Berlin looked over her shoulder. The tramp was almost on her.

The plastic slid open to reveal a kid clutching a metal spike, her eyes wide with terror.

'Quick,' she shouted. 'The ogre!'

Berlin shoved herself sideways through the gap and the kid thrust the plastic back into position and peered through a hole in it. She brandished her spike.

'Fuck off!' hissed the kid.

The derelict's shadow darkened the plastic. He stood very still, bending forwards: a hunchback listening.

As Berlin's eyes adjusted to the purple-tinged gloom, she could see the kid's weapon of choice was a tent peg. But it was a big one, intended to anchor a marquee. It had been honed to a sharp point. Lethal.

The girl addressed her in a gabbled whisper. 'Don't worry, he won't come in, he knows what he'll get if he does,' she said, waving the spike around. 'He puts sandwiches and stuff in a tin. I gave them to the dogs the first time and they were okay so I eat them, but it doesn't mean anything. I know what he wants but he's not getting any.'

Berlin could see goosebumps on her thin arms and the hand that gripped the spike was trembling.

It was also emblazoned with a crude version of a symbol that Berlin recognised from long ago: the phoenix that decorated Cole Mortimer's fist. She was her father's daughter.

This was Princess.

28

The girl bore little or no resemblance to the soft-featured innocent in the photo in Berlin's pocket. This kid was all angles; a head of hacked, badly bleached hair atop a sharp little face, eye sockets blue-black from sleepless nights. Her reedy body was all bony arms and legs.

Berlin offered her hand.

'Berlin,' she said.

They shook hands.

'Princess,' said the child.

They stood side by side, waiting for the ogre to move on.

Berlin was impressed with the way the kid had set up the container; the string of cans was a smart move.

The bag on Princesses' back was emblazoned with faded symbols wonkily executed in felt-tip pen: pentagrams, a staring eye in a pyramid, Celtic crosses. A legacy of Sonja's hippy predilections: a universe of auras and karma. Sonja had said the kid made things up. Something else she'd inherited.

Berlin couldn't abide that sort of pseudo-mystical claptrap. It lulled children into thinking that there was another world over the rainbow, or that the fairies could save them. Don't bother clapping. Tinkerbell is dead.

But this kid wouldn't be surprised to hear that. She had a mind of her own.

It dawned on Berlin that getting the ten-year-old delinquent back to Sonja wasn't going to be easy. She had imagined a few gentle, reassuring words about her mother's love and then a walk hand-in-hand into the sunset. Now it occurred to her that the runaway might not want to go home. It could get ugly.

'It's okay,' said Princess, apparently mistaking Berlin's frown for fear. 'I'll protect you.'

Somehow she had to get the kid to go with her without a fuss, or else attract a lot of unwanted attention.

'He tried to grab me the other night,' said Princess, meaning the ogre. 'These others were after me, too. Anyway, I got out.'

She gestured to the rear of the container. If there was a hole back there only a kid could wriggle through it. Princess was no fool.

'There must be safer places than this,' said Berlin.

'Like where?' asked Princess.

'Home?' said Berlin, making sure the emphasis was on the interrogative.

Princess snorted. 'Where's your home, then?' she said.

'I ran away a long time ago,' said Berlin. It was the truth.

'Adults don't run away,' said Princess, scornful.

'I said it was a long time ago,' said Berlin. 'My dad was dead and I didn't get on with my mum, so I took off.'

'Same here,' said Princess.

'You don't get on with your mum?'

Princess nodded. 'And my dad's dead, too,' she said.

The sweat trickling down Berlin's spine suddenly ran cold.

She glanced sideways at Princess, whose finger was unconsciously tracing the rough shape of the phoenix on the back of her hand.

'That's tough,' she said. 'About your dad.'

'Yeah,' mumbled Princess. But when she looked up, her crooked smile implied it might not be all bad.

The ogre was sitting in the entrance to his container, watching. Berlin yanked the purple plastic back into position behind her, and limped over.

'If you go near her, you'll be sorry,' she said.

He leant back, taking his weight on his hands, and squinted up at her.

'Who the fuck are you?' he responded gruffly. 'The fucking social?'

'No. I don't have their scruples,' she said. 'So if you want to crawl out of here without kneecaps, you're going the right way about it.'

'What's it to you?' he said.

She stood up and took a step forwards. Her Peacekeeper boot came to rest firmly on the fingers of his left hand. He gasped and squirmed.

She had always worn knee-high Cossack-style boots. Then a man she realised too late was more than a friend had been blown away by a suicide bomber. All they found were his boots. Peacekeepers. Now she wore them too, and whenever she kicked someone or stomped on a sensitive part of their anatomy, she thought of him. It was a kind of homage.

'If I get back and the kid tells me you've been hassling her, I'll be crushing more than your fingers.'

Princess watched the exchange through her peephole with satisfaction. The ogre sucked his fingers as Berlin walked away. She was old, but she was different. People always raised an eyebrow or laughed when Princess told them her name, but she hadn't.

She said she'd be back and Princess believed her. *Anyway, she's got nowhere else to go*, she thought. *Just like me.*

29

It was apparent from the state of Sonja's room that things were going downhill. It had never been a palace, but the mess was a sign of growing desperation. Whatever she was using had run out. Berlin knew Sonja would have to score. Even if it was talcum powder and speed.

Now Sonja sat on the edge of the bed, arms wrapped around her thin body, self-protective.

Berlin stood over her. She'd used the front door instead of coming in through the window. The old bag had clocked her but Berlin couldn't care less. She was going to extricate herself from this business before it got any messier.

'What the fuck, Sonja?' she said. 'You drag me into this with some bullshit story and say Cole is out of the picture. Then his mates beat you up because he's gone missing. Now I find out he's dead.'

'Who told you that?' whispered Sonja.

It was the only confirmation Berlin needed.

'Tell me the truth or I'm going to the cops,' she said, and meant it.

'You've found her, haven't you? Where is she? Why haven't you brought her home?' asked Sonja.

'For Christ's sake,' said Berlin, pacing. 'What the hell's going on here? Just for once be straight with me.'

'Where is she?' demanded Sonja.

'Why didn't you just say Cole was dead?' retorted Berlin. 'God knows the world's a better place without him, so why all this crap about him being long gone?'

'Did Princess tell you he was dead? I told you she makes stuff up all the time. It's not true. Why would I lie?'

But it was too late for her to backtrack now, and Berlin could see Sonja knew it. She stopped pacing and got in Sonja's face.

'I don't know. You tell me,' Berlin said.

'She said it, didn't she?' said Sonja.

'I'm going to the police unless I get the truth,' said Berlin.

'You wouldn't do that. They'd take her away from me and put her in one of those homes.'

'You're confusing me with a bleeding social worker,' snapped Berlin.

'She'd be abused!' said Sonja.

'And what do you think is happening to her here, you worthless fucking junkie?' said Berlin, her attempt at self-control deserting her. 'For the last time, is Cole dead?'

'Yes,' said Sonja quietly.

Berlin shook her head in disbelief.

'So why not just say so?' she said.

Above them a jet roared, soaring into clean, cool skies. The rumble died into an empty silence.

'Because I killed him. I fucking killed him,' said Sonja.

They sat either side of the small table and drank strong, sweet tea from chipped mugs. Sonja kept staring at an old piece of carpet, purporting to be a rug, near the sink. Berlin got up and kicked it aside. A dark, irregular patch stained the worn floorboards. She felt a heaviness in the pit of her stomach and was seized by the sensation she was sinking into a tight space that she would never escape.

'Jesus Christ, Sonja. Why?' she heard herself ask.

Sonja turned her back on Berlin and slipped off her T-shirt. Her thin shoulders were scored with deep welts that ran across her back. Some were a faded pink, old blows, and others were scarlet. Some were still weeping. A grid of pain.

Berlin's hand rose to the scars at her own throat.

'Princess was there. She saw everything,' said Berlin.

Sonja nodded. 'It had been going on for years,' she said. 'I just snapped. Grabbed a knife and stabbed him. I didn't mean to kill him. It happened so fast, there was so much blood. Then it was over.'

'What did you do with the body?' asked Berlin.

'One of those old cars out the back is ours,' said Sonja.

'You don't mean —' said Berlin. For a moment she could see Cole, still in the boot, liquefying in the heat.

'No. He's gone,' said Sonja.

Berlin didn't want to know where.

'Jesus, Sonja,' she muttered. Her hand went to her woolly hat. Her scalp was hot and itchy but that wasn't it. She touched the morphine caps stowed underneath it in the small Ziploc bag. Talismanic.

Sonja reached out and gripped Berlin's arm.

'What are you going to do? When are you going to bring Princess home? You won't turn me in, Cath, will you? You're not a grass.'

'This life, Sonja – the kid.' She tugged her arm away.

'I know!' said Sonja. 'Don't you think I want to get away from it? Get clean, do something right for Princess.'

Sonja's urgent tone didn't impress Berlin. 'Get clean?' she asked, sceptical.

'This is our chance, mine and Princess's, to get away from this shit once and for all,' said Sonja. 'I couldn't do it while Cole was around. He would never let us go. But now it's different. We have to get away from here, from this dump, from London, from the blokes looking for him.'

Berlin picked up her tea and drank it down, longing for something stronger.

'He owes them money and they won't stop,' said Sonja. 'If I tell them he's dead they'll want to turn me out to cover the debt. I'm too old to go on the street.'

Berlin nudged the carpet back into place with the toe of her boot.

'You'll help me, won't you, Cath?' pleaded Sonja. 'For the kid's sake, not mine.'

'Give me the car keys,' said Berlin.

30

Berlin was too preoccupied to pay attention to the police car outside her block of flats as she drove past looking for a parking space. It was hardly unusual in Bethnal Green. The sound of sirens was a perpetual melody against the traffic drone: urban muzak.

She needed to get home, take a cap and try to come up with a sensible plan to address the various messes she had created by failing to mind her own business.

Not the least was what to do about the murder of Kylie Steyne. She really wanted to speak to the brother before she went to the police, but in all conscience she couldn't leave it any longer. She would pick up Parr's licence and family photo and go straight to the station as soon as she had sorted Princess.

That she was about to embark on a criminal conspiracy to conceal another murder seemed almost trivial. She didn't want to see Cole's demise come to light. If Sonja went down, the kid would suffer.

Sonja could probably get away with manslaughter: loss of control or self-defence. The scars on her back would bolster her case. On the other hand she was a junkie, she had disposed of the body, and only Princess could say whether Sonja had really been in fear for her life when she stabbed Cole.

Berlin would bet London to a brick that Sonja would do time, and then it would be straight into care for Princess. The kid's life would be even more of a bloody disaster if that happened.

One thing was certain. She couldn't leave Princess in that battered shipping container another night; she had to go back there and somehow get her to a safe place.

Sonja had lost it after Berlin announced she wasn't going to bring Princess straight home. She only calmed down when Berlin described what would happen if Princess kicked off in the street as Berlin dragged her back to her mother: someone would call the cops. The last thing Sonja wanted.

The kid needed time to accept what had happened. That might be a challenge. What effect would it have on a child to see her mother kill her father? Even if she hated him, would that make it any easier to deal with? No matter how tough she was, a ten-year-old would find a load like that difficult to carry.

Adults were often compelled to unburden themselves, against all self-interest. The whispered secret inside the kid could become a roar. If the kid needed to talk about it, she could choose badly, confiding in some low-life at Love Motel who might exploit the situation. Which was another good reason to get her out of there, fast. The warning to the ogre would last only as long as the daylight.

Berlin thought about her own dad. The conversations he and her mother conducted in low, strained voices, that she would struggle to decode. The times she witnessed exchanges with his 'associates' that he implored her not to mention to her mother. But it was no time to go there. Her feelings about her father were a quagmire. She had to focus on the job at hand.

She had told Sonja she would stow Princess in a safe place, but she had no idea where. How many people did she know who could be trusted to care for a kid and watch her twenty-four seven? It would be a very short list.

She also had to figure out what she was going to do with Princess and Sonja once they were reunited. They'd have to be well out of the reach of the authorities, Cole's thuggish associates and Sonja's heroin connections. Which meant far, far away. Abroad. A two-week package on the Costa del Sol wouldn't cut it.

If Sonja was serious about getting clean, it would take time and money. Berlin had neither.

How the hell had this become her problem?

She had to park well down the road and walk back to the flats. The door of the police car opened as she passed. The kids in the street stopped kicking the ball to watch.

'Excuse me,' said an officer, putting on his cap. Berlin stopped. She noticed he was a sergeant.

She also noticed that his offsider, who got out of the other side of the vehicle, was a very young Police and Community Support

Officer. Her uniform was so new it squeaked when she moved. The more cynical warranted officers in the Met sometimes referred to PCSOs as chimps: can't help in most police situations.

'You need to come with me. Us,' said the sergeant.

'What?' said Berlin.

'You're under arrest. Don't give us any trouble,' he said, although she hadn't moved a muscle.

'What for?' asked Berlin, stunned.

'Stalking,' said the sergeant.

The door of a nearby van slid open and a woman got out.

'Yes,' said Mrs Demir. 'That's her.'

Berlin stared.

Murat was in the driver's seat.

At the station, Berlin deployed her sharpest legal argument.

'This is bullshit.'

The weary, grizzled old constable rolled Berlin's fingers across the scanner and sighed. It was clear he agreed.

It was also clear that Murat had pull with the arresting officer. No doubt Berlin wasn't the only one being paid off by a member of the Demir family, although a sergeant wouldn't come as cheaply as she did.

He hadn't been remotely interested in the fact that Mr Demir was employing Berlin to watch his wife, and, of course, she didn't have a contract to back up her claim.

'I'll be glad to retire,' said the constable. 'How we get involved in this sort of rubbish I'll never know.'

Although she suspected he did. There was at least one rotten apple in every station and everyone always knew who it was, although no one did anything about it. You kept your mouth shut and held the line, which was already stretched to breaking point.

Sweat ran down the constable's forehead and disappeared into his bushy grey eyebrows. The air conditioning had broken down and there was a two-week wait for the contractor.

Berlin overheard someone say the traffic boys were looking for an air-conditioning mechanic to pull over for a minor offence. Which would turn into a big one if he didn't fix the station system quick smart.

'It's a civil matter, if you ask me,' grumbled the constable. 'Do you want a cuppa?'

'How about a nice cold lager?' suggested Berlin.

He smiled.

'Come on, love, we'll get you signed out.'

The constable steered her down a corridor towards a secure door with a wire-reinforced aperture. Before they reached it, the locking mechanism clicked and a bloke walked through. As they approached he politely held the door open.

Berlin had to exercise every ounce of self-restraint as she walked past. It was one of the thugs she had seen at Sonja's. The skinny one with the glasses.

'Thank you,' she muttered, eyes averted. She felt his breath on her cheek as she squeezed past.

'How are you, Jack?' he said to the constable.

'Very well, thank you, Detective Kennedy,' responded her escort, rather coolly, as he followed her through.

Sonja had conveniently forgotten to mention that the blokes looking for Cole were cops. No wonder she didn't want the police involved in the hunt for Princess.

Berlin had recognised the detective, but there was no reason he would recognise her.

The door clicked shut behind them and she relaxed.

Kennedy felt a surge of optimism at his new prospects; he took off his glasses and cleaned them, patted his knee to calm the tremor and considered his options. He had wondered whether he could believe

Sonja's story, that the limping woman was an old friend with a habit: a professional investigator she had asked to find her runaway daughter.

When pressed, Sonja admitted that the kid had taken off after a parental punch-up during which Cole had given Sonja a good belting. According to Sonja, Cole went after the kid and never came back.

Naturally, he had taken the recent shipment of heroin with him.

Sonja thought Cole could be worried that the authorities would pick up the kid and the police would get involved. He might also fear she would report Princess missing and tell them why she had run away. It would be the first thing any mother would do.

In any event, Cole hadn't come home and the chances were that he wouldn't if he thought the place was under surveillance.

Which it was. Of a kind.

This was the first time Sonja had provided an explanation for Cole's disappearance, and it made sense. Sort of. But something about it didn't quite ring true: the part about Cole being concerned that Sonja would go to the police to report the domestic violence or Princess running away. It seemed unlikely that she would report it, or that Cole would think she might, given their proclivities and criminal histories. She'd never reported him before.

And they were already 'involved' with a police operation. Of a kind.

But the kid was a different story. Kennedy thought it was more likely that Princess had scarpered after Cole had belted her, not Sonja, and that Sonja was afraid the kid might be taken away if child protection got wind of it.

Which it would if Kennedy had anything to do with it. He'd made a few observations about the environment Princess was exposed to when the kid had been around during previous visits, but Cole and Sonja had seemed oblivious. Typical junkies.

Apart from that, Sonja's story was plausible. Princess had run away, Cole had gone after her, and neither had come back. So Sonja had someone out looking for her. A maternal instinct, of a sort, had finally surfaced.

Now he had the limping woman within reach. Time to step up.

The door of the Community Response Sergeant's office was ajar. Kennedy gave it a perfunctory knock and entered.

Sergeant Harvinder Pannu sat behind his desk briefing two of his PCSOs. The gist of it was that a Darby and Joan in their nineties were being harassed by vandals, whose latest trick had been to turn on the garden tap and shove the hose under the back door, flooding the kitchen.

'All right. Off you go, and sort it,' said Pannu.

His charges left with enthusiasm. They'd been assigned the crime of the century.

Pannu turned his attention to Kennedy.

'What can I do for you, Detective?' he asked.

'How's business, Pannu?' asked Kennedy with a grin.

'What can I tell you?' said Pannu. 'We're failing to stem the tidal wave of crime that's sweeping the capital.'

It was a recent quote from an editorial in one of the broadsheets.

'Diversification is the key to survival,' said Kennedy.

'How do you mean?' asked Pannu, suspicious.

Kennedy laid a business card on the desk. It was embossed with the words 'London Superior Systems'.

Pannu got up and closed his door.

'What's your problem, Kennedy?' asked Pannu. 'One in ten Met officers has got a second job. It was in the paper.'

'Yeah,' said Kennedy. 'And that's just those that appear in the register of police business interests.'

Pannu didn't sit down again.

'I applaud enterprise, Pannu. This country needs more of it,' said Kennedy. 'There must be a great – what do they call it – synergy between your day job and this little outfit.' He tapped the business card. 'I understand you offer the best after-sales service available.'

'What do you want?' said Pannu.

31

The queue at the custody desk moved slowly. When she finally got out, Berlin left the station as fast as her leg would allow, clutching the documents that demanded she appear at the Thames Magistrates Court the next day. She could ask for an adjournment, but she had to attend or they could issue a bench warrant.

Before she was even five yards from the station a van pulled up sharply beside her. Berlin took an involuntary step back as she recognised the driver. But when he beckoned it was clear there wasn't much point arguing. She got in.

Detective Sergeant Kennedy formally introduced himself and informed her that he wasn't interested in the stalking matter. He drove away from the station at speed, while making the point that he had nothing to do with the sergeant who had arrested her. He was investigating the murder of Kylie Steyne, and had recognised Berlin from Billy Steyne's description.

Twig. The scarring had given her away.

Billy had given him a pretty good idea of what went on that night and her role in it.

Berlin said as little as possible as Kennedy rattled on. He was nervous, which meant he was playing out of school.

She glanced over her shoulder at the rear of the van and confirmed her impression that it was set up for surveillance. It occurred to her that she had been overly confident at the station; perhaps he had seen her at Sonja's.

She shivered despite the heat. The sergeant who had arrested her, and from whom Kennedy was at such pains to distance himself, had confiscated her morphine caps. He had refused to return them until he'd made 'proper enquiries', even though it would only take a quick call to Rolfey. Murat Demir wanted to put the squeeze on her and she was powerless to squeeze back.

Now she was taking a ride with one of the men who had roughed up Sonja.

'Who was he, the paedophile in the alley?' asked Kennedy, as the van took a sharp corner. He seemed keen to put distance between them and the station.

'A family man. I kept his driving licence and a picture of his kids. They're at my flat.'

'If you broke his arm he would have had a problem strangling the girl,' said Kennedy. 'Although I suppose it's possible. A bloke could knock her out with one blow and choke her with one hand. But it seems very unlikely. He would have been in agony.'

Berlin didn't respond. She had to agree.

'Which leaves you as one of the last people to have seen her alive,' said Kennedy.

'Why aren't we doing this at the station?' she asked. 'I came in yesterday to report my involvement, as soon as I heard about the girl found by the canal. You can check the waiting room CCTV tapes.'

'I will,' said Kennedy. 'But there's no statement on record, is there?'

'I had to leave. There was a long wait and . . . I had other commitments.'

Kennedy gave her a look. She waited for him to ask what was more important than reporting information that might catch a child's murderer. But he didn't.

'So why aren't we at the station?' she demanded.

He softened his tone. 'Look, it was the end of my shift, all right? I could have been stuck there for god knows how long waiting for your brief or a free interview room. We can take a formal statement another time.'

Berlin didn't buy it. He was a nervy type who didn't really have the swagger that accompanied corruption. He wasn't used to playing the heavy. That was Fatty's role.

The streetlights flickered into life. Twilight was fading and she had to get back to Princess. She tried to put it together, searching for an angle that would help her get out of Kennedy's clutches, fast.

Cole's violent cronies were policemen. For obvious reasons Sonja didn't want to tell them he was dead. Kennedy and his mate were letting Cole stay in business for a slice of the action. But now Cole had gone missing and they thought he was doing the dirty on them.

A loud horn behind them made her jump. Kennedy jumped too and when he looked in the rear-vision mirror she saw him blanch. He pulled over.

'What the fuck are you playing at, mate?' demanded Bertie.

'What the fuck are you doing following me?' said Kennedy. He glanced up and down the road, acutely aware of the interest that two grown men having a spat might attract. It wasn't like Bertie to make a scene and create unnecessary risks.

'Are you trying to avoid me, Grant?' said Bertie.

'Of course not,' said Kennedy.

'Jack told me he saw you pick up some woman outside the station,' said Bertie. 'You took off pretty fast. Who is she?'

Kennedy could see Berlin watching them from the van. He went on the offensive.

'I have to do my day job, you know. She's a witness in the Steyne case.'

'Jack said she was a stalker,' Bertie said, grabbing his arm.

Always one fucking step ahead, thought Kennedy.

'That's just some crap dreamt up by Pannu. Doing a favour for one of his extracurricular clients. Some domestic bullshit. She's a private investigator,' said Kennedy.

'So why aren't you interviewing her at the station?' shouted Bertie.

Kennedy had to placate him, and quick. The last thing they needed was someone calling the police. He lowered his voice, conspiratorially. 'Sonja's kid is missing, did you know that?'

Bertie frowned.

Kennedy indicated Berlin. 'She's been looking for the kid at Sonja's behest.'

'Why did you say she was a witness in the Steyne murder then?' asked Bertie.

Kennedy knew there was no point bullshitting. The heat might be getting to Bertie, but it hadn't shrunk his brain.

'Because she is. She doesn't know that I'm anything to do with Sonja or Cole.'

He could see Bertie processing it.

'You think Cole took the kid as insurance against Sonja telling us where he is?' he said.

'It's possible,' said Kennedy.

'Find the kid and you'll find the dad,' mused Bertie. 'Yeah.'

Kennedy nodded. 'What's more,' he said. 'I think this woman knows where the kid is, but she's not saying.' He drove home his advantage. 'So just let me work on her, Bertie.'

'How are you going to get her to give it up?' asked Bertie, more respectful now.

Kennedy smiled.

'I'm taking her for a drive,' he said.

Bertie licked his lips. 'I'll come with you,' he said.

Kennedy gave the fat fingers clenching his arm a friendly pat.

'Leave it to me, mate. You've done more than your fair share lately.' He winked, trying to maintain an air of confidence.

'I suppose you're right, mate,' said Bertie. Then added with a sigh of envy, 'Enjoy yourself then.'

It was stifling in Kennedy's van. Dogs and infants were dying all over London as their owners left them in locked cars to cook while they did the shopping or played bingo in air-conditioned comfort.

Berlin swore. This couldn't have happened at a worse time. She had to get to Princess before her warning to the predatory vagrant wore off. Lengthy jail term and beatings from other inmates didn't deter paedophiles, so the effect of a few crushed fingers would be transitory.

Kennedy seemed relieved when he got back in the van after his altercation with Fatty. He slammed the vehicle into gear and pulled out into the traffic. She'd tried to hear what they were arguing about – she was clearly a topic of conversation – but couldn't catch it.

'Is he your boss?' she asked.

'Bertie?' said Kennedy. 'Not any more. But he's having trouble adjusting to the new arrangements.'

He reached into his jacket pocket, brought out the Ziploc bag of morphine capsules and tossed it to her.

She was astonished.

'Call it a token of good faith,' he said. 'You're going to have to trust me.'

Hell will freeze over first, thought Berlin. Which was very unlikely in the current climate. The gesture was an assertion that he was in charge.

'Where are we going?' she asked.

'Your place,' said Kennedy. 'No need for directions.'

He had done his homework. She was relieved Sonja's car was parked well away from her flat in case it was familiar.

'You've been a registered heroin addict for over twenty years,' said Kennedy.

'That's a rather old-fashioned term,' she retorted.

'You've no criminal convictions though,' he continued. 'Which is a miracle considering the shit you've been involved in. And you're not a bad investigator.'

'So I passed the audition,' she said.

Kennedy's laugh was hollow.

32

The heat was killing Bertie and he couldn't wait to get inside. He loved going home.

He opened his front door and paused, waiting for her usual greeting to ring out: 'Did you bring my treats?' But it didn't come.

He glanced up the stairs. That's where she was. Reassured, he closed the front door behind him, switched on the light and plodded down the hallway.

The girth of DCI Maurice Burlington had expanded in direct proportion to his disappointment in life. It was substantial.

He had been called Bertie from birth, and often wondered why his parents hadn't just christened him Albert in the first place. When he started school, the teacher read out the class register, and all the little Johns and Marys had dutifully answered 'Here, miss'. When she called 'Maurice' he had remained silent, in complete ignorance of his proper name.

'Aren't you Maurice?' asked the teacher.

'No, miss, I'm Bertie. Bertie Burlington,' he had replied, in all innocence.

The rest of the class had burst out laughing and the teacher had given him a clip round the ear for being cheeky. The incident had set the tone for his school days.

Bertie was the horrid fat boy in every playground. Too big to belt, a bully, shunned by all. He was destined to become a copper.

His dad, a bus driver, had died of a heart attack when Bertie was eleven, and his mum had clung to him, and he to her, for the next thirty years. When he got teary or lonely, she gave him some of her pills. They shared everything.

Although he had opened all the windows the oppressive, putrid air hung about him, a thick, sticky blanket. The stench was overwhelming. The heat obliged him to use talcum powder to prevent his sweaty skin becoming inflamed. He hated the talc because it seemed girly, but like so many things it had become a necessary evil.

He stripped off and dropped his clothes on the floor. He'd tidy up after his soother. He wasn't a slob. He kept the house neat, the way she liked it, and the cupboards well stocked with their favourite snacks and biscuits.

Bertie tightened the belt around his arm. The drought was a worry, but he had a bit put by for rainy days. The incongruity of the thought made him chuckle as the needle pierced his flesh. Bliss flooded his brain and a quiet confidence dispelled the anxiety about the recent disruption to his arrangements.

The natural order would be restored, and he would be on top. Just the way Mum liked it.

33

Berlin went straight to the shelf, removed the creep's driving licence and family photo from the book where they were hidden, and handed them to Kennedy.

But he didn't leave. He sat down at the table, his right knee working like a piston.

'Derek Parr,' he read from the licence.

She remained standing and checked out his shoes. Was it his trainer that had left its mark on Sonja's face? His Nikes were old, probably knock-offs, and the soles lacked tread. They were worn and thin. Just like him.

'Will you make a sworn statement?' he asked her.

'Of course,' she said.

'Even though you were carrying an offensive weapon and committed grievous bodily harm?' he said.

'Who's going to charge me?' she said. 'You?'

It was clear he wanted her cooperation. This wasn't going on the record, that much was obvious. 'If he's charged with anything, he'll plead to it, rather than risk publicity,' she said. 'He wouldn't want to see me in court.'

Kennedy brought out his notebook and flicked through it, looking for the page he wanted. 'You should have broken his neck, not just his arm,' he said. 'But we won't be looking at him for her murder. After Billy told me his story I checked the crime reports for that night.' He pointed to a name in the notebook. 'There was one report that fit the bill. It was made by a bloke who alleged he was mugged near Liverpool Street station by a young black man. The complainant was your Mr Parr.'

She contemplated the misfortune of being young, male and black in Britain. A soft target.

Kennedy slipped his notebook back into his pocket with Parr's licence and the photo. She could hardly object.

'He spent the rest of that night in A & E,' continued Kennedy. 'I talked to the hospital. He sat there for four hours before he was seen by a doctor for a fractured ulna. CCTV will verify it. He didn't have time to kill Kylie, or the two-handed grip used to strangle her. It's NFA on Mr Parr.'

No further action. A phrase she was familiar with.

'I'd like to speak to her brother,' she said.

Kennedy didn't respond.

'I feel, I don't know . . . responsible somehow,' she said.

Kennedy looked at her for a long moment. 'Billy says his sister had the money you "confiscated" from Parr. How much?' he asked, not sparing her feelings.

'About five hundred,' she mumbled.

Kennedy made a small noise of disgust. 'That kind of cash. Word would have spread fast if she was after drugs.'

Berlin nodded. She'd already come to that conclusion herself, and it didn't make her feel any better.

'Billy thinks she might have gone to the Halal Southern Fried Chicken place in Brick Lane,' said Kennedy. 'Apparently she loved their spicy mix. A lot of street kids hang around there. They beg from City types who are slumming it after they've had a skinful.' He sighed. 'They love throwing chicken legs in the air and watching the kids fight over them. The pavement is thick with tiny bones.'

There was an awkward silence as they both contemplated the image. Kennedy was genuinely appalled. He was not the hardened cynic she expected.

'The cash was well gone when we found her,' he said. 'And there wasn't any sign of chicken in her stomach. She was fourteen. Ain't life grand?'

At last he stood up. Berlin went to the front door and opened it.

'Billy's at the shelter in Westminster,' he said, and walked out.

34

Billy shuffled into the common room, which was deserted because it was so stuffy, and sat down on the threadbare, rickety sofa next to Berlin. She couldn't help thinking of him as Twig.

'Got a smoke?' he asked, without making eye contact.

'Do you remember me?' said Berlin.

Billy nodded.

'Come on, then. You can't smoke in here,' said Berlin, standing up.

She hadn't relished the idea of driving about in a vehicle that was practically a crime scene, but she didn't have much choice. She needed to move fast in case Billy was moved, or just disappeared onto the street. Then she had to get back to Princess.

Billy dutifully shuffled after her and out onto the concrete steps at the front of the building, where they joined other sleepless residents, smoking, drinking or just escaping the stifling heat inside for the heat and traffic fumes outside.

Berlin never went to a hostel or a prison without a pack of cigarettes. She thought it was a disgusting habit, but then some people took the same view of heroin.

'I'm sorry for your loss,' she said as she handed him a smoke.

'Yeah, thanks.'

'How are you doing?' she asked, reigning in her impulse to get straight to the point. She couldn't afford to get Billy offside.

'They've got me on all these zombie drugs,' he said. His hands trembled as he lit the cigarette.

Berlin nodded. *And you were so alert before,* she thought.

'They're trying to put me on methadone,' he said. 'That stuff's horrible.'

Berlin had to agree. But she was on a tight timeframe here and in no position to discuss the merits of opiate substitutes. She asked the question that she knew he wouldn't answer if asked by a policeman. He wouldn't burn someone he might need one day.

'Who was the dealer, Billy? The dealer she went to buy from that night,' she asked.

'Dunno, miss, honest,' he said.

'Come on, you can tell me. I'm looking for a connection.'

Billy looked nervous.

'Really?' he asked.

She nodded.

He looked her up and down. She was still wearing the rough sleeper outfit she'd donned for Love Motel. It wouldn't hurt her credibility.

'Did she always buy for you?' she said.

'She looked after me, miss.'

Tears began to dribble down his cheeks, quickly joined by a long string of snot.

'You're not gonna hit me, miss, with that stick?'

She realised he meant the Asp.

'No. No, of course not. Look, Billy, I want the shithead who did this as much as you do.' She said it with a vehemence even he could recognise.

'I'm sorry, miss. The thing is, I dunno where she tried to score. It couldn't have been the usual bloke, he's got nothin'. I dunno where she went or who she saw, but she just never came back.'

He began to cry in earnest. She wasn't going to get anything else out of him, so she stood up and dropped the pack of cigarettes in his lap.

'Thank you, miss,' he said and began to sob.

Berlin was about to leave.

'That's cold,' she heard someone mutter.

She sat down again and put an arm around Billy's shoulder. He collapsed into her. She patted him.

'It will be all right,' she said. They both knew it was a lie.

'She looked after me, miss. Who'll look after me now?'

Berlin remained silent. *Typical junkie,* she thought. *His sister has been choked to death but it's all about him.*

'Who looks after you, miss? Where do you get your gear?' asked Billy.

You sly little bugger. The question hung out there. He was clinging to her.

'Billy, I'm sorry, I've got to go,' she said, trying to gently extricate herself.

Billy's expression turned from pitiful to malevolent in a flash.

'Fuck off then. You're just like everyone else. Everyone's got someone to look after them except me.'

Berlin caught hold of his wrists, sensing that any minute he might clobber her.

'I look after myself, Billy. Now you're going to have to do the same instead of pimping your little sister.'

'Liar! You're a fucking liar. What about that bloke?'

'What bloke?'

'The bloke who was with you,' shouted Billy, struggling to free himself from her grasp.

'What are you going on about? I haven't got a bloke, for god's sake.' Berlin tried to keep it down, acutely aware of the growing interest of the other residents.

It was pointless. Billy was apoplectic.

'Bull-fucking-shit! He was there, I saw him. We both did. He was watching your back the whole time. Let me go, you bitch.'

She released his wrists and stepped away, but Billy was on a roll.

'You think you're so tough but he was there to protect you. You and him, you were in it together. You fucking killed Kylie!'

35

Twig hadn't given her a description apart from 'just some bloke', who he said was hanging back in the shadows watching her that night.

There was nothing she could do to follow that up right now; the ogre's confidence would grow with every moment Princess spent alone. When he finally made a serious move a sharp spike wouldn't keep him at bay.

Berlin knew there could be a problem if Princess recognised the car, but it was a risk she had to take to get the kid out fast.

At that time of night the traffic wasn't too bad heading away from central London. She drove down Grove Road, through Mile End to Stepney, then veered right at East India Dock Road. At Canning Town she took the fourth exit onto Silvertown Way.

In the distance the soaring towers of docklands glimmered: banks, investment houses, financiers. Masters of the universe who strode across the landscape, never gazing down at the destruction they wrought.

The price of bailing out the strongest had been paid by the weakest. *We haven't come far from the days of baronial tithes extracted from poor tenants*, thought Berlin, as she pulled up near the yard.

From the road, the giant, rusty boxes gave no hint of the misery they contained. Out of sight, out of mind.

Sparks drifted up from the pit of a forty-four-gallon drum and again Berlin was assailed by the smell of frying. When had she last eaten? The food in the battered pans had probably been rescued from bins at the back of supermarkets and restaurants, but she knew that real hunger beats squeamishness any day.

People were huddled around their camping stoves, backs to the yard. Privacy was a need in even the most deprived circumstances.

The atmosphere was subdued tonight, apart from the usual distant singing.

She wound her way through the labyrinth to the row of containers where Princess was hiding. The purple plastic was still drawn across the entrance. A good sign.

She tapped on it and glanced over her shoulder.

The ogre's eyes glinted. He was watching.

'What?' said Princess. Not who.

'It's me,' said Berlin.

The plastic slid open.

Princess devoured the chocolate bars Berlin had brought.

'It's too dangerous here,' Berlin said.

'It's as safe as anywhere else,' said Princess, through a mouthful of chocolate. 'I can handle him,' she added, meaning the ogre.

Berlin tried another tack.

'It's overdue for a raid,' she said.

Princess stopped chewing and focused.

'Why would the cops come here?' she asked.

Berlin was taken aback by the sudden hard edge. The police were a foe to be taken seriously.

'I should think there would be more than a few people here

with outstanding warrants. It would improve the cops clear-up rate without too much effort.'

Princess pondered this.

'Yeah, but where can we go?'

Berlin felt a surge of optimism at her use of the word 'we'. Maybe they could just walk out of here together.

'Couldn't we try your mum's?' said Berlin, keeping it low-key.

'No,' said Princess.

'Why not?'

Princess looked away. The subject was closed.

'Okay,' said Berlin. 'Let's just go. I know a place. If you don't like it, we can always come back here.'

A noise outside attracted their attention. Princess put her finger to her lips, commanding silence.

Suddenly there was a loud crack and the air was filled with shards of purple plastic. The ogre filled the gap.

'She's not going anywhere,' he said.

Berlin saw Princess whip the sharpened spike out of the waistband of her jeans and run straight at the ogre with a bloodthirsty war cry. Her intent was plain.

Unsure who she was saving from whom, Berlin launched herself between them and felled the ogre with a tackle that jammed them both in the narrow gap.

She felt Princess scramble over her back as she struggled to hold the ogre down. The close quarters didn't allow for any punches to be thrown, which was just as well, as he was strong. They tussled, his hands gripping her shoulders, trying to shove her off.

She used her boot for leverage and felt it connect with something soft. He grunted and relaxed his grip for a moment, which gave her a chance to scramble to her feet and take off as fast as she could manage.

A small figure darted out from between two containers.

'Come on, this way,' hissed Princess, grabbing her hand. They fled down the narrow passages, deeper into the dark warren.

In the distance, Berlin heard the whump of a muted explosion. A dull orange glare briefly illuminated the slit of sky above them.

She had stumbled into a war zone, but had no idea how to identify the enemy.

36

Rita always enjoyed her chats with Mr B. He brought her a decent class of spirits and didn't try to fob her off with that supermarket-brand stuff. She had a mature palate and Mr B respected that.

'She only ever goes as far as the petrol station. Fading away she is. There wasn't much of her in the first place,' said Rita. 'She's had the odd visitor, if you take my meaning, Mr B. Lorry drivers, probably. Cash in hand, I should imagine.'

'What about the kid, Reet? Seen the kid about?'

'Not since that night. She shot out of here, like I told you. Not seen the cheeky little bugger since,' said Rita.

'Who went after her?'

'How do you mean?'

'Did anyone chase after her? Mum? Dad?'

Rita shook her head.

'I should think they were glad to see the back of her. Nothing but trouble.'

Bertie reached into his pocket, unfolded a sheet of paper and handed it to her.

'Ever see her around?' he enquired.

Rita peered at the printout from the police computer. She picked up her reading glasses and took a closer look. Above a set of finger-prints was a digital headshot of Limping Woman, glowering.

Rita took off her glasses.

'No,' she said.

'Are you sure, Rita?' said Bertie.

'On my life, Mr B.'

It was too much, too soon, and Rita knew it the moment it was out of her mouth.

Bertie's fist smacked into her temple and knocked her off her chair and onto the floor. Dizzy, ears ringing, Rita tried to crawl under the table, but Bertie grabbed her by the ankles and yanked her out.

'Let's try that again,' said Bertie, snatching up the printout from the floor. 'Have you ever seen this woman around here? Is she one of Sonja's visitors?'

Rita nodded. 'He told me not to say,' she said.

'Who? Kennedy?'

She nodded again.

'And that's another thing you forgot to tell me about. His special visits.'

Rita knew it didn't matter what she said now, she was in for it. She knew that look in a man's eye. Someone was going to cop it. It was going to be her.

'You take orders from me, Rita, not him. Understand?'

He reinforced the message with a backhander.

Rita's teeth flew out of her mouth. Her tears mingled with the blood pouring from her nose. She didn't know what CHIS stood for, but she knew what it meant. There was another word for it in her world, and it wasn't very complimentary. Deep down she wasn't surprised it had come to this.

It was just that the pension didn't go far these days.

'I'm sorry,' was all she could manage, 'I'm sor—'

Outside the door, Sonja heard Rita's apology cut short by a series of short, sharp smacks. The stupid old bag should know better. Grassing for those bastards, as well as playing footsie with one behind the other one's back.

She wasn't going to hang around to be next on Bertie's visiting list. On the other hand, she wasn't supposed to leave the room at night.

A moan from Rita helped Sonja make up her mind.

She tiptoed out of the front door and made for the petrol station. The bloke there was okay. He'd let her hang about for a bit if she bought a Pot Noodle. She had to eat, didn't she?

37

'You're bleeding.' Princess touched her own neck, indicating the spot.

Berlin put her fingers to the place beneath her jaw. It had been difficult to graft there because of the constant movement. Her hand came away bloody. The collar of her coat was soaked. The scar tissue, already stretched thin, had split during her scuffle with the ogre.

There was a noise behind them. Someone was coming. Berlin felt woozy. She realised she could be losing a lot of blood and would be too weak to fend him off. She put her hand on Princess's shoulder for support and they took off, Berlin in her awkward fashion, the child jogging just in front of her.

They made it to the last row of containers at the edge of the yard, where the security lights created pockets of illumination. She no longer cared if Princess recognised the car. If she had to flatten the kid to get her into the vehicle she would do it. Whatever it took to get away from the fucking pervert.

They crawled through the container that opened onto the fence. Princess kicked the concrete post aside, they stepped through and hurried across the lumpy, barren wasteland.

Berlin stumbled forwards, blinking to clear her vision. She could see a dull orange glow in the distance. An acrid smell hung in the air. The unmistakable fumes of burnt vinyl and petrol. They slowed down as they approached the smouldering wreck.

Sonja's car was completely gutted, the buckled chrome still glowing from the intense heat of the fire.

Oh shit, thought Berlin. *At least all traces of Cole's body will be well and truly gone.*

And then she fainted.

33°C

38

Kennedy was woken by the buzz of the mobile under his pillow. It was a text message from Hurley: *Billy Steyne dead. Get yr arse down there & keep an i on it frm our end.*

Down the hall he could hear his little boy labouring to breathe. He crawled out of bed.

Berlin was woken by a bright light.

'Feeling better?' asked the nurse, directing a small torch beam into each of Berlin's blinking eyes.

The uniform was familiar. The Royal London Hospital. She touched her neck, which was bandaged.

'You were lucky,' said the nurse. 'After the transfusion they packed the wound with a special antibiotic gauze. You won't need more surgery.'

'How did I get here?'

'Your daughter called an ambulance.'

Berlin sat up and looked around. There was no sign of Princess.

'Don't worry. She wouldn't leave your bedside all night, but we persuaded her to go down to the canteen to get some breakfast. You owe me two quid.'

Berlin tried to get out of bed, but the nurse placed a firm hand on her chest and pushed her back, none too gently.

'If you're going to leave before a doctor signs you out, you're not doing it until I've gone,' she said. 'I've worked two straight shifts and I don't need the bloody grief.' She glanced at her watch.

'I'm off in fifteen minutes.'

The nurse left and Berlin tried to think through what had happened.

She needed to find the kid and get them both out of there before anyone started asking questions. She grabbed her phone, threw off the bedclothes and swung her legs out, then realised she was wearing only a white hospital gown. Before she could make another move, a smiling young man approached the bed.

'Hello,' he said. 'My name's Bryan. That's with a "y". I'm a social worker. I've had a word with your daughter. I understand the two of you have been sleeping rough.'

Bryan perched on the edge of the bed as if they were old friends, and opened his crisp new file. Behind him, at the other end of the ward, Princess peeked around the door.

Berlin could tell Princess had encountered the Bryans of the world before. The kid wasn't going to get any closer.

'Can we do this some other time?' asked Berlin.

Bryan frowned. 'There are some concerns we need to address – about your daughter's situation,' he said.

'Fine. I just need to go to the toilet,' she said.

'Oh, sorry. Yes, of course,' said Bryan. 'I'll be right here.'

Berlin had a vision of herself running through the hospital with her gown flapping open at the back, the escaping lunatic. But when she got out of the ward and turned into the corridor, Princess was standing beside the door marked Ladies clutching a neat, rolled bundle.

Berlin's cards, cash and front-door key were still tucked in her boot. She found her woolly hat rolled up in the other boot, but the Ziploc bag containing her morphine was gone. The paramedics would have handed it over when she was admitted. If she wanted to leave now, without a fuss and a lot of hassle, she would have to forget about it.

She dressed quickly, then they took the stairs and went out the back way, into the narrow street behind the old part of the hospital. Princess seemed familiar with the area.

Although Rolfey's clinic was nearby, Berlin doubted it would be open yet. Whatever they'd given her at the hospital was still working. Her pain was under control, but that was all. She would have to come back later.

First, she needed to stow Princess somewhere safe while she worked out how to persuade her that Sonja loved her, or at the very least, that she really wanted her to come home.

After that, she had to get Sonja and Princess out of the country before Kennedy and his obese partner realised Cole wasn't coming back and they were going to be permanently out of pocket. It would only be a matter of time before they began to wonder how he'd managed to drop out of sight so effectively.

She had never asked Sonja how she'd disposed of the body, but given the state she must have been in at the time, she probably hadn't done a great job. It was likely to be in the river, which meant Cole would surface eventually.

After the air-conditioned hospital the temperature on the street was oppressive, but Berlin kept her coat on and her collar turned up to hide the bandage around her neck. They were conspicuous enough: a scruffy woman wearing a dusty overcoat, jeans and boots, all black, during a heatwave, and a skinny kid with bleached hair.

'Where are we going?' asked Princess.

Berlin wasn't in the mood for twenty questions. They crossed Whitechapel Road and descended into the Underground. Nobody cared what you looked like down there, as long as you got out of their way.

Berlin grabbed Princess's hand so she didn't get lost in the crush and they fought their way onto a train.

'Berlin,' said Princess quietly.

Berlin looked down at her.

Princess was at eye-level with some unsuspecting bloke's back pocket. His wallet protruded. She wiggled her fingers and indicated Berlin should give him a bump while she lifted it.

Berlin glared at her and took hold of her free hand.

Princess shrugged. A missed opportunity.

Berlin sighed, despairing. The progeny of a violent drug dealer and battered junkie mother. Was it any wonder?

Rolfey had lain awake all night, and so arrived at the clinic early. There was already a queue on the concrete ramp. He unlocked the doors and deactivated the alarm. His patients shuffled in behind him.

He was fairly certain that Berlin hadn't seen him. But he'd seen her and Sonja's daughter legging it across Whitechapel Road. He had a feeling Berlin wouldn't be attending her usual appointment.

His instinct was to follow them, but he couldn't leave his patients waiting. Their desperation trumped his concern. When the receptionist arrived he told her to hold the first client.

He went into his office, shut the door and took out his mobile.

Sonja was woken by a relentless banging. She came around slowly, stiff and cold. The trill of her phone added to the racket. She stumbled to her feet and struggled to open the door.

She had fallen asleep in the petrol-station toilet. As she stepped out an irate lorry driver shoved her aside. 'Fucking junkie,' he said.

She bounced off the concrete wall and dropped her phone. It stopped ringing.

Rita's front door was closed. Sonja hesitated: was the nosy old cow lying in there bleeding to death? Not much else would keep her from sentry duty. Then she heard a muffled version of Rita's usual raucous voice. It sounded as if she was on the phone. So she was alive and conscious.

Sonja tiptoed away. She was tired and irritable, her mouth was dry, her lips were cracked and sore. She felt feverish, but it wasn't the flu.

She unlocked her door and slipped inside. A snarl greeted her. 'Where the bloody hell have you been?'

'Nowhere. The petrol station,' she said. Her back was to the door, but there was no point in running.

'Who have you been talking to?' came the demand.

'No one.'

The air was rank with menace.

'Give me your phone.'

39

Berlin rang the bell to avoid smudging the highly polished brass knocker. The windows of the neat corner terrace were clean, the net curtains spotless.

The door was opened by a woman who appeared to be on her way to an important appointment. Her grey hair was permed, she wore modest gold jewellery and her blouse was crisply pressed. Her bearing was erect, her lipstick fresh. She was old, but it was impossible to guess how old. That was the way she liked it.

She glanced at Berlin. 'Hello,' she said, then looked down at Princess. 'And who's this pretty fairy?'

'Princess,' said Princess.

'I'm Peggy. Do you like cakes?'

Princess seemed bewildered by this adult: she addressed her

as if she were a child, so Princess tried to act like one. 'I do like cakes, thank you,' she stuttered. Berlin thought the kid might curtsey.

'Well, you'd better come in then,' said Peggy, and extended her hand. Princess stared at it.

She looked up at Berlin, who shrugged.

Princess took Peggy's hand and the two of them walked off down the hallway.

'Hello,' said Berlin. 'My name's . . .'

'Shut the door behind you,' called Peggy.

Berlin sat on a stool, sipped her tea and watched Princess through a hatch that opened onto the dining room. She was staring at a jigsaw puzzle with wonder, as if she'd never seen one before. It occurred to Berlin that maybe she hadn't. What she would make of 'The Hay Wain' as it emerged from one thousand pieces Berlin could only imagine.

'Keeping busy?' said Peggy.

Berlin sighed. 'You?' she asked.

Peggy gave a hollow laugh. 'I'm not exactly rushed off my feet. It's not as if I have grandchildren to babysit.'

Berlin couldn't believe she was going to start on this so soon.

'Princess will cure you of that aspiration,' she said.

'I thought you were joking when you rang. Ten years old. Where are her parents?'

'Does it make any difference?' said Berlin. 'She needs a safe place and I can't watch her all the time. I've got some arrangements to make, and then I'll come back to get her. Okay?'

'Oh it's easy come, easy go with you. As always.'

'Can she stay or not?' said Berlin.

'What choice do you give me? She's an innocent child caught up in your shenanigans, I suppose,' said Peggy, looking pointedly at Berlin's attire. 'I can't let her suffer.'

'Oh, for Christ's sake,' said Berlin. 'My shenanigans, as you refer to them, happen to be how I make a living.' For a moment she thought better of it; it was a stupid idea. But she had to get going and there was no one else she could trust with the kid.

'Fine,' she said. 'Don't let her out of the house, and don't tell anyone you've got her.' Passing over the Battenburg and jam tarts, she grabbed a handful of chocolate bourbon biscuits and stuffed them in her pocket. 'And watch out, she's a bit . . . unpredictable.'

'Are you going to say goodbye to her?' asked Peggy.

Berlin slid the hatch closed and left the kitchen.

Princess looked up as she heard the front door shut.

'She had to go, but she'll be back for you soon. We're going to have a lovely time. Come with me,' said Peggy.

Princess followed her up the stairs to a landing with three doors.

'That's the bathroom,' she said. 'That's my room, and this is yours.'

She opened a door and ushered Princess inside. The single bed was crowded with teddy bears. Books and games were piled high on a bookshelf, and the walls were covered with old posters of pop stars and bands.

'Jimmy Page,' exclaimed Princess, pointing at a life-size poster in psychedelic colours.

She ran across the room, leapt onto the bed and played a wild air-guitar riff. 'Ladies and gentleman,' she screamed. 'Led Zeppelin! The greatest fucking rock band in the universe!'

The bears scattered.

40

Kennedy had a problem with dead children. They reminded him too much of the fragility of his own son. He didn't want to look at Billy Steyne's body; as wasted as it had been in life, it was even less substantial in death.

He returned to the front of the building, where the denizens of the shelter were lined up, ready for interview. The uniforms had taken the names of everyone who had seen Billy last night, and sorted out anyone who had something of value to say.

They were all of No Fixed Abode, so it was a matter of getting to them now, before they wandered off and joined the anonymous, transient mass of the London homeless.

Three detectives were sitting at makeshift tables, working their way through the standard questions. Kennedy was there as liaison. A different team would conduct the enquiries.

It wasn't even clear yet that the circs were suspicious, but given the recent death of his sister, the local team would treat it as such. If it was murder, you'd have to think the two were linked.

Kennedy listened at each table. The wits were all telling the same basic story: Billy was seen arguing with a woman. After that, no one remembered seeing him again. A profound sense of unease came over Kennedy as he listened to the witnesses describe her. When his mobile rang he answered, still preoccupied with what he had heard.

'Yeah?' he said, distracted.

'Khan here.' Khan was the Crime Scene Manager on the Kylie Steyne case. 'There's something from the scene you should take a look at.' Khan cleared his throat. 'Something that was missed the first time round,' he said, apologetic.

Kennedy wasn't surprised. The so-called experts had missed a body in the attic of a suspect a couple of months ago.

'Hurley's on his way,' said Khan.

'Okay. I have to have a word with someone first,' said Kennedy. 'I'll meet you at the lab.'

En route to Bethnal Green, Kennedy tried to estimate how long it would be before one of the detectives on Billy's case read the boy's statement about his sister's murder, and put his description of 'the nice lady' together with the descriptions of the woman seen arguing with him at the shelter last night.

Kennedy was the only point of contact between the two cases: he was the conduit, and in theory he should report the similarity of the descriptions immediately. Which was the last thing he was going to do. The problem was, it wouldn't take Einstein to go the extra mile and review the file on Kylie. Then the hunt for the unknown woman would get serious.

The first question would be why Kennedy didn't notice the 'co-incidence' of the two distinctive descriptions. The next question would be how exactly 'the nice lady' had found Billy.

The team would be busy for a while, tied up with the witnesses at the shelter. But sooner or later someone would put the two descriptions together, *if* Billy's post-mortem revealed evidence of foul play.

He died with a needle in his arm, and if the results didn't indicate violence, it would get written off as an accidental overdose. The brass would jump at the chance to pull the resources devoted to someone as insignificant as Billy.

It was all about politics, perception and the so-called public conversation. Law and order rhetoric was popular, but serious policing cost real money. Kennedy had to keep his fingers crossed that it wouldn't be spent on Billy Steyne.

It was callous, but if Berlin was picked up she might name

Kennedy as the source of her information about Billy's location. That would lead to questions about how Kennedy found her, and why he kept it quiet.

The whole fucking house of cards would come tumbling down. His and Bertie's connection to Cole and Sonja would be on the table. Berlin would do a deal. Self-preservation.

It would get ugly.

But right now no one knew who 'the nice lady' was. There was no connection except through Billy's statement. And poor Billy wouldn't be available to positively identify her.

Kennedy spotted a parking space and felt lucky. As long as Berlin's identity was his little secret, he was safe. Probably.

The wheezy bloke behind the counter looked anxious when Kennedy showed him his ID.

'Murat Demir?' he said.

Kennedy thought the poor man might have a heart attack on the spot. He gasped for breath and took three good pulls on his inhaler. Kennedy, who knew a bit about breathing difficulties, was alarmed.

'My son isn't here at the moment, officer,' Mr Demir wheezed between puffs.

A woman appeared from out the back, said something in Turkish and then spoke to Kennedy.

'I won't be a moment,' she said as she took the breathless man by the arm. He tried to wave her away, but she insisted on leading him out the back. 'I'm sorry,' she said to Kennedy. 'My husband's health is very fragile.'

'I understand, madam,' said Kennedy. He could hear her scolding Mr Demir in a low voice. In a moment she returned.

'How can I help you?' she said.

'Do you have any idea when your son will be home?'

She shrugged.

'Perhaps I could ask you then, Mrs Demir, very quickly, about your son's affidavit in this stalking matter? Which I understand involves yourself.'

'Affidavit?' she said.

'His statement. You both made statements concerning the alleged activities of Ms Catherine Berlin?'

Mrs Demir nodded. She glanced back at the beaded curtain through which she had steered her husband. Kennedy could hear his rasping breath.

'Your son's statement concerns her movements. Do you know how he came by this information?'

A change came over Mrs Demir.

'May I ask your connection to this matter, officer? I understood the sergeant at the station —'

Kennedy recognised the instinctive reaction of a mother whose child is threatened. She stood a little taller. Her jaw set.

He flashed his ID again.

'Detective Sergeant Kennedy, madam,' he said, emphasising detective. The public were generally under the impression that detectives were superior to uniforms, even when they were of the same rank.

'No,' she said. 'I don't know how he came by the information.'

It wasn't a hesitant or dilatory response. A customer entered and hovered behind Kennedy. Mrs Demir moved to one side so she could eyeball the customer and ignore Kennedy.

'Madam?' he said, ducking back into her line of sight.

'You will have to ask him yourself,' she said, and began serving the customer.

The conversation was over.

'Perhaps you could ask Murat to call me when he gets home?' he said, thrusting his card into her hand. 'I'm asking nicely. This time.'

*

The Thames Magistrates Court was a building redolent of sixties brutalism, but inside the chaos was pure twenty-first century.

The usher called Berlin's name for the third time, but it was lost in the din outside the courtroom: a dozen Chinese purveyors of 'Gucci' handbags were discussing plea options with a harassed lawyer; a bunch of police officers were arguing about the football; youths were milling about waiting to be sent back to the Children's Court, if they were lucky; and a clutch of junkies on minor possession charges paced and squabbled.

The scene was replicated outside each of the eight courts in the building.

The usher scored a line through Berlin's name and moved down to the next defendant on her list.

Berlin limped up the steps and into the waiting arms of the security guard, who obliged her to take off her dusty overcoat and undergo a pat down for weapons.

She was late, which meant she'd have to try to wheedle them into putting her back on later in the day. She was also aware that her current outfit wasn't going to do her any favours in court. She hadn't had time to go home and she certainly wasn't going to borrow anything of Peggy's.

The sullen clerk was as thick as the glass behind which he skulked. He mumbled that her case was to be heard in Court Two.

Berlin joined the throng and waited for the usher to emerge. When she appeared, flicking through a wad of documents, she began calling Chinese names in a thick Glaswegian accent.

'Chang Kai-shek, Lu Shao-chi, Hu Jintao, Wen Jiabao . . .'

Berlin thought one or two of the names sounded familiar. Pushing through the crowd she touched the usher on the shoulder as she turned to follow the line of famous Chinese politicians into court.

''Scuse me, miss,' said Berlin, adopting her best forelock-tugging, downtrodden underclass idiom. 'Did you call me? I was in the Ladies.' She affected a look of bewilderment.

'Name?' snapped the usher.

'Berlin.'

She flicked through her papers. 'Too late,' she said.

'Oh dear,' said Berlin.

'Are you going to plead guilty?'

'No,' said Berlin.

The usher sighed.

'I can put you back on today if you want to plead,' she said. 'It's a lot quicker and you'll get a better result than if you plead not guilty and end up being convicted.'

Berlin stared at her, suppressing the urge to suggest that making this recommendation wasn't really in her job description. This was British justice in an overburdened system. An usher could dish out cheap and cheerful legal advice in the service of efficiency.

'I'm innocent,' Berlin said.

'You'll be given another date. Ask at reception,' said the usher, and disappeared back into the courtroom.

Before the door swung shut behind her, Berlin heard a querulous voice demanding to know why nobody had booked an interpreter for Chang Kai-shek.

Murat put his mobile back in his suit pocket and offered Sergeant Pannu a cigarette, which he declined.

'Not on duty,' he said. 'Too many busybodies about.'

'Make sure you pick up an extra carton next time you're at the shop,' said Murat.

'Yeah, thanks,' said the sergeant. 'Very kind.'

Murat glanced around him. The pavement outside the Magistrate's Court on Bow Road was wide, but crowded. No one was paying them any attention. Another copper with his witness, waiting to be called.

'My mother tells me a detective has been at the shop,' said Murat.

The sergeant looked surprised. 'About this matter?'

Murat nodded.

The sergeant frowned. 'Kennedy,' he said.

'That's right,' said Murat. 'How did you know?'

'It's nothing to worry about,' he said.

'He was asking about the Berlin woman,' said Murat. 'Why would he be interested in her?'

'She's a junkie,' said the sergeant. 'When I arrested her she had a pocketful of morphine. Kennedy came to get it back. I couldn't say no because it was on prescription. She's his snout, he works a lot of drug cases. He has a vested interest in keeping her happy and on the street.'

'Can he interfere in this?' asked Murat, indicating the court behind them.

'Nah,' said the sergeant. 'Due process. They're not going to lock her up, in any event.'

'Oh,' said Murat. 'You never know your luck.'

41

Kennedy hurried down the corridor of the forensic unit. He hated the chemical smell that oozed from the walls of places like this. Morgues, labs and hospitals seemed to share the same odour. He thought he might be allergic.

He pushed open a pair of opaque plastic swing doors and was

greeted by a glare from Detective Chief Inspector Hurley.

'Sorry, boss. Traffic,' said Kennedy.

Khan hovered behind a bench spread with litter, mostly condoms and cigarette butts.

'You're looking at 72 square feet of rubbish from under the canal bridge,' said Khan. 'Useless.' He picked up a bagged item and offered it to Hurley. 'Apart from this.'

'What took so long?' asked Hurley.

Khan looked sheepish. 'Er . . . it was found in the second sweep.'

'The second?' said Hurley.

'The first team finished their shift, there was no overtime authorised for this job, so . . .'

'So everyone fucked off and came back the next day,' barked Hurley.

'The scene was secure,' protested Khan.

'Yeah, right,' said Hurley. 'How? With a bit of tape and a sleepy PCSO in a car parked on the bridge.'

Khan fiddled with his pen.

Hurley thrust the bag at Kennedy.

A printout was attached to it; the results of a fingerprint scan.

Kennedy followed Hurley out of the lab.

'Get a warrant,' said Hurley.

'I thought you might want another opinion on the prints first,' said Kennedy.

'Well,' said Hurley, 'I might.' He looked at Kennedy, expectant.

'We've lost a couple of big cases on fingerprints lately,' reasoned Kennedy. 'Challenges to the science and that sort of bullshit.'

'These crime-scene numpties have already cost us twenty-four hours,' protested Hurley.

'Exactly, sir,' said Kennedy. 'Khan's admitted there may be an issue with the integrity of the scene. Strike two against us.'

They emerged from the air-conditioned building into the sweltering car park.

Hurley mopped his brow, frowning.

'Perhaps we should get our ducks in a row first,' suggested Kennedy. 'An arrest means time starts running. I know you like to follow best practice, sir.'

Hurley was fretful. 'We could bring her in to assist with enquiries,' he ventured.

'It's up to you, boss,' said Kennedy airily. 'But if we've got no *solid* physical evidence it'll just be no comment at interview, the CPS will run for cover and so will the suspect.'

'Yeah,' said Hurley. 'That's what I was thinking. Get another opinion on the prints. But let's find her and have an informal chat. Put a flag in the system. We don't want anyone fleeing the jurisdiction. Best practice.'

'Good thinking, sir,' said Kennedy.

When Berlin finally emerged from the court foyer after a lengthy monosyllabic engagement with reception, Bow Road was crowded.

Defendants, lawyers, uniforms and detectives, the latter apparent by their ill-fitting suits, all jostled for space in which to talk, smoke and eat.

Among them Berlin caught sight of Murat and the sergeant who had arrested her on the stalking charge. As she watched them, the sergeant answered his mobile. He listened, then began to scan the crowd.

Berlin's own mobile rang as she made her way down the steps.

'Berlin,' she said.

'Are you at the Mags?'

She recognised Kennedy's voice, although he had spoken softly.

'Just leaving,' she said, edging through the press of bodies.

'Keep going,' he said.

The sergeant and Murat had separated now. Murat had gone to the top of the courthouse steps. From this vantage point he scanned the crowd. The sergeant was roaming through it.

They were looking for someone.

'What's all this, Kennedy?' she asked.

'You're wanted for questioning,' he said.

'I just spoke to the listing clerk. They're putting me on again next week.'

'For god's sake, Berlin. It's got nothing to do with stalking,' snapped Kennedy.

'What is it then?' she asked.

His voice dropped to a hiss, no more than static on the line.

'Murder.'

42

Berlin was moving up in the world. She was a person of interest in a murder inquiry, just a notch below prime suspect. But promotion to those dizzy heights was only a matter of time, according to Kennedy.

The money in her boot wouldn't get her far, so she went straight to the nearest cash machine and withdrew everything she had, which wasn't much. It was too soon for them to implement alerts or have her mobile tracked. They would have to submit requests, make a case and negotiate layers of authorisation for that. But she wanted to get ahead of the game.

She dumped her coat and woolly hat in a skip behind a ke-bab shop. Further along Whitechapel Road the market was open. She bought a white T-shirt emblazoned with the words 'I Love

London', a Union Jack scarf, a baseball cap bearing the Underground logo, and knock-off, oversized Oroton sunglasses. The Whitechapel Art Gallery was open and she ducked inside to change in the toilets.

In the cubicle she sat on the toilet lid and took a couple of deep breaths. She tried to stop trembling. The pounding in her chest subsided but, as the adrenaline left her system, the pain flooded through the damaged nerves in her neck and jaw.

Twig was dead. The news had shaken her. Kennedy had not broken it gently. His perfunctory announcement was a poor disguise for his own distress at the loss of another young life. She could hear it in his voice. His fear was palpable, too.

Rolfey's clinic was nearby, but she would have to rely on Scotch and low-dose over-the-counter codeine until she managed to get there. That could be a while.

Gingerly she wrapped the scarf around her throat, hiding the bandage, then jammed the cap on her head and slipped on the glasses.

When she stood up and looked in the mirror, she didn't recognise herself.

She was a tourist in her own town.

43

Kennedy walked the perimeter of the British Library. The high red-brick wall reminded him of a prison. He thought of the special wing prisons had for crooked cops and kept walking past the entrance. The third time around he took the plunge.

You had to admit it was a clever choice of venue. It was highly unlikely he would bump into any of his colleagues or associates in here. They were neither scholars nor tourists. He went upstairs to the café, as directed, and found an empty table. He waited.

When the woman sat down opposite him his first instinct was to tell her the seat was occupied. Then he looked again.

'Christ,' he said. 'You look like a walking bloody souvenir.'

'I'll take that as a compliment,' said Berlin. 'Two fig rolls and a black coffee. Grande.'

In the queue, Kennedy suffered another bout of trepidation. If he was smart, he'd call for back-up and take her in. But she was smarter. She knew this wasn't a trap or she would never have come.

If arrested, she could say that he had questioned her off the record then told her Billy's location. Despite the air conditioning he was sweating so much his glasses kept slipping down his nose.

The coffee and cakes cost a small fortune, but he reminded himself of the much higher price he would pay if he didn't go through with this. If she were picked up, he would have to explain how he had identified her from Billy's statement in the first place. Luck wouldn't cut it as an explanation. Why keep this critical intel to himself?

He'd be finished. Somehow he had to persuade her they were in it together.

Berlin watched Kennedy in the queue and smothered her anxiety. She reminded herself that he was alone, and he was exposed.

But her real ace was that she knew about his dealings with Sonja and Cole. She didn't really believe that Kennedy had simply recognised her at the station on the basis of Billy's description. If she had seen Kennedy at Sonja's, then he may well have seen her. He had certainly had the place under surveillance, watching for Cole's return.

He didn't know it would be a bloody long wait.

They were all dancing around the same corpse.

Kennedy put the coffee and a muffin in front of her. She took off her sunglasses and looked at him.

'They'd run out of fig rolls,' he said.

'I didn't kill him,' said Berlin. She didn't have time for niceties.

Kennedy sat down quickly and lowered his voice.

'You were arguing with him shortly before he died,' he said. 'And people heard him accuse you of killing Kylie.'

'He was angry. He didn't mean it literally, and if that's all they've got it doesn't add up to much of a case. Prospect of a conviction unlikely, I would have thought.'

Kennedy gave her a long, hard look and with a flourish took a document out of his suit pocket and laid it on the table in front of her.

It was a forensic report, a list of items found at a crime scene. One item had been scored through with pink highlighter. Berlin read it once, then again.

She looked at Kennedy. An emptiness unfurled in her chest.

'This can't be right,' she said.

'There's no mistake,' he said. 'I've just come straight from the lab. The prints matched those taken when you were arrested on the stalking charge. Now it's just a matter of matching the DNA when they catch up with you, and it's all over.'

Berlin felt as though she were seeing and hearing everything from a great distance. So much for her ace. Kennedy had a full house.

She gazed at the report: an empty Scotch bottle found under the canal bridge was covered in her fingerprints, and hers alone. It was the brand Mr Demir always gave her.

For a moment Berlin was back in the alley with the pale child and the creep. She could almost smell his sweat and feel the Asp clenched in her hand.

'Steady,' said Kennedy.

He touched her wrist and she realised she was crushing her cardboard cup. Coffee trickled across the table. Kennedy mopped it up with paper napkins.

'I thought you were talking about Billy,' she said. 'It never occurred to me that you meant *her*. His sister.' It came out small and flat. The words died in her throat.

All her energy was focused on subduing her panic.

'The witnesses in Billy's case aren't the most reliable and could be discredited in court,' said Kennedy. 'And it might be tricky to make murder fly, given the circumstances. But Kylie, well, the bottle together with Billy's description of the nice lady . . .'

He let it hang out there, waiting for her response.

She tried to process what he was saying, but she couldn't think fast enough to react, so she let him continue to the inexorable conclusion.

'I'd say there's a good chance you'll be looking at two counts. Him and her.'

She couldn't find her voice.

'You haven't touched your muffin,' he said.

'I'd like some more coffee,' said Berlin.

When Kennedy returned from the counter, she was gone.

44

Morpheus, son of night and god of dreams, often brought Berlin the same vision. A towering wall, which somehow she could see over, and beyond it dead people calling to her. She could never hear what they were saying. Her father was always one of them.

Morphine had nothing to do with her reverie as she slumped in the back seat on the upper deck of the bus. Shock had been succeeded by fury, then replaced by dread; now she had succumbed to an anguished trance. Kylie and Billy stood behind the wall, reproachful.

If Billy's death was ruled a homicide Kennedy was right, she would be looking at two counts of murder: the vicious slaughter of a brother and sister.

She was suddenly cursed with perfect recall of famous cases in which innocent people had been convicted on the basis of forensic evidence that at the time seemed damning: the Birmingham Six, the Guildford Four, the Maguire Seven. Even when it wasn't particularly damning.

There seemed to be a terrible inevitability about her guilt; the trajectory of culpability led straight to her, even if she hadn't actually killed anyone. She felt anguish and panic yield to resignation. The fault lay with her. It always did.

The bus passed her father's old shop on Bethnal Green Road. Lenny Berlin had been a jeweller. When she was seven her mother and father bought a terraced house in Leyton with a shiny brass knocker. She and her mother moved in, but Lenny always stayed in the flat above the shop.

That her parents had separated was never mentioned; Peggy took the bus every day to work in the shop, then returned to Leyton in the evening. Her father went upstairs to the flat. Lenny never set foot in the house in Leyton, and her mother never went upstairs at the shop.

The shop's latest incarnation was as a payday loan operation. Legal loan sharks. Berlin sat on the bus, reassured by the sensation of movement but unable to think clearly about where she was going, or why. She longed to dissolve the fear that infested her veins and to slow the sharp, relentless wheels turning in her brain as she went over it again and again. The loop took her back to the same place each time. Heroin. She craved a hit.

45

'This is a bad business, Sonja,' said Rita.

Sonja gulped from the grimy tumbler of spirits. 'Tell me about it,' she said.

Rita poured her another. She knew desperation when she saw it, so she had invited Sonja in for a drink. Sonja had nowhere else to go. A friend in need was a bloody good opportunity, and Rita was going to make the most of it.

If she spoke slowly, her dentures didn't slip and slide about too much. The vodka didn't seem to be affecting the superglue. She poured herself another shot. They'd run out of ice long ago.

They raised their glasses and drank.

'It's time you and I were straight with each other, love,' said Rita, pouring more of the oily liquid from the half-gallon plastic orange juice container. It was home-brew from a lock-up in Plaistow. The distillery was run by a couple of Russian blokes. Rita figured they knew what they were doing. They had invented vodka.

'The two cops. You're their snout,' said Sonja.

Rita nodded. 'For my sins,' she said. 'Look where it's fucking got me.'

Her scrawny arms were black and blue. She lifted her blouse to reveal the unmistakable imprint of a trainer on her ribs. It matched the one fading from Sonja's face.

'You bruise easy at my age,' said Rita.

'Yeah. But what can we do? Call the police?' said Sonja.

'You know what they want, love,' wheedled Rita. 'They just don't believe you when you say you don't know where he's hiding. I'm sitting here night and fucking day, terrified that I'll miss him when he does come back, and then that fucking Bertie will take it out on me.'

'He's not coming back, Rita,' said Sonja.

Rita considered her next gambit.

'My grandson's been helping me out, you know,' said Rita. 'Terry. He's in number four upstairs. He has his moments. He snaps, like.'

She hoped the threat wasn't too obvious. Or too subtle.

'There's no point threatening me,' said Sonja. 'They've already tried. Cole's gone for good.'

'Bullshit!' shouted Rita. 'They're going to get him eventually so give him up and save us both a lot of grief.'

Sonja leapt to her feet and threw her tumbler across the room. 'Fuck off, Rita. He's not coming back!'

Rita was almost tempted to believe her. Sonja was so strung out she couldn't remember her own lies. Rita knew all the signs.

'Why don't we just sort this out between us, woman to woman?' said Rita. 'We can put a lot past these blokes if we work together.'

Sonja seemed to consider this for a moment.

'I know it's the kid, Sonja,' said Rita.

Sonja grabbed her by the hair and thrust her face into Rita's.

'Leave my fucking kid out of this. I'm warning you. I'll fucking kill you if you breathe a word about her to anyone. Understand?'

She banged Rita's head down on the table and left.

Rita would have smiled if she wasn't afraid her dentures might fall out. That was all she needed to know. It was definitely the kid.

46

The double rap on the knocker echoed through the house. Peggy wiped her hands on her apron and hurried down the hall. She glanced up the stairs.

The bedroom door was ajar and she could see Princess bent over the little desk, beavering away with her felt-tip pens. Peggy had tried to interest her in the old plastic-bead bracelet kit she'd found stuffed in the top of Catherine's wardrobe. Another disdained Christmas present. Princess's reaction had been similar.

Princess heard the knock. She was dying of boredom. Peggy had tried to get her to make a charm bracelet from some old box of plastic beads because she said it had her name on it: 'Fun for a Princess'. Bollocks. It was just advertising.

She leant back in her chair so she could see the front door. She saw Peggy open it. There was a bloke standing on the step, but she could only see his legs from this angle. He said something she couldn't hear and then Peggy said, 'You'd better come in.'

The man stepped into the hall and Peggy showed him into the front room. Princess caught his profile as he turned.

He followed Peggy up the stairs, hard on her heels.

The bedroom door was closed. Peggy knocked on it out of habit and an ingrained sense of propriety. Her view was that you couldn't expect children to behave correctly if you didn't do so yourself.

Lenny had been more inclined towards the 'do as I say, not what I do' school of child-rearing. It had been nearly impossible to stop Catherine from burping loudly at the end of a meal, just as her father did. That wasn't the only bad habit Peggy had acquired from him.

When she tried to reprimand their daughter, Lenny would back her up with a gruff 'Listen to your mother', but it was unconvincing. She'd watched, helpless, as Catherine grew up with a fierce sense of injustice. If her father could do it, why couldn't she?

Peggy knocked again.

'Princess,' she called. Perhaps she had fallen asleep.

She turned the handle and peered around the door.

The room was empty.

The man pushed past her, took in the situation and swore.

'Is there a back way?' he demanded.

Peggy nodded.

He ran down the stairs, taking two at a time. Peggy heard him run through the house. She went to the open window and peered down, saw him reappear in the empty garden, then turn and run back inside. His footsteps thundered up the hall, then there was a crash as the front door banged against the wall.

Peggy turned away from the window.

The bedroom door swung back to reveal Princess. She was standing behind it with her finger to her lips, cautioning Peggy to remain silent.

Her warning was backed up by the gun she held in her other hand.

Berlin turned into the road just in time to see a man in a suit emerge from Peggy's gate. The house was on a corner and he took off down the side street.

Instinctively she picked up her pace and broke into an awkward jog. When she reached the house the front door stood wide open and there was no sign of Peggy.

'Peggy!' Berlin shouted.

Down the hallway and through the silent house she ran, checking each room. Nothing had been disturbed. Returning to the stairs she took them as fast as she was able.

When she reached the landing she saw Peggy standing stock-still in the middle of Berlin's old bedroom, her gaze riveted on something behind the door. As she watched, a trickle of urine ran down Peggy's leg. Berlin hurried to her, wondering if she was having a stroke or something. After all, she was eighty-something and on a lot of tablets.

'Peggy? Are you all right?'

She turned around, following Peggy's frozen stare.

Princess stood there with her bag on her back and her feet planted wide. She was clutching a gun in both hands; it was a heavy piece and it wobbled up and down.

Her finger was on the trigger.

'What the fuck do you think you're doing?' said Berlin.

Princess glowered at her, all defiance.

There was a small, whimpering noise. Berlin realised it came from Peggy.

'It's okay, Peggy,' she said very quietly. 'It's not real.'

Princess exclaimed, enraged by this disrespect. She squeezed the trigger with all her might, the gun recoiled and a deafening noise enveloped them.

Peggy crumpled to the floor. Berlin's ears were ringing as she dropped to a crouch beside her.

'Mum!' she cried. A cloud of plaster dust settled around them.

Berlin felt for the pulse at Peggy's throat. It thudded under her fingers, strong and steady. She had just fainted. Berlin touched her cheek.

'You'll be fine, Mum,' she said, and glanced up.

Jimmy Page had copped it right between the eyes.

Her taut nerves snapped. Rage replaced fear. She leapt up, grabbed the gun with one hand and a handful of Princess's hair with the other. She yanked the kid's head back hard, forcing her to look Berlin in the eye.

'What the fuck do you think you're doing?' she shouted.

'He came for me!' cried Princess.

'What are you talking about? Who came?'

Princess looked beyond Berlin.

'The ogre,' she whispered.

Berlin tightened her grip on the gun and turned around.

There was no one there.

Peggy lay at her feet in a puddle of urine. Berlin had a lethal weapon in one hand and a dangerous child in the other. It was one of those moments that life can't prepare you for; she laughed, and knew it was shock. Then she heard a siren. Her next decision wasn't conscious: it was visceral.

'Sorry, Mum,' she mumbled as she slipped the gun in the waistband of her jeans and yanked Princess in the direction of the door. The kid had no will of her own, and Berlin still had her by the hair. She dragged her down the stairs, along the hall and out the front door, slamming it behind them, then released Princess's hair and grabbed her arm.

She had no idea where they were going, but it seemed sensible to head in the opposite direction to the approaching siren. They ran around the corner.

Tyres squealed, car doors slammed and heavy boots connected with concrete as they fled. Berlin heard Peggy's front gate clang, then someone used the shiny brass knocker in a fashion that Peggy would find rude and unnecessary. If she had come around in time to hear it.

Berlin and Princess took off as if pursued by the devil.

He dug in his heels and followed.

47

Peggy sat on the edge of the single bed between the ambulance lady and a senior constable. She looked from one to the other, humiliated by the fact that she had soiled herself, and embarrassed that the floor was coated in a thin film of white dust. She couldn't think what to say.

'I just vacuumed in here yesterday,' she said. It was the best she could do.

A young PCSO entered carrying two mugs.

'Here you are, Mrs Berlin. A nice cup of tea,' said the senior constable, taking one and handing the other to Peggy.

'Oh,' said Peggy to the PCSO. 'You should have used the good cups and saucers. And there are some chocolate bourbons in the cupboard on the right.'

'Senior?' said the PCSO, in a tone of mild protest that indicated he felt he was meant for better things.

'You heard,' the constable said. The PCSO stomped out of the room, colliding with a bouncy scenes of crime officer coming in.

'Hey ho,' said the SOCO, snapping on her disposable gloves. 'Firearm discharged?'

The senior constable pointed to Jimmy Page. The SOCO got to work.

The ambulance lady finished taking Peggy's blood pressure. 'You're fine,' she said to Peggy.

'I'm fine,' said Peggy to the senior constable, who promptly got out her notebook. The ambulance lady smiled and left.

'Now, Mrs Berlin, let me see if I understand this,' said the senior constable. 'Your daughter, Catherine, brought a young girl to stay with you, and she fired the weapon?'

Peggy nodded. 'The other policeman said she fitted the description of a missing child. He wanted to talk to her. But when we came upstairs, she was gone. That is, we thought she was gone,' said Peggy.

'He wasn't in uniform?' asked the senior constable.

'No. My daughter had told me not to let anyone in, but well, he showed me his identification. He was a detective, so I thought, well, you know, it's official. You can't really say no, can you, when it's the police.'

The senior constable looked doubtful.

'Are you sure he was a police officer?' she asked.

'He was very polite,' said Peggy. 'Very neat.'

The SOCO had taken down the poster of Jimmy Page and was digging a bullet out of the wall. Peggy found it distressing. Plaster was going everywhere.

'Let me just go and get a dustpan and brush,' she said.

'Did his ID look like this?' The senior constable produced her warrant card.

Peggy peered at it and nodded. 'Similar,' she said.

The SOCO gave a grunt of satisfaction as a bullet popped out of the plaster.

'The thing is, Mrs Berlin,' said the senior constable. 'We can't find any record of a detective tasked with enquiries that would involve paying you a visit about a missing child, because no child answering that description has been reported missing.'

Peggy looked stricken.

'Oh no,' she said. 'Catherine will kill me.'

48

Kennedy had left the British Library and gone straight home. He rang the station and called in sick. He was sick. Sick to his stomach. He had put himself on the line, risking everything – and she had run out on him.

He went and sat beside his son's bed. The little boy smiled at him from behind his oxygen mask. His bravery nearly undid Kennedy. He had to remember: he was the daddy. Everyone was depending on him and he had to show some guts and follow this thing through. He flicked open his mobile and dialled Berlin's number. Voicemail.

'I stick my neck out to give you a heads-up and your reaction is to leg it,' he said. 'We can help each other. Call me. We need to talk.' He hung up with a heavy heart.

If he was wrong about this woman it meant he'd thrown in his lot with a child killer.

His son lifted the mask from his face.

'Is it a crim, Dad?' he asked. Every word cost him, but he was always eager and curious about everything.

Kennedy shook his head and tried to smile.

'I'm going to be a policeman when I grow up,' said his son.

Kennedy slipped the mask back on him gently.

'Come on now,' he said, his own chest constricting with despair. He wanted to buy the boy a special vibrating vest that would help clear his lungs. It wasn't available on the National Health Service. They cost thousands.

His phone rang and he jumped, startled. That was quick. But when he checked the ID it was Bertie, not Berlin.

He only hesitated for a moment, then slipped the phone back in his pocket. That was it then. He'd made his choice.

He stroked his son's damp forehead.

Bertie slammed the phone down on his desk. He was suffering and feeling peevish. His mood hadn't been improved by the news that Kennedy had called in sick. Now the prick was ignoring his calls.

The product meant nothing to Kennedy, he was only interested in the extra cash. Bertie could hardly believe that the gutless wonder was doing the dirty on him, getting information from Sonja and Rita without passing it on. Kennedy seemed to be forgetting his place.

Berlin's crumpled face lay on the desk in front of him. He smoothed out the creases. The interfering cow was involved with the murder Kennedy was working and, according to him, she was looking for Sonja's kid.

A polite cough made him jump. A young DC, one of his outside team, was hovering in front of his desk.

'Fuck,' said Bertie. 'Ever heard of knocking?'

The DC gave him a funny look.

'I did knock, sir, but the door was open and I —'

'Get on with it then,' snapped Bertie.

The DC offered him a document.

'What's this?'

'There was a shout in Leyton, boss. It's just come through on the system. They're looking for that Berlin woman you flagged. Looks like she's armed.'

Bertie snatched the piece of paper out of his hand.

'Okay, I can read. Bugger off,' he said.

The DC backed out. Bertie quickly scanned the report.

It had to be Sonja's fucking kid that she had in tow. Rita was right. The kid was in the middle of all this and now Berlin had found her. A fact Kennedy had signally failed to mention.

He knew what drove a weak-kneed, good family man like Kennedy. He also knew what drove Catherine Berlin, and it wasn't heroics. The drought had them all trapped like fish in an ever-diminishing puddle, gasping for oxygen.

No doubt if he reeled in the little fish, the big fish would follow. He picked up his phone.

'Detective Chief Inspector Burlington here. Get me Commander McGiven.'

He chewed his thumbnail while he waited for his connection.

'Jock? Bertie here. I thought you'd be interested to learn that there's a suspect in a child murder running around with another kid. Looks like she's got a weapon.'

He listened for a moment.

'No, it's not my case. It's Hurley's. You know him, don't you? A right fucking nervous nelly – everything by the book. I thought it would be an opportunity for your crew to cover themselves in glory. For a change. Interested?'

There was a pause.

'Righto. I'll send over the details. Don't thank me. What are mates for?'

He hung up. Jock's outfit were looking for a soft target and a bit of good publicity since they'd managed to gun down a couple of unarmed individuals who turned out to be foreign students.

He wouldn't be sharing this initiative with Kennedy, either.

The minnow didn't know how close she was to the hook.

49

Berlin had turned her T-shirt inside out and dumped the sunglasses, which she didn't need anyway in the twilight. She couldn't do much about the Union Jack scarf, but it was less conspicuous than her scars. She had plonked the baseball cap on the kid's head, making her look a bit like a boy. It wasn't much, but it might throw off a casual observer.

The kid hadn't said a word since they'd left Peggy's, just trotted along beside her, getting on and off buses without asking any questions, apparently unconcerned with where they were going or what the fuck they were going to do now. Princess had her issues, but she wasn't delusional. Bad men were after the kid. Ogres. It looked like she was on the money with that characterisation.

The bloke in the suit at Peggy's was clearly looking for Princess: he'd pursued her when he thought she'd snuck out. Peggy wouldn't have let just anybody into the house, either. He must have been able to convince her he was legit.

Berlin didn't want to think how mortified her mother would be when she came around to find she had wet herself and the house was full of coppers. They'd only recently been back in touch after years of 'no speaks', except for polite exchanges at birthdays and Christmases.

Peggy had come and sat with her often during the long months when she was in hospital, and with her jaw wired she hadn't been able to tell her to go away. At least, that's what Berlin told herself.

She took out her mobile and dialled. The call was flicked to voicemail. Maybe they had taken Peggy to hospital, as a precaution.

She took a deep breath and struggled to think of something to say. 'Sorry,' just didn't seem to cut it. She hung up.

The heat was still merciless, the day's accretions of traffic fumes and dust a grimy veil hanging in the still air. Berlin touched her throat, as raw inside as it was out. She needed a drink.

The Blind Beggar was no stranger to fugitives.

'Where did you get the gun?'

Princess barely paused between mouthfuls as she devoured her third packet of crisps. 'It was my dad's,' she said.

Thanks for the heads-up, Sonja, thought Berlin. *Your kid could have killed me.*

'Did your mum know about it?' she asked, aware of the weight of the weapon tucked into her jeans. It felt snug in the small of her back.

Princess frowned, as if unsure how her mum had got into the conversation. She shook her head, but Berlin couldn't tell if she meant 'no', or 'I'm not going there.'

The beer garden was heaving with beefy men in baggy shorts and tight T-shirts, their faces, shins and forearms scorched pink. Berlin and Princess sat in the corner on a piece of artificial grass, their backs to the wall.

Despite a steady stream of true-crime tourists who came to see where Ronnie Kray blew away George Cornell in 1966, visitors didn't linger. It wasn't that sort of pub. Berlin felt relatively comfortable; she knew that now, as in the sixties, eyewitnesses and snitches were not welcome here.

'Look Princess, let's get real here,' said Berlin. The Scotch and the pint of Stella had gone straight to her head and she didn't have the energy to finesse this situation.

'I've got my own problems and I can't have you hanging around. That bloke who came after you at Peggy's, I strongly suspect he's actually looking for your dad. And since your dad's dead, he isn't going to find him, is he?'

Berlin waited a moment to let this sink in, but Princess didn't react, just squinted into the sun and slurped her lemonade.

'You need to go home. You'll be safe there,' said Berlin, although she didn't believe it for a moment. *Safe compared to what?*

Princess shot her a scornful look.

'What's really the problem between you and your mum?' asked Berlin, struggling to keep the note of exasperation out of her voice.

'She doesn't want me.'

'Yes, she does.'

'How would you know?' said Princess.

'Because she sent me to find you.'

Berlin knew it was a tactical error the moment she said it, but she'd run out of options. And patience. She saw every muscle in the kid's body go taut, although she didn't move an inch.

'You don't know her,' said Princess.

'I knew Sonja and Cole before you were even born,' she said.

She caught the merest hint of movement as Princess prepared to bolt. Berlin grabbed hold of her wrist.

Princess stared at her, her eyes empty, giving nothing away, shutting down in the face of another betrayal.

Berlin moved closer to her and lowered her voice.

'I know Sonja did it. She realises that scared you, it was a terrible thing for you to see, but she really wants you to come back. If you go home, I'll do everything I can to get you both far away, somewhere safe. You can make a fresh start. She loves you.'

It was the best she could do. She let go of Princess, who immediately stood up and took a backward step.

'She's a lying cunt and so are you!' she shouted, and tossed her drink in Berlin's face.

For a moment Berlin thought the kid was going to glass her, and so did the drunks around them, their blank faces suddenly alive at the prospect of violence. But Princess flung the pint pot to the ground and stormed off.

'She needs a good hiding,' said some wag in the crowd, his heavy gold rings glinting as he brandished his fist.

His mates laughed.

What the hell was she going to tell Sonja? She had been a fool to alienate the kid now, when they had come so far. She limped down Whitechapel Road, sticky with lemonade, cursing herself as she tried in vain to figure out which way Princess would run. Every bone in her body ached. The kid was fleeing back onto streets where her chances of survival diminished on an hourly basis.

Berlin checked her phone, which had been vibrating in her pocket at regular intervals. Missed calls and messages. All from Sonja pleading with her to bring Princess home. *Fuck it. Fuck it. Fuck it.*

She weaved through the crowd thronging the broad pavement. The moist smell of rotting melons hung in the air, undercut with the tang of crushed turmeric and chilli. Market leftovers. It made her eyes water. Fat, sweaty babies in floral sunhats screamed for mercy. Listless men hung about in the doorways of mini-cab offices, playing games on their mobile phones.

She hadn't got more than a hundred yards from the Blind Beggar when a sharp cry made her turn.

Princess was running towards her, pursued by a man in a suit. He was gaining on her fast.

The ogre.

50

The golden arches provided a demilitarised zone for their negotiations. Berlin gazed at the man sitting opposite her. The transformation from derelict to suited-and-booted respectability was dramatic. Only the swollen fingers of his left hand and the plaster on his ear remained as evidence of his former incarnation.

His new persona hadn't fooled Princess. Berlin thought the kid had probably clocked his eyes, which were a strange coppery colour, almost amber. He was lucky he hadn't lost one to her spike. He was even luckier that he hadn't lost his life to her Glock.

His ID lay between them. He was with the National Crime Commission, the most recent incarnation of over a decade of law-enforcement agency mergers, shuffles and closures.

The process had begun years ago with the establishment of SOCA, the Serious Organised Crime Agency, which had soon gained a reputation as Seriously Disorganised. SOCA had been formed from the merger of six other law enforcement bodies, or at least, some of their functions, although it wasn't always clear which, especially to those working for it.

After a few years SOCA had been merged into the commission. It was on the cards that one day the NCA too would be reduced to ashes in response to political, rather than law enforcement, interests. The process was ongoing.

The people who had survived the various waves of toe-cutters neither knew nor cared what the chain of command might be on any given day. This was the agency to which the ogre belonged. It was an operational free-for-all.

He extended his hand, which was very decent of him given that the last time they met she had kicked him in the bollocks. His impression of a pervert had been very convincing.

'Joseph Snowe. With an e,' he said.

She had the feeling that no one would get away with calling him Snowy, although it would be irresistible, particularly because he was black.

'Berlin,' she said. But she was sure he already knew that.

'You should never have let her out of your sight,' he said. Berlin could scarcely believe he was reprimanding her. On the other hand, he was dead right. Neither of them were making that mistake twice.

Princess was watching them from a table just out of earshot, where she sat with a burger, fries and thickshake. It had taken Berlin fifteen minutes to calm her down and convince her that they were in no position to let him have it right between the eyes. The panic that had seized the kid when she saw Snowe approaching had trumped her outrage at Berlin's deception. Any port in a storm.

'When she ran out of the Blind Beggar I had no option but to blow my cover,' said Snowe. 'I knew if she saw me the chances were that she would run straight back to you. It indicates she trusts you – as much as she trusts anybody – and that's what we need.'

'We?' said Berlin. His speech was clipped, precise. Oxbridge perhaps, management fast track. He had probably missed the action so had himself assigned back to the street. Or perhaps he was just a lone ranger. Some people spent so much time undercover they could never readjust to normal operations. Or normal life.

'We need to clear up a few matters,' continued Snowe. 'First, where's the weapon?'

Berlin didn't like his tone. She leant back and folded her arms.

'I dropped it down a drain.'

She didn't give a shit if he believed her or not. She was reasonably confident he wasn't going to search her in the current circumstances. He had driven Princess back into her arms, instead of just grabbing the kid and calling Social Services. Which meant he needed her, and the kid, for something.

'Second, I need you to brief me on your relationship with Sonja Kvist and Cole Mortimer.'

Berlin glanced at Princess to make sure she couldn't hear them. She winked to reassure her they were in this together. Princess gave her the finger. So much for trust. It was going to take some work to repair that relationship.

Berlin turned her attention back to Snowe.

'Why don't you just cut this officious bullshit and tell me what's really going on here?' said Berlin.

Snowe's jaw tightened. For a moment she thought he was going to produce handcuffs and snap them on her. Then he scratched his chin and pinched his nose, as if he was telling his face to relax. His coppery eyes softened and his expression changed to a wry smile.

'I should know better than to shit a shitter,' he said in his posh voice. 'Let's take this somewhere more private.'

Somewhere more private turned out to be a hotel in Limehouse. Princess had been taciturn during the cab ride, but after Snowe checked them in, excitement overcame her surliness: a TV and minibar hidden in cupboards, lights that dimmed, free stuff in the bathroom. She couldn't hide her delight.

After Sonja's it must seem like the Ritz, thought Berlin.

Princess made a beeline for the minibar and helped herself to orange juice and a cellophane packet of expensive muesli cookies.

Berlin took a Coke.

'That stuff'll kill you,' said Princess.

'Says who?' said Berlin.

'Sonja. It's full of sugar. Pure, white and deadly.'

Berlin had once known a junkie who fed his dog a vegetarian

diet because he thought meat was unhealthy.

'Go and have a bath,' said Berlin. 'It's a spa.'

Princess looked sceptical. She went to investigate.

Snowe and Berlin went out onto the tiny balcony.

They were on the tenth floor. It was the first time Berlin had felt a breeze on her face for days. She unwound the scarf from her neck and let the air soothe the taut, febrile scar tissue. Snowe didn't give it a second look.

'I'm going to ask my boss to authorise your registration as a CHIS,' he said. 'It won't protect if you do anything illegal, but it means that if you're picked up at any time they'll come straight to me.'

Berlin doubted it would help if she were charged with murder.

'How did you get onto me?' she asked. 'If you've been staying so close to the kid?'

'Kvist's phone. I receive logs of incoming and outgoing numbers, date, time and who's calling. All the best tramps carry a smartphone.' He smiled.

Berlin didn't.

'I ran your name through PNC,' he said. 'You haven't got any convictions, although even if you had that's no barrier to being a Covert Human Intelligence Source.'

'What about the outstanding matters?' she asked.

'As I said, to date you have avoided conviction.'

Which meant he was up to speed on her current status as a person of interest, and he was prioritising his case over the others. Berlin loved inter-agency cooperation.

'So what's the upshot?' said Berlin.

'Putting together your background and the sequence of events, it seems reasonable to assume that Kvist engaged you to find her daughter.'

He was being economical with the truth: in his job it wasn't 'reasonable' to assume anything. Intelligence had to come from a reliable source before it was actionable. Which meant they were actually listening to Sonja's calls, not just logging them, and Snowe was receiving transcripts. Or he had a snout. Or both.

'Why did you try to stop me from getting her out of Love Motel?' she asked.

'Because I couldn't follow you in that get-up without you spotting me,' he said.

'You didn't have to torch the car,' she said.

Snowe didn't react. 'I backed off when the ambulance arrived, then just enquired at with the hospital and picked you up when you left.'

'Why were you following the kid in the first place?' she asked.

'Mortimer and Kvist are under investigation,' he said. He was hedging.

'And?' she asked.

'There are other targets,' he said. 'Police officers.'

She didn't press him. Bertie and Kennedy.

'So why are you staying so close to her?' She gestured at Princess.

He turned to look back into the hotel room. She followed his gaze. Behind them the sun was sinking into the river. It cast a pink radiance over the glass, bathing the tableau beyond, a reclining Princess, in a soft rosy glow.

'Because there's half a key of heroin in her backpack.'

51

Snowe stood with his back to the view and watched Princess sprawled on the bed watching TV. Berlin stared at the river below: it was the silent custodian of so many secrets.

Snowe had been monitoring the activities of Sonja Kvist, Cole

Mortimer and two Metropolitan Police detectives for some time.

He was unaware that Berlin knew who the officers were. She would keep it that way. There was nothing in the record about her contact with Kennedy. He wasn't the senior officer in either Kylie's or Billy's case. It was doubtful, anyway, if Snowe would know what other cases Kennedy was working on. He was only interested in busting Cole and the two corrupt coppers. Then Cole would give up his source, probably someone abroad, to reduce his sentence and the operation would go transborder.

The glint in Snowe's weird eyes was familiar: he had a job to do and he would do it, whatever it took.

He had mentioned that the senior of the two bent detectives had a history of 'cutting corners' and was old-school, with extensive contacts in the law-enforcement community. He was also a clever delegator. There was always a sucker to carry the can. But at the moment Snowe had nothing concrete on the pair. They had the best cover that money could buy: running their own legitimate operation on Kvist and Mortimer.

Berlin reflected that it was a story as old as cops and robbers: the bad guys pay a tax to stay in business. If they failed to pay, they would be busted. And who among them was going to complain that he was actually in possession of a kilo of smack, not half a kilo, at the time of his arrest?

It was more efficient all round if a deal was done up front. No messy raids or arrests were required. Just hand over a percentage of the profits or the product, or both. Everyone went home happy.

When Snowe fell silent it was clear he was waiting for her to reciprocate with the history of her relationship with Sonja and Cole. She kept it brief, emphasising that it was ancient history until very recently. She left out the juicier bits. Like the fact that Sonja had killed Cole. She simply said that she and Sonja had reconnected by chance because they both attended the same clinic.

There was no point in disguising her status as a user.

Snowe listened to her account and then in a quiet, neutral voice explained Princess's role in her parents' activities.

Disgust rose in Berlin's throat: the bile of guilt and self-loathing. For more than twenty years she had been able to persuade herself that she wasn't implicated in the relentless, unforgiving machine that fed addiction. She couldn't deny it any longer.

She had played her part.

'Princess had a critical role in distribution. She was Mortimer's most trusted mule,' he said. 'He sent her out on the street.'

'With a Glock 17,' said Berlin. 'Which is what the police use, isn't it?'

Snowe nodded.

'One of the detectives has to have been the source of the gun,' Snowe said. 'Given the people Princess had to deal with, she must have been terrified half the time. It's a miracle she's still walking around. God knows how Cole managed to keep her in line.'

Berlin knew how. If Princess played up, Sonja suffered.

'I was watching their place when she came running out that night,' said Snowe. 'I knew Mortimer's shipment had arrived. Sonja and Princess had been out to collect. Whenever the drugs were in transit the child always carried them. I went with her.'

'You took a chance. She might not have had the heroin,' said Berlin.

Snowe shook his head. 'My source confirmed it.' His intel had obviously been solid.

'She went straight to the container yard and stayed there,' said Snowe. 'I was sure the drugs were in her bag, as usual. But beyond that, I had no idea what was going on. I'd reached a dead end.'

'It could have been a lot deader if she had used the gun,' observed Berlin.

'Indeed,' said Snowe. 'I didn't know about the gun. I might

have taken a different approach if I had.' His smile was wan, self-deprecating.

Berlin was struck by this. There was a kind of collegiate respect in his frankness, which she didn't deserve. She saw herself collecting bread, milk and Scotch from a distressed shopkeeper, and felt ashamed.

Snowe continued his story, staring at his own reflection in the balcony doors now that it was dark outside. Berlin realised that it wasn't vanity. He was using the opportunity to debrief. The real conversation was with himself, about the job.

'It was all quiet on the western front after that,' he said. 'Mortimer must have taken off soon after Princess, but he didn't follow her or I'd have seen him. When you appeared and moved in on the child I thought you were her connection.'

He turned to face her. For a moment she saw him entertain the possibility that this might still be the case – that she'd known about the smack all along.

'Why did you take her to your mother's?' he asked.

'She wouldn't go home. She's a runaway, remember? I needed some time,' said Berlin.

'But Sonja knows you've found her, so why hasn't Mortimer resurfaced?' asked Snowe.

Berlin glanced down at the river. She couldn't afford to hesitate. This was the sixty-four thousand dollar question. She looked Snowe in the eye.

'Because he's done a runner,' she said.

He gave her a hard look. 'I don't believe it,' he said.

Berlin shrugged. 'That's what Sonja told me. I certainly haven't seen hide nor hair of him. Have you?'

'Why would he walk away from all that gear?' asked Snowe.

'Maybe he was on to you. Maybe he sent Princess out so he could take off while you were busy following her. You would nick

Princess and Sonja and he would live to fight another day.'

Snowe dismissed this suggestion with a flick of his hand.

He would be a difficult man to sell a bill of goods.

'No. Nothing has compromised this operation to date, and nothing will,' he said.

He was a true believer. The most dangerous kind.

52

Sonja waited in the shadows, just out of range of the bright lights of the petrol-station forecourt. It was late, business was slow. The attendant, securely locked inside his perspex box, was dozing between customers.

An old Mondeo pulled in and stopped at one of the pumps. Perfect. No electronic locking mechanism. The scruffy young driver got out, yawned and began to fill up. He looked like a student. He stopped the pump at ten quid – strapped for cash, probably. Enough fuel to get him home.

When he went to pay, Sonja flitted across the forecourt, ducked low behind the Mondeo, opened the door and reached inside. His mobile was on the passenger seat. *When would these people learn?* She grabbed the phone, shut the door with a quiet click and ran.

Standing beneath the silent overhead rail line, Sonja waited for her call to be answered. Across the road she could see the flicker of Rita's television, faint through the dirty windowpane. 'Come on, come on, please answer,' she muttered. She felt as if she'd spent her whole life chasing, pleading, running, hiding, waiting. Waiting.

The sound of water on shingle drifted to her across the still night.

The tide's coming in, she thought. *Easing the shore's burden.*

At last her prayer was answered.

'Were you asleep?' she asked. 'I'm sorry. I'm sorry, I know what we agreed. But I can't do this any more.'

A dog slunk out from behind a skip overflowing with rubbish, its eyes yellow in the moonlight. It stared at her as she listened.

'I know!' She took a deep breath and tried to keep her voice under control. 'I know that. But it's not easy. You understand. Please. I'm begging you. Meet me behind the petrol station.'

She hung up, lacking the strength to argue any more. She tossed the mobile in the skip and went back to the petrol station. To wait.

The dog trotted on.

Berlin sat in the dark watching the sleeping child. Or rather, her backpack. Sweet salvation lay an arm's length away.

She still wanted to believe in Rolfey's approach: the talking cure and a gradual reduction in morphine, so she could experience life without dependence. A normal life. Whatever that was. So many people seemed unable to let go of something, or someone. Even when it was killing them.

She'd seen amputees, people who had lost a leg because of smoking, sitting outside the hospital attached to drips and still lighting up.

What was Snowe's weakness? Risk. He wasn't oblivious to the gamble he was taking by leaving Princess with her. But he didn't have any choice if he wanted to run the job his way. The hierarchy would never condone it.

Snowe wasn't interested in just taking half a kilo of smack off the street and putting a kid into care. He wanted the big score.

He was relying on the assumption that she was an addict of a different order from the Sonjas of this world. Was it a reasonable assumption?

If she took the heroin from the bag she was no better than the people who had put it there. Princess would wake up, there would be a struggle and she would hurt the kid, who would hate her.

Why did she care?

She didn't even have to use the stuff. She could just offload it and use the money to start again. Or for someone to start again. It cast a new light on Sonja's desperation to get Princess back. Sonja could pay off Bertie and Kennedy. Half a kilo of smack would be worth a small fortune on the street during the drought. It would be stepped on three or four times, with lactose, glucose, or even brick dust, before it reached the user.

All at once Berlin was engulfed with pity for the terrible regime that mother and daughter endured. She swore to herself she would get them out before the shit-storm broke. It was surely coming.

If Berlin could say she wanted to get clean, what right did she have to be sceptical of Sonja's intentions?

The fact that Sonja hadn't mentioned the heroin.

Snowe lay wide awake, staring at the ripples of light on the ceiling, reflections off the river. He'd spent nearly every penny of his salary on this tiny glass box in sight of the Tate Modern. The proximity to culture was his substitute for a proper life.

He went over it again; he'd really had no choice but to leave Berlin and Princess at the hotel. It was either that or take Berlin into custody and put the child in care. Which would have put paid to his operation. He only needed to keep Berlin under wraps for about twelve hours, just enough time for him to get the paperwork and his team sorted.

The main thing was that she was off the street and wouldn't be picked up until it suited him.

He switched on the light and made a call.

'Snowe here. Any activity on that mobile?' he asked when the call was answered.

He listened.

'Okay,' he said, disappointed. 'Let me know as soon as there is.'

He hung up. He had to be patient. Give her some time to think it through. Inciting betrayal was a tricky business. Treachery could become a habit.

He switched off the light.

Berlin slid open the door and went out on the balcony, restless with doubt. From up here she could look out over the twinkling domain that was Silvertown. A world where, at night, crane gantries were transformed into soaring parapets and flyovers became magic paths of light in the sky.

Everyone wanted the kid for the wrong reasons: Bertie and Kennedy, Sonja, Snowe. He was the worst somehow. He wanted to use her as bait.

'So what do you want me to do?' Berlin had demanded. 'Tie her to a picket and smear her with blood to attract the predators?'

'Unless you can think of a better way to apprehend the targets *in flagrante*,' came his cold response.

'You're as bad as Cole,' she'd muttered through clenched teeth, unable to shout in case Princess overheard. 'She's just a fucking kid.'

He had been adamant.

'Call Sonja and tell her you're bringing Princess home tomorrow. I'll see that Sonja is bailed once I have the other three locked up.'

Berlin remained silent. Three. Would Snowe be satisfied with nicking the two coppers or would he escalate the hunt for Cole when he was a no-show?

He had given her until the morning.

She made a call. It was answered on the second ring, as always.

'It's me,' she said.

'Hello. How's your missing-kid thing?' asked Del. She was grateful he didn't expect small talk.

'I found her,' said Berlin.

'That's a result. Congratulations,' said Del.

'Have you ever come across a bloke called Snowe? Joseph Snowe. With an "e". A black guy.'

'Never heard of him,' said Del.

This was a good sign. Del had once worked for police complaints and had a voluminous knowledge of wayward coppers in the capital.

'Could you look into him for me?'

She heard him sigh.

He had resources aplenty at work but had to log every inquiry and bill someone for it. It wouldn't be her.

Del was burdened with an aversion to injustice, which he had inherited from his mum, who was Jamaican, and his dad, who was Jewish. He was also very loyal. Both qualities made him a sitting duck for Berlin's machinations. She tried not to push it, but she nearly always needed something from him, and didn't have much to offer in return. One day she would make it up to him.

'Okay,' he said.

When she slid open the balcony door and stepped back inside, Princess murmured in her sleep and rolled over. The bag rolled with her.

How could the kid sleep with that uncomfortable weight on her shoulders? Berlin knew she would wake up if it were removed. It could be a terrible awakening for both of them.

53

Kennedy sat in the hotel lobby and wondered whether the CCTV was recording. He could flash his ID at the security guard and check it out, but he really didn't want to call attention to himself.

There was a bar in the lobby and a few hardened drinkers were avoiding turning in. Perspiration was steaming up his glasses, but his sweat had nothing to do with the heat. It was chilly in here. He could barely sit still; his leg was going fifteen to the dozen. His beer slopped all over his trembling hand as he picked it up from the sticky table.

Berlin had called at two in the morning as if it were normal business hours. Odd didn't begin to describe her. But a murderer? Kennedy just couldn't see it. He knew a fit-up when he saw one, and a bottle with her fingerprints on it at the scene had more than a whiff about it. She was too smart for that. She wasn't your average chaotic junkie.

Someone wanted to put Berlin in the frame, and that someone had killed the girl, or was there when it happened. Between them, he and Berlin should be able to work out who had motive and opportunity.

If he found Kylie's killer, he would move up in the world. Promotion. A decent pay rise. What's more, Berlin would owe him. She would keep her trap shut about his other business interests. And once that matter was sorted, and the money was in the bank, he was going to tell Bertie he was out of it.

He just had to solve the murder first.

Berlin watched Kennedy from the car park. She didn't want him to realise she was staying at the hotel by emerging from the lift, and she wanted to make sure he had come alone.

You didn't need an interpreter to read his body language. He was a man with a lot on his mind. He had challenges. The trouble was, he knew hers.

She walked into the lobby, fresh from a long, hot shower, and wearing an expensive black linen shirt over her black jeans. The concierge had been prevailed upon to produce the shirt and happily, now she was a CHIS, it would go on Snowe's bill. Princess was sound asleep. Berlin had left her a note: *call me as soon as you wake up.*

Kennedy looked surprised when he saw her, and she realised she looked almost respectable.

'Drink?' asked Kennedy.

'Talisker. A double. No ice. No water,' she said.

He stood up to go to the bar, but hesitated.

'Don't worry. I'll still be here when you get back,' she said.

When he returned with their drinks and sat down his knee started to jig again. She got straight to it.

'Let's not fuck about, Kennedy. I know you and Bertie are shaking down Cole Mortimer. I know he's gone missing and you want the product.'

'So we're even,' said Kennedy. 'I'm a corrupt copper and you're a murderer.'

'The big difference is that I didn't do it, as you well know, but you're in it up to your neck,' said Berlin.

Kennedy's knee jigged faster, but he came straight back, jabbing his finger in her direction.

'No. The big difference is that you'd be convicted on the strength of good forensics, but I would walk because there isn't a scrap of physical evidence against me. And who's going to provide credible witness evidence? A pack of junkies?'

No, thought Berlin. *Another copper, you idiot. There was the fatal flaw for you. Hubris.*

'I have to admit you've got me there,' she said.

Kennedy looked pretty pleased with himself. 'But look,' he said. 'If we work together to find Kylie's killer you'll be home free. And all I'm asking is that you tell me first when you find the kid.'

She didn't react.

He gulped his lager. She could see he was hesitating before going any further. He wiped his mouth with the back of his hand and jumped in.

'Sonja gave me the heads-up,' he said, and took another long drink.

Berlin waited. Let him take his time.

'She told me how Cole used Princess to move the stuff, and that the kid ran off with it when he belted her, the bastard.'

He leant forwards, in earnest.

'Find her before he does, Berlin. I won't let any harm come to her.'

So the honest cop wanted to use Princess as bait and the bent cop wanted to protect her. Sonja must have realised Kennedy had a soft spot for kids and exploited it.

'Does your ex-boss know?' she asked.

Kennedy shook his head.

So he would let Bertie keep thinking Cole had absconded with the heroin. And if Cole didn't reappear, that was the end of it. Then Kennedy could do a deal with Sonja and cut Bertie out. No honour among thieves or dodgy policemen.

Kennedy thought he had all his bases covered.

She savoured her Scotch and considered her trump card: Snowe. When she finally told Kennedy he was under investigation he would be begging her to keep the kid well away from him and let Bertie have everything: the gun, the heroin, the long prison term.

She was going to wait and drop that on him when the time was right.

The lift doors opened on the other side of the now-empty lobby and Princess stepped out. She strolled over and sat down.

'Hello, Mr Kennedy,' she said.

Kennedy looked at Berlin.

Suddenly the time was right.

*

Marion Kennedy had long got over complaining when her husband was called out in the small hours. But when she was woken late that night by a knock on the front door she went cold.

She hurried downstairs and peered through the spy-hole. His boss was standing on the doorstep. She stepped back and caught her breath. This was the moment she'd always dreaded, the moment every police officer's partner feared. She opened the door.

'Hello, Marion,' said Bertie. 'Can I come in?'

'Kennedy?' repeated Berlin. He had turned a funny colour, and it wasn't just the lighting in the hotel lobby. She could see the pulse in his neck fluttering, a tiny blue insect trapped beneath his pale skin.

'How long have they been watching us?' he croaked.

'Long enough,' said Berlin.

Berlin had given Princess all her change and sent her to play the fruit machines in the corner of the lobby.

Kennedy was looking at the kid as if it were the plague she was carrying, rather than half a kilo of heroin that could send him straight to prison. He found his voice.

'I would never, ever have laid a hand on her,' he said. 'I wouldn't have had a clue what to do with the stuff. I haven't got the contacts or the know-how. I went along with Bertie, that's all. What am I going to do?'

He looked around wildly as if addressing someone who might be eavesdropping, someone who might swoop out of the shadows any moment and nick him.

Berlin let him sweat.

His voice rose a register. 'What am I going to do?'

He buried his face in his hands.

She gave him a long moment, to let it all sink in.

'Trust me,' said Berlin.

He lifted his head and stared at her.

'I'd like another drink,' she said.

Resignation replaced despair on Kennedy's face.

'Of course,' he said.

While Kennedy was at the bar Berlin beckoned Princess over and took the opportunity to have a quiet word.

'Do you ever do as you're told?' she said. 'You were supposed to ring me if you woke up.'

'You're not the boss of me,' said Princess, pouting.

Berlin took a deep breath. To Princess she was just the lesser of two evils, able for the time being to keep her out of the hands of the law. Berlin didn't want to jeopardise this uneasy truce.

'You've put me in an awkward position with Kennedy,' she said.

'Why?' asked Princess.

'You do know he's a detective?' said Berlin.

'Yeah. But he's our detective,' replied Princess with a smile.

It could have been Cole sitting there. It gave Berlin the willies. Could a ten-year-old be playing her?

When Kennedy sat down again he addressed Princess as if she were one of his own kids.

'Your mum's very worried about you,' he said.

'Did she say that?' said Princess.

Kennedy nodded. 'She wants you both to make a fresh start. She wants to get clean.'

Princess frowned at Berlin. This was exactly what she had said. Berlin shrugged, disclaiming any collusion between her and Kennedy.

'What about Cole?' asked Princess.

For one awful minute Berlin thought she was going to give the game away.

'Don't worry about him,' said Kennedy. 'He won't hurt you any more.' He leant forwards and gave Princess a wink. 'I'm a policeman.'

He turned to Berlin with a twitchy, tentative smile. His silent plea was unmistakable: *we're on the same side. Aren't we?*

54

Berlin had another drink after Kennedy left, attempting to assuage her fatigue and irritability.

Princess had fallen asleep in her chair.

Why do all hotels smell the same? The muzak was disconcerting too. Very little traffic noise permeated the double-glazed picture windows, which were blank in the still darkness. The skies were empty. The City Airport operated on a curfew until six-thirty a.m.

She thought about going abroad. Would she be stopped on her way out? She knew nothing about border security, except that it didn't work very well. Anyway, her passport was about twenty years out of date.

She shivered in the dank, artificial air. The Scotch couldn't reach the part of her that felt the chill. She knew that now she was involved in the most dangerous game of all: playing coppers off against each other.

Weighing up the two men from a strategic point of view, it appeared she had the most to gain by protecting Kennedy from Snowe, because he was working Kylie Steyne's murder.

On the other hand, Snowe's persistence, which reminded her of her own foolish reluctance to let things lie, meant he wouldn't be satisfied with just nabbing Bertie.

There was nothing noble about this reckless pursuit of the truth; it was just a determination to know, to not be beaten by the people trying to stop you. To get a result.

It was unfortunate that in this particular situation Snowe was chasing the truth and she was determined to stop him. He hadn't bought her story that Cole had done a runner.

Whatever her sense of Snowe's character, and she was still waiting for Del's verdict, she had to work on the assumption that his intentions would conflict with her interests: he wanted her to make a call that could only lead to disaster. When neither Cole, nor Kennedy, turned up for the kid's homecoming, Snowe would want answers.

She dragged Princess from the chair and led her, half-asleep, to the lift. They rode up, still pursued by the muzak. If she were arrested for Kylie's murder, there would be nothing she could do to help Sonja and Princess.

She would keep Kennedy out of Snowe's grasp. The neurotic detective seemed genuinely concerned about protecting the kid, unlike Snowe. And only Kennedy could help her avoid going down for murder. It had to be him.

Princess was fully awake by the time they reached their room. It was almost dawn. Berlin drew the curtains and lay on the bed.

'Keep the TV down,' she said. 'I need a couple of hours sleep.'

In her half-dream, populated by the voices of cartoon characters and daytime TV talk-show hosts, Berlin heard her father, who sounded a lot like Homer Simpson, telling her to 'break for the border'. It was a common refrain that ran through all his advice, which included 'get going while the going's good' and 'take the money and run'.

Lenny Berlin had loved gangsters: James Cagney was his favourite. He often greeted Peggy with, 'Top of the world, Ma!' To which she would respond, 'I'm not your mother.'

He'd do a poor Cagney imitation and Peggy would say, 'I wish you'd stop that'; his response would be a quote from *The Public Enemy*: 'There you go again with that wishin' stuff. I wish you was a wishing well, so that I could tie a bucket to ya and sink ya.'

It had cracked Berlin up when she was a kid, but her mother

never laughed. The problem with her dad was that he hadn't drawn the line at films; he loved gangsters, period.

Anxiety swept through Berlin and she shuddered, seized by an agitation that made her skin crawl. This lack of ease was familiar. There was only one cure. It wasn't talking.

34.5˚C

55

Murat sat on the edge of his bed listening to his father shuffling about. The old man wasn't usually so active. After raising the shutters he would usually retreat to his stool behind the counter, where it would take him the next twenty minutes to recover his breath.

Murat ran his fingers through his thick hair and scratched at his stubble. His mother wanted to cut their losses, but he couldn't face all their hard work going down the drain. She kept talking about going home.

For some reason the prospect filled him with disquiet. The truth was that he'd been born in England and home was an abstraction for him. His real home was more an ideology than a place.

Loud wheezing heralded his father's approach. He had on his old suit, as if he were going to a funeral.

'I'm going out,' he announced. 'You will watch the shop.'

Murat sprang off the bed. 'Where are you going? Don't be stupid. You can't go out!' he shouted.

His father turned and shuffled away. 'This is not your concern,' he said. 'She may be your mother, but she is my wife.'

Murat groaned. He heard the shop door slam, ran out and saw his father getting into a cab.

Murat ran back to his room to find his phone.

Berlin gave Princess strict orders not to venture out of the hotel room.

'Where would I go anyway?' she asked, affecting wide-eyed innocence.

Berlin dragged a comb through her hair, which was damp and tangled from a cold shower that had failed to wash away her agitation.

'So, what about breakfast?' asked Princess, querulous.

Berlin tossed the comb away. She didn't have time for this.

'Do you know about room service?' she asked.

Princess frowned.

Berlin showed her the menu and how to order. The kid's face lit up.

She had unleashed a monster, but that would be Snowe's problem.

It was another blistering day. Berlin walked up to Limehouse Rail Station.

For the time being she could travel relatively safely; Kennedy had told her they were still waiting for the expert opinion on the bottle. Hurley was risk-averse and wouldn't escalate the alert for her until he had confirmation.

The train was sticky and uncomfortable, even though it was above ground. With a change at West Ham, she would be at her destination in half an hour. She paced up and down the empty carriage, the hiatus of the journey forcing her to confront the source of her discomfort.

Her physical injuries were healing and she knew that Rolfey was obliged to reduce her pharmaceutical support. He had as good as admitted he didn't believe that long-term abstinence was anything other than the latest rhetorical flourish in a policy driven by politics, not public health.

If professionals like him were sceptical about its value as a way of managing addiction, then why should she adopt it? Her use of heroin did not automatically make her mad, bad or criminal. But a nagging voice insisted it was tyranny. She was bound to agree.

Berlin hurried through the leafy streets of Upminster, anxious to arrive before her quarry left for work. She was reasonably confident that he would keep executive's hours. His routine would involve a journey into the City.

She had a lot to do and very little time to do it; Snowe had her on a short leash. If he was intercepting Sonja's phone he would know Berlin hadn't called her. It would be too risky for him to let the situation drag on, so he would be forced to take the kid and the heroin and be satisfied with arresting Sonja. Then he would turn in Berlin, as an afterthought.

When he'd asked why she hadn't taken Princess home in the first place she had said she wanted her safe at Peggy's while she sorted things out. The kid was reluctant to go home and he knew that Berlin had to appear on the stalking charge. What he didn't know was that the kid was reluctant to go home because she'd seen her mum kill her dad.

They hadn't discussed Berlin's involvement in the Kylie Steyne murder. Blind Freddie could see it was a fit-up. A bottle at the scene with her fingerprints? Come on. She knew exactly where it had come from: her neighbour's dustbin. And she knew exactly who had planted it at the scene, someone with the treble: knowledge, motive and opportunity. If it had been any old bottle she would have had her doubts. The brand was the clincher.

Snowe wasn't remotely interested in helping her out of that situation. But she and Kennedy understood each other. He would help Berlin find Kylie's killer, the same person who had set her up for the murder. She would be off the hook and Kennedy would be a hero. In return she would keep him informed about Snowe's operation so he could stay clear of it.

Win-win.

She could rely on Kennedy's self-interest.

Probably.

Kennedy strode into Bertie's office. From the look of it Bertie hadn't slept a wink. That made two of them.

'Good morning, Grant,' said Bertie. 'Marion's looking well. She passed on my message then?'

56

Berlin's target didn't live far from the station. She watched from behind a tree on the other side of the leafy street, a very different world from the one in which she had last encountered him.

A woman emerged from the house and herded three kids into a Mercedes SUV. Mrs Parr. Derek followed her out, shut the door behind him and used a remote device to activate an alarm. Then he waved goodbye to his family with the arm that wasn't in plaster.

The Mercedes drove away and Parr set off on his stroll to the station. He stopped dead when Berlin emerged from behind her tree.

'Boo,' she said.

Parr stared at her as if she had stepped out of his worst nightmare. She had.

'You have a lovely family,' said Berlin.

He glanced up and down the road, then advanced.

She stood her ground as he gave her both barrels, rapid-fire.

'What do you want? Money? No one will believe you. Who are you going to tell, anyway? I already told my wife, and the police: I was mugged while I was engaged in an indiscretion with a lady of the night.'

Berlin was taken aback by this extraordinary anachronism. She almost laughed. His outburst seemed rehearsed, as if he always knew this moment would come.

'And did you tell her that this lady of the night was fourteen years old?' she asked.

'There's nothing to connect me with that girl,' he said.

He fell silent as she displayed his licence and the family photo, which Kennedy had returned to her.

She watched as sweat bloomed through his crisp white shirt.

'You can't prove I was with her,' he stammered.

'Yes I can. Because she died with your semen all over her.'

'I didn't kill her. I couldn't have, I was at the hospital for god's sake!'

She thought he might faint.

'You'd better come in,' he said.

The Parrs' living room was an expanse of quality: generous wool carpet, a discreet but top-of-the-range home-theatre system, stylish standard lamps that would confer a warm glow on the domestic scene during long winter evenings.

Berlin had a fleeting vision of Kylie on her knees in the cobble-stoned alley.

Parr sat opposite her on a cream leather sofa, hands clenched in a position of prayer. A supplicant.

'Isn't that a bit impractical, with three kids?' she asked him, indicating the sofa.

He was completely flummoxed.

'I . . . we bought it before we had them.'

'Do you like kids then?' she said. She might just as well have plunged a dagger into his heart. He winced.

'Oh god. No. You don't understand.'

'Tell me everything about that night,' she said.

Parr bit his bottom lip and nodded, a schoolboy about to try extra hard.

Berlin sat through Parr's self-serving story with a non-judgemental demeanour, ensuring that he didn't omit any little detail. But she felt sick to her stomach.

It was the predictability of the litany that depressed her: he had no idea of the girl's age; she had come on to him; he was drunk; he wasn't a paedophile; his wife didn't enjoy oral sex; and on, and on, and on.

But when he came to describe his encounter with Kylie, his voice dropped to another register. He couldn't disguise his excitement.

The putrid odour of decay in the stifling alley seemed to catch in the back of Berlin's throat once again. She asked herself how it was even possible, in a civilised society, that a child could come to this? The greater mystery was how a civilised man could justify giving free rein to the depravity that lurked inside him. The banality of the act appalled her.

She smothered her rage. He was lucky she didn't have the Asp with her. Of course she did have the Glock. She leant back in the chair and felt its cool promise against her skin.

When he got to the part where Berlin had appeared in the alley, he didn't hide his resentment. It was apparent that he thought she had been unfair; that the punishment she had meted out didn't fit his crime.

Berlin didn't argue. Instead, she asked him to move on from what she had done. To look past her. What did he see at the end of the alley?

Parr studied her for a moment. Her enquiry was too eager.

'Will you leave me alone then?' he asked.

She didn't reply.

His licence and the family photo lay on the table between them. 'What about my stuff? Will you let me have it?' he wheedled.

He was a man who liked to bargain.

Berlin was glad to be leaving the suburbs behind. Misery was contained there, kept behind three-panelled oak front doors or in the dim corners of conservatories. She preferred it to be out where she could see it.

Parr had confirmed Billy's story. There was someone else there that night.

'I just assumed he was your backup,' he had said. 'That's why I knew you weren't police officers. You did well out of that night. There was at least five hundred quid in my wallet.'

She'd kept her temper and pressed him for a description.

'He looked – I don't know – solid. The next thing I knew, you hit me. I didn't see anything except stars after that,' he said, petulant.

Berlin wished she had hit him a whole lot harder.

The picture was sketchy. There was little light in the alley and, like Billy, Parr's perception was dulled. Eyewitness descriptions were notoriously unreliable, but although the details he had given her might not pass the beyond-reasonable-doubt test, it was good enough for cash, as her father would say.

Time to come out swinging.

57

Sonja woke up and lay very still, waiting for the grinding ache to seize her, body and soul.

Nothing happened. She found that she was remarkably clear-headed, and was amazed to find that she felt dirty. She stumbled out of bed and went to the bathroom.

The gentle stream of hot water from the shower was a miracle. She had asked him to top up the prepaid gas-meter card, and he had. He was a bloody marvel, really.

She gazed down at her body. She barely recognised it. Emaciated, mutilated, hollow where her heart should be. She was weak and tired. She had betrayed everyone who had ever loved her. Even the people who had used her had little use for her any more.

She hadn't noticed the jolt when she hit rock bottom, but she was sure that was where she had arrived. It had taken her a bloody long time, more than twenty years, to get there.

Something long-neglected stirred: a sense of decency that belonged to the woman she had once been. Another miracle. What happened to her now was unimportant. There was only one thing that mattered, one thing of which she was absolutely certain: she had to stop Berlin from bringing Princess home.

58

The shop was closed. Berlin banged on the door. Nothing. She went to the rear and peered through the fence. That door was shut too. The place was deserted. She hurried back to the front.

'There's no one there.' The woman who ran the laundrette next door was standing in her doorway.

Berlin could hear the rolling thunder of washers and dryers. The hot air drifted past, thick with the smell of burnt cotton. Perspiration ran down the woman's neck in rivulets and dripped off her bingo wings.

'Foreigners,' said the laundress, in a thick Polish accent. 'They just run off and leave their business. We should all have a holiday.'

'What happened?' said Berlin. Then she added with a note of disgust, 'They owe me money.'

'I'm not surprised,' said the laundress. 'These people. They had a row. I heard the son and the father. The father went off. Then the son. Just locked up.'

'Did you see her at all this morning, the mother?' asked Berlin.

The Polish laundress was insulted.

'What? You think I'm watching them all day? I'm run off my legs. I mind my business,' she said. 'Not like some people.'

It was quicker to walk than catch a bus. The traffic on Cambridge Heath Road would be backed up, and anyway she could take a shortcut through Sainsbury's car park. It was a route she often took to Rolfey's clinic, popping out for morphine and Fairtrade Arabica coffee. She tried not to think about that. Her phone rang. It was Kennedy.

'How's it going?' he asked.

'How's what going?' she said.

'Give it a rest,' he said. 'I gave you Parr's stuff, didn't I? I imagined you'd be paying him a visit sooner rather than later.'

'Are you checking up on me?' she said.

'Are you paranoid?' he replied.

'Yes,' she said. She had to learn to be more trusting. It was part of her rehabilitation, according to Rolfey.

'Parr confirmed that someone else was there,' she said. 'He thought he was my backup.'

'Right. Well, that's what you needed, wasn't it? Confirmation. You couldn't rely on Billy.'

She had nothing to say on that subject.

'Did you leave him in one piece?' continued Kennedy.

'Physically,' she said.

'So what's next?'

'I have to find this bloke that Parr saw,' she said. 'The bastard who set me up.'

'It's a big city,' said Kennedy. 'Where are you going to start?'

'I've already started,' she said. 'I'm on my way to Whitechapel.'

'Don't do anything stupid,' he said.

She hung up, catching a glimpse of herself in a shop window as she passed. She paused to take another look. She barely recognised the haunted woman who gazed back at her. Was she the predator or the prey?

Kennedy had told her not to do anything stupid, but she wasn't at all sure she had a choice. She had a bad feeling that free will was an illusion. She clung to the belief that whatever she did was what she chose to do. But how would she know the difference? It was the dilemma of addiction.

For Christ's sake, she thought, *I haven't got time for an existential crisis*. And moved on.

It wasn't just a flat. It was the luxury penthouse at the top of a converted school, and it was very secure: a camera at the bottom of the glass-enclosed stairwell captured the street and the main entrance.

She pressed the buzzer. A camera focused and she heard static as the entry phone came on.

'My name is Catherine Berlin,' she said to the intercom. 'I'm looking for Mrs Demir.'

Mum would know where her little prince was hanging out. It seemed rude to arrive when she and the doctor would no doubt be at it, but needs must.

There was no response.

Berlin imagined clothes being hurriedly thrown on.

'If you don't let me in, I'll have to call the police. I believe Mrs Demir may be able to assist with —'

It was sheer bluff, but the door clicked open.

She stepped inside and took the lift.

When she got out on the third floor she faced a solid timber door with security hinges and a sophisticated deadlock. She heard the bolt on the deadlock disarm. She pushed the door and it swung back. The whole system was automated. There was a camera in the vestibule and a motion detector.

She followed the hallway into a spacious living room. A monitor on the wall above the sofa captured feeds from the cameras outside. A burqa lay in a heap on the floor.

The first surprise was the sight of Mr Demir. He was sitting on a chair, his face grey, his forehead beaded with sweat. Mrs Demir stood to one side of him.

The second surprise, which was a big one, was that Murat stood on the other side, with one of his hands on his father's shoulder. Comforting or controlling?

Across the room stood a tall, elegant woman. She regarded Berlin with an intense expression and for a fleeting moment, Berlin thought she must be the doctor's wife, recently apprised by Mr Demir of her husband's infidelity.

Then the penny dropped. She was the doctor.

Poor work, Berlin, she berated herself. *Why shouldn't Mrs Demir's lover be a woman?*

Three suitcases were stacked near the door.

'Sit down,' barked Murat, pointing to a chair beside his father's.

Mr Demir's cheeks were damp with tears. 'I'm so very sorry, Miss Berlin,' he wheezed. For people engaged in a family punch-up they were all strangely composed, apart from him.

Berlin ignored Murat's order.

'What are we going to do with her, Murat?' said Mrs Demir. It was curiosity, not concern.

Something was very wrong. Murat, Mrs Demir and the doctor were all as cool as cucumbers.

Then it came to her. They were the professionals. She was the amateur.

And this was no love nest.

Murat must have seen her put it together. He made a move, but before he could get to her she had the Glock in her hand. He stopped dead.

Everyone froze.

Jesus Christ, thought Berlin. *What now?*

59

Princess lay on the hotel bed surrounded by plates of half-eaten food, sachets of tomato sauce and a tower of the funny metal things, like flying saucers, that were used to cover the plates. To keep the chips hot on their way up. She was beginning to get the hang of hotels.

A knock at the door heralded another moment of glory. The food was okay, but the best part was being called madam and writing your name on the screen of a tiny computer with a stick. The man said it was called a stylus.

'Yes?' she answered, in an imperious tone.

'Room service.'

She took her time. She stood up, stretched, and strolled to the door. It was heavy and took two hands to open it. But this time it wasn't a problem. As soon as she turned the knob, the door burst open. She was knocked off her feet and before she could scream a hand was clamped over her mouth.

She fumbled for her spike, but it was snatched away. She kicked, clawed and squirmed, to no avail.

The tower of flying saucers tumbled.

60

Berlin had never pointed a firearm at anyone in her life. She was surprised at how profoundly it changed the atmosphere. The air crackled with uncertainty.

Murat's jaw was clenched with anger, not fear. The doctor was alert, but not alarmed. She had obviously seen a gun up close before. Mrs Demir seemed almost resigned.

Mr Demir was watching Berlin in a kind of trance.

'So whatever it is, it's not adultery,' she said to him. 'I'm sorry I didn't do a better job.'

Mr Demir sighed and gazed at his wife.

'It may seem strange to you, Miss Berlin, but in one way I'm relieved.'

Strange didn't come close.

'Okay. Everyone on the sofa,' she said. She needed time to work out what the hell she was going to do. 'You can stay where you are, Mr Demir,' she said. He didn't look as if he could make it from the chair to the sofa.

The others went to the couch and sat obediently. Could they possibly believe she would gun them down in cold blood? It meant they thought she was a serious threat to their operation and that she wasn't acting alone.

'Who do you work for?' demanded Murat.

'Your father,' she said.

Murat sneered and shook his head in disbelief. 'What do you want?' he demanded.

'I just want to know what happened to Kylie Steyne.'

It was momentary, but she was sure Murat faltered. He knew

exactly who she meant.

'I don't know what you're talking about,' he said.

Berlin heard herself snarl, her throat taut with suppressed rage. She advanced on him, levelling the gun at his head. She suddenly understood what was meant by an itchy trigger finger.

The only sound was Mr Demir's ragged wheeze.

The doctor snapped at Murat in Turkish. He muttered something in response. It was clear the doctor wasn't impressed. It made Berlin nervous.

'Enough talking. I've got the gun. Do you understand?'

Murat and the doctor fell silent. Berlin's heart was pounding so loudly she thought they must be able to hear it. Sweat dripped into her eyes and plastered her hair to her head.

If I have a heart attack at least there's a doctor in the house, she thought.

She took a step towards Mrs Demir, levelled the gun at her head, and spoke to Murat.

'The truth,' she said. 'Now.'

She pushed the barrel into his mother's temple.

'I didn't kill the girl,' said Murat.

Then a movement on the monitor above their heads caught Berlin's eye and she was seized with the sudden desire to leave.

The back of the apartment offered no way out. A door off the kitchen led onto a wide balcony, a vision of polished granite stones, bamboo and white canvas sunshades. Berlin peered over the balustrade, careful to stay out of sight.

Three storeys below a fully kitted officer stood by a vehicle, talking into his radio. She had to get out. The sound of a shot came from somewhere inside the apartment, followed by the tattoo of an automatic weapon. Suddenly it all seemed academic. There was no way down. She should just surrender.

Berlin knew an Armed Response Vehicle when she saw one. There were three officers in a unit. She had seen the other two on the monitor approaching the building and now they were inside. No other units had arrived yet. The apartment building and the street hadn't been secured.

The Demirs' activities were nothing to do with her. She would explain that Murat had killed Kylie, or had seen who had, and she would be in the clear. It seemed unconvincing.

She thought about Sonja. The pair of them giggling as they squeezed through the skylight out onto the squat roof as the police came through the front door. The Nordic Fairy laughing until she was cross-legged, white-blonde hair flying, milk-blue eyes sparkling.

Berlin looked up.

61

Rita noticed straight away that there was something different about Sonja. It took her a while to work it out, but eventually she realised it was her smell. Or lack thereof. The acrid odour of stale sweat and the whiff of old mattress from unwashed hair had gone.

'I wonder if I might borrow your phone, Rita?' she said. 'The credit's expired on my mobile and I need to make an urgent call. Please.'

The body of a wasted junkie was standing in her doorway, but the person inhabiting it seemed somehow different.

'Urgent, eh?' said Rita. She folded her arms.

'I'm really very sorry about the other day. It was the drink, you know what it's like. I've been under a lot of strain lately.'

Rita kept a stony silence.

'Please, Rita,' said Sonja, exasperated. 'I can't tell you how important this is. It's a matter of life and death.'

That did it. Rita was a forgiving soul, after all. This was a turn of events that should be reported. If she could find out who Sonja wanted to call concerning such a serious matter, all the better.

'Be my guest, love. I'll take a turn around the premises to give you some privacy.'

Rita stepped aside to let Sonja enter, then strolled away. As soon as she turned the corner into the corridor, the stroll turned into a scurry.

Keeping an ear out, she found the key to Sonja's room on her ring and pushed open the door. The window was wide open, the sheets were hanging over the sill to dry, and there was something different about the room. Although not exactly spick and span, it was tidy.

Sonja took a deep breath and steadied her voice. She had to try to convey the gravity of the situation and that she knew what she was doing: she was rational.

The robot invited her to speak after the tone.

'It's me. Whatever you do, don't bring Princess here. To Silvertown. Get in touch as soon as you can, but keep her somewhere safe. I can't explain now, but this is really important, Catherine. Please, please, do as I ask. Do not bring Princess home.'

It was the best she could do. She hung up and waited for Rita to return.

Wandering around the room, she peered at the faded sepia portraits hanging on the wall. Rita's forebears. Stalwarts in First World War uniforms. They had all had mothers.

Rita's bedroom door was ajar and Sonja could see a beautiful old-fashioned quilt on the bed. It had been a long time since she had noticed anything so simple and elegant. It was incongruous amongst the detritus of Rita's life, but inexplicably it gave Sonja hope. She pushed open the door to take a closer look.

A noise that seemed to come from the wall above the iron bedhead made her jump. It sounded too big for rats. She took a few steps closer. Someone was shuffling around. The noise was coming from the ventilation grilles high up on the wall, which went through to the room next door.

The room next door was hers.

When Rita returned, a bit flushed, Sonja was sitting at the table.

'This heat!' Rita exclaimed. 'When will it ever end? Everything all right then, love?'

'Fine. Thanks, Rita,' said Sonja, standing.

'Think nothing of it, love,' she said. 'Feel free to come in and use it any time.' Rita made an expansive gesture. She couldn't help herself. She was generous and forgiving.

62

Sirens wailed, alarms shrieked, bells clanged. It was the cacophony of disaster. Berlin crouched between two large air-conditioning units on the roof of the building.

The stanchions supporting the canopy on the balcony were steel and had easily taken her weight. She thanked god for her Peacekeeper boots, which had given her enough swing to kick away the chair on the table without breaking her foot.

She had crawled onto the canopy and across it onto the roof proper, but now she was stuffed. Her damaged tendon was screaming and she thought she might throw up from fear and exhaustion. As the adrenaline left her body, the shakes set in.

Doing a runner across the rooftops may have been a laugh when you were in your twenties, but it could well kill her now. If it didn't, no doubt the Met would be happy to finish the job.

Mr Demir's request had seemed so simple. Find out what his wife was up to. Money, or rather Scotch, for old rope.

Now she was caught up in a raid when she was already sought by the police to assist with their enquiries. She didn't believe in coincidence, but in this case there was no other explanation.

She struggled to quell her panic and get her priorities sorted. First, get off the roof alive.

Time to bring in the cavalry.

Kennedy was in the canteen when his phone rang. He answered, but didn't say anything. He sipped his tea.

'Kennedy, it's me' came Berlin's voice.

'Yeah. How did it go?' asked Kennedy.

'There's a problem.'

'What sort of problem?'

'I need you to give me a hand,' said Berlin.

'How's that?' asked Kennedy.

'I'm in Whitechapel. You know what's going on?'

Kennedy glanced up at the TV on the wall. The sound was muted. Special Operations were swarming all over a building. Bomb disposal was there; a body was being stretchered out.

'Yes, it's on the TV now,' he said.

'I'm on the roof,' she said.

Kennedy's tea slopped all over his shirt. He looked around the canteen: the custody sergeant was doing a crossword, two PCSOs were arguing about the legitimacy of a penalty shootout. He wasn't dreaming.

He stood up and approached the TV, as if he might be able to see her.

'Are you serious?' he said.

'Perfectly,' came the reply. He could hear the distant thrum of a helicopter through the handset.

'What the hell can I do about it?' he whispered.

There was a long silence. The sound of the helicopter got louder.

'You're a fucking policeman, aren't you?' she said.

Bertie had just walked back into his office and was gulping down cough medicine when in stormed Jock.

'What the fuck are you playing at, you fat muppet?' he shouted.

The deputy assistant commissioner was right behind him.

'I beg yours?' asked Bertie as he swallowed hard and screwed the lid back on the bottle.

'A female with a single firearm and a kid in tow, you said.'

'That was the original intel,' said Bertie. 'To which I alerted you as a professional courtesy.'

'Well, she turned into a Turkish bloke with an automatic weapon and a state-of-the-art surveillance system. What does that fucking tell you?'

Bertie looked at the deputy assistant commissioner. If she was here, it was political. Political made the brass very, very nervous. The golf courses were littered with the bodies of senior officers who had made the wrong call in a terrorist-related incident.

'What was the intel on the address?' asked Bertie in an even tone, as he put his desk between himself and the enraged Scot.

The deputy assistant commissioner was all ears, waiting for Jock's answer.

Jock stared at Bertie. They both knew his blokes wouldn't have bothered to wait for more information. Berlin was wanted for questioning about a murder, not terrorism. They weren't counter-terrorism, anyway. They were just plods deployed in ARVs.

Send in the clowns.

The deputy assistant commissioner speed-dialled a number on her mobile.

'Get me the director of media and communications,' she said.

'Your suspect —' said Jock.

'Not mine,' broke in Bertie. 'DCI Hurley's. I believe I mentioned that. You conferred with him, of course?'

The look on Jock's face was enough of an answer.

'No? But then I take it your female target is either in custody or in a body bag?'

'They're still searching the building,' came Jock's guarded response.

The deputy assistant commissioner was in damage control on the phone. 'Say we can't disclose that at this time,' she said. 'Just use something like "known subversive organisation", right?'

Jock's hand went to his chest.

If my luck's in, it might be a heart attack, thought Bertie.

'The suspect was reported to be in Whitechapel,' insisted Jock.

'By whom?' asked Bertie.

Jock hesitated. 'It was an anonymous tip,' he said. 'Confirmed by CCTV.'

'I see,' said Bertie gravely. 'Anonymous.'

He glanced at the deputy commissioner as she hung up.

'And no checks were run on the address?' he added, rueful. 'Looks like there's been a cock-up somewhere.'

Jock took a step forwards, as if he might leap across the desk and choke Bertie there and then. 'I've got a man down, on top of the other casualties,' he shouted. 'I want your fucking phone records Bertie. Landline and mobile!'

Bertie looked shocked. 'Of course, be my guest. I'll co-operate fully with any inquiry.' He addressed the deputy commissioner. 'There will be another inquiry, I imagine?' he said.

It was a none too subtle reference to the history of Jock's crew.

This time Jock made a move.

The deputy assistant commissioner put a restraining hand on his arm, but it was Bertie she had in her sights.

'Yes. There'll have to be a *full* inquiry,' she said.

Bertie looked at her, then at Jock, then back at her.

'I'm going off sick,' said Bertie. 'Stress. Talk to my union rep.'

Berlin stayed flattened against the air-con units as the helicopter cruised the perimeter of the scene, which would be well and truly secure by now.

Her mobile had logged a missed call. Probably from Sonja or Snowe. Sonja would want to know when she was bringing Princess home. Snowe would want to know too. He might have already run out of patience. She had to check.

Berlin called the hotel room. It rang out. She cursed. She called again and this time spoke to reception. Would they please send someone up to check on the occupant of the room? They weren't answering the phone and she was concerned.

There was a pause. The lobby muzak drifted down the line. Berlin could hear the soft clack of a computer keyboard.

'I'm sorry, madam, that party appears to have checked out,' came a voice trained to communicate a bright, corporate smile.

'Did you see them go?' asked Berlin. Snowe would have brought a female uniformed officer with him.

The smile hesitated.

'Are you the cardholder to whom the room was charged, madam? Because there seems to have been a misunderstanding . . .'

Berlin listened to the smile rabbit on.

A leaden blanket of cloud hung so low she felt its suffocating weight bear down on her.

Heavy footsteps approached across the roof.

She hung up.

A masked face appeared in the gap between the two units.

63

The young constable was amazed by the number of forensics people and senior brass going in and out of the apartment building. There were dogs and vehicles everywhere to add to the chaos, and he couldn't hear a word anyone said because the helicopter was still circling.

He checked the ID of the figure in a disposable forensic suit and mask who emerged from the posh apartment building. How come terrorists could afford digs of this standard, when he could hardly manage the rent on his shoebox in Croydon? He ticked the exit box against Detective Kennedy's name and noted the time on the log.

Thirty minutes later two officers left the scene. One, whom the constable recognised as Kennedy, went past stripping off his disposable suit and talking on his mobile. Confused, the constable checked his log.

Meanwhile the other officer, who was shrouded in suit and mask, kept going.

'Sir, your ID?' the constable called after Kennedy.

Kennedy signalled that he'd only be a moment; he was busy with his call. He kept talking and walking.

The constable ran after the other officer.

'Hang on! I need your ID,' he said.

The officer stopped, yanked off his mask and dragged his badge out from inside his suit.

The constable ticked him off the list and noted the time.

By the time he turned around, Kennedy had gone.

The constable knew he'd fucked up somewhere. Kennedy had

left twice. He could have missed him going in again. The same number of officers had gone in and come out, according to the log.

Everyone was very touchy about terrorist incidents. Shit would rain down on him if he admitted to making a mistake. But no one would know if he didn't tell them. There was no way of telling from the paperwork.

He'd worked long hours as a volunteer before he finally got into the Met. His career would be over before it began.

What should he do?

Nothing.

No one took any notice of a woman in a pair of white paper overalls. It was London. She was five minutes from a hospital and five minutes from a crime scene. It was like being six feet from a rat. It went with the territory.

Kennedy was astounded when Berlin got into the back seat of his car and pulled a gun on him.

'What the fuck?' he said.

They were in an ill-lit corner of an enclosed car park near Petticoat Lane, where they had agreed to meet. He couldn't believe it. So this was how she repaid him. The dim light obscured her face, but he could see the rage gleaming in her eyes. It wasn't a good look.

'Let's have it, Kennedy,' she said. 'And don't bullshit me, I'm not in the mood.'

It occurred to him that whatever substance kept Berlin's addiction under control might have run out. He cursed himself for ever getting involved with a junkie. They were just so fucking unreliable.

'I don't know what you're talking about,' he said. 'I just saved your arse, didn't I?'

'Because it wouldn't suit you if I was nicked,' she said.

'Get that thing out of my face. Please.'

Berlin kept the barrel level with his head.

'What? What?' he shouted.

Berlin squeezed the trigger.

They were tucked into a corner of a filthy car park, littered with used needles and condoms. The place where he might end his days. He thought about the trusting face of his little boy, gazing at him from behind his oxygen mask. He lost it.

'I haven't got her!' he screamed.

'Only two people knew where she was,' she shouted back. 'You and Snowe.'

'Put a gun to his head then,' yelled Kennedy.

Berlin pressed the Glock into the soft spot under his jaw, jabbing at the place where her own throat was blotched by tender cords of scar tissue.

'Snowe doesn't check out of hotels without paying the minibar bill,' she said quietly.

Kennedy knew the steady roar of the traffic would drown the shot and he had no doubt she was capable of pulling the trigger. The buzzing in his ears was probably his blood pressure going through the roof.

'You don't know what it's like,' he said. 'My son needs specialist treatment just to stay alive. My wife can't cope and —'

'Get to the fucking point,' she said.

'It was Bertie,' said Kennedy, miserably.

'So you told him Princess was at the hotel.'

Kennedy nodded. 'I had no choice. He wanted to know where you were too, to get you out of the way. But you have to believe me, I didn't know he was going to set you up like that. I had no idea he would involve armed officers.'

'What? Do you mean they were after me, not them?' asked Berlin, incredulous.

'He threatened my family! When I got home from meeting you at the hotel my wife was freaking out.'

'So much for bloody coincidence,' she said, and resolved to drop trust from her rehab programme.

He didn't like the way she was staring at him. There was something cold and impenetrable at her core.

There was a long silence.

Kennedy drove through the narrow back streets of the East End. Berlin sat behind him. An unmarked police vehicle was probably the safest place for her to be right now.

Kennedy reached for his hanky, but she jabbed him with the gun. She'd moved it from under his jaw to the back of his head.

'I just want to wipe my face,' he said. The sweat from his forehead was running into his eyes.

'Use your sleeve,' she said.

He did as he was told.

'I read Murat Demir's affidavit and I spoke to Pannu before all this went down,' said Kennedy.

'Who?' she asked.

'The sergeant who arrested you on the stalking charge. No one, including Pannu, could have known that Murat had more to hide than you did. No wonder he was watching you.'

She didn't respond.

'So, did you get anything from him?' he asked tentatively.

'My interrogation was rudely interrupted,' she said.

Kennedy's phone rang. He glanced in the rear-view mirror. Berlin nodded. He answered the call.

'Kennedy,' he said. He listened for a moment. 'Yeah, okay. Thanks for that,' he said, and hung up.

The traffic lights ahead turned red. He glanced over his shoulder at Berlin.

'The toxicology on Billy just came through,' he said. 'It was an overdose of Special K. No sign of a struggle. Definitely self-administered.'

'Where did he get the cash?' she said.

'Maybe someone made a generous donation,' he said.

'Yeah,' said Berlin. 'Maybe.'

64

Sonja sat at her table staring at her phone. She waited for a call or for someone to come.

Her fear was so great that she felt one more shock, no matter how small, could finish her. She would fracture and disintegrate into a thousand tiny fragments.

All the king's horses and all the king's men would never put Sonja together again.

An awful vision was seared into her brain: a photo of Princess had been sent to her phone. Her daughter was bound and gagged, her eyes wide with terror. Did they have Berlin too?

Paralysed, she sat and waited. Someone would call. Someone would knock.

Bertie's front door was on the latch. A note pinned on it read *Gone to the shops. Back in five minutes, love Mum*. The ink was faded, the paper weathered. The note had been there a lot longer than five minutes.

Berlin gave Kennedy a nudge in the back with the gun and he pushed open the door. The minute they stepped into the hall they were assailed by the smell.

'Jesus Christ,' said Kennedy. 'Bertie?' he called.

'Up here,' came the muffled response.

Towering mounds of newspapers and milk cartons lined the walls, forming a tunnel that had to be negotiated with care.

Dank gloom swarmed in as they filed up the stairs. The reek of decay grew as they reached the first landing. Berlin heard the skittering of rats in the walls. Every window upstairs was sealed behind mountains of old handbags, overcoats and clothes. Hoarders.

A door on the small landing stood ajar.

Kennedy hesitated. Berlin pushed him forwards.

Kennedy's hand went to his mouth as he pushed the door wider. The stench hit Berlin like a punch in the guts.

A single bed against one wall was heaped with blankets and covered with sheets of thick plastic.

'I'm in here,' came Bertie's voice from somewhere above them.

They backed away from the door, crossed the landing and took the final three stairs to the top of the house. Kennedy entered the attic first. The dirty skylight was closed, bathing the room with a yellow stain.

'You took your time,' said Bertie.

Berlin was right behind him.

Princess was gagged and tied to a kitchen chair. Bertie was pointing a sawn-off shotgun at her head. Berlin could see the stock was slick with sweat.

Bertie didn't seem surprised to see her.

The floor was littered with empty blister packs of medication and bottles of cough syrup.

'Give him the gun,' Bertie ordered Berlin. 'And get over there against that wall.'

She offered Kennedy the Glock. He took it without looking at her. He was staring at Bertie with loathing and horror. Berlin went and stood where she was told.

Bertie relaxed once Kennedy had the gun and Berlin had backed off. He took a step away from Princess.

'You can let the kid go now, Bertie,' said Kennedy. 'Then we can all go downstairs.'

'Mum likes company,' said Bertie, with a chuckle.

The silence that followed was broken by the scrabbling of tiny claws across the sheets of plastic in the room below. Berlin and Kennedy stared at the floor, their eyes following the sound.

Bertie had his mum's body tucked up down there.

'Let the kid go, Bertie,' said Kennedy.

'No,' said Bertie, and cocked the shotgun.

Berlin watched the blood drain from Kennedy's face.

Princess began rocking back and forth on the chair, rolling her head, struggling to spit out the gag.

Berlin tried to send a message with her eyes. *It's okay. Take it easy. Calm down. Don't provoke him.* Bertie was on the shortest of fuses.

Kennedy took a step towards Princess.

'Where is the fucking dope?' said Bertie.

'In the kid's bag, like always,' said Kennedy.

'No, it isn't!' shouted Bertie, waving the shotgun about. His finger was still on the trigger.

He reached down, snatched Princess's backpack from the floor and up-ended it. Stuff flew everywhere: pens, books, beads, feathers, stones, charms, an old lipstick and eye makeup, dirty hankies. But no package.

Bertie pointed the shotgun at Berlin.

'Where is it, you cunt?' he demanded.

Berlin tried to find her voice, but her tongue felt dry and swollen, stuck to the roof of her mouth. She swallowed hard and struggled to think of something to say.

'I haven't got it. Do you think I would be standing here if I had half a key of smack?' she said.

'Yes, I think you would,' said Bertie. He swung around and smacked Princess hard with the back of his meaty hand. Her chair wobbled with the impact, but didn't tip over.

Berlin flinched, as if the blow had struck her.

'Bertie! No. Not the kid,' shouted Kennedy.

'Shut up, you fucking girl's blouse,' sneered Bertie.

Kennedy was shaking so much Berlin thought he might fall down.

'We could belt *her* all we like,' said Bertie, indicating Berlin. 'She would never give it up. But I'm guessing she's sentimental about this little blighter.' He swung again and caught Princess full in the face.

Blood began pouring from the kid's nose and soaking into the gag in her mouth. She struggled to breathe. Berlin felt something inside her snap and she lunged across the room.

But Kennedy was closer. He raised the Glock, shoved it under Bertie's chin, and fired.

65

Snowe cursed himself for the umpteenth time. Berlin and Princess were in the wind and he had no damn idea where. The housekeeper at the hotel had told him the room had been a mess; her description was consistent with a struggle, which was inconsistent with the kid and Berlin taking off together.

That was bad enough. But now Berlin had been involved in what was being described by the brass as a 'debacle' and as a result he was here, instead of doing his job. As he approached Thames House he gazed up at the floodlit figures of St George and Britannia. They protected the denizens of this grey building, who in turn protected the wilful inhabitants of the British Isles; no one would protect him.

His instructions were to 'negotiate a positive outcome for the commission'. The Whitechapel incident had been triggered by a sighting of his CHIS, so it was down to him. He had no idea why she was there; it involved the family who had alleged she was stalking them. But nevertheless he had to deliver a solution that would satisfy the competing agendas of all the so-called stakeholders; every agency and their dog were involved.

He slipped off his shoes and stepped into the explosives detector. He didn't understand how Princess could have been snatched from the hotel. No one knew she was there. He hadn't logged it or mentioned it in any email or verbal briefing.

If Berlin had told someone, it wouldn't be anyone she knew was a threat. Unless she had staged the struggle to throw him off. That didn't make sense. She could have just taken the heroin and left the child.

He finally made it through the interminable layers of security and slipped his shoes back on, then took a seat in a vestibule, as directed.

After a while, a door opened. A uniformed officer of the Metropolitan Police, a sergeant, emerged. He practically crept past Snowe; head down, shoulders slumped. Snowe glanced at the name on the man's visitor's pass: Harvinder Pannu. It didn't ring any bells.

The tall, austere figure who had shown Pannu out beckoned Snowe and stood aside to usher him into the conference room.

The men and women at the table ignored him, murmuring among themselves, making notes, texting on smartphones. Some were dressed for dinner, some were in tracksuits. All had been dragged out of their clubs or gyms or armchairs to form a committee. An ad hoc committee: it would never be given a title or have its deliberations minuted.

Border protection, customs and excise, SO15, MI5, MI6, the mayor's office and, of course, the Met. Task forces, command units, operational teams, directorates, advisers. Uncle Tom Cobley and all with a single aim: to manage the fallout from another bloody cock-up in policing the capital.

An officer had died and another was wounded; the families were screaming blue murder. Two women, one a doctor, the other a nurse working at the Royal London, both suspected terrorists, were dead. Londoners were asking if they were safe.

An abortive raid had been undertaken on the spur of the moment without a proper risk assessment; a team had gone in without intel on the address or its occupants – not that there was any intel, anyway; there had been miscommunication at every level of command.

A representative of the political wing of a Kurdish organisation had accused the British government of carrying out assassinations at the behest of the Turkish government.

MPs were already rising to ask what the enormous counter-terrorism budget was being spent on. If the apartment had been booby-trapped the whole of Whitechapel could have been blown sky-high.

They had to get ahead of the news cycle.

Snowe cleared his throat. His inquisitors looked up.

No one smiled.

66

'I'd better call this in before the neighbours do,' said Kennedy. 'You should make yourselves scarce.'

Berlin extricated herself from Princess and turned her towards the door. But the kid resisted. She wouldn't leave without her stuff.

Berlin crouched down and swept it all into the backpack. Princess took it from her and slipped it on. It was her security blanket.

And it contained the things in her chaotic existence that she could rely on. Things that were truly hers, that were worthless to anyone else, that nobody would want to take from her. Not the heroin.

'The heat does funny things to people,' said Kennedy.

He wiped the gun down carefully, placed it in Bertie's grip, then let it slide to the floor, where it lay beside the shotgun he'd dropped as he fell. Kennedy righted the chair and scooped up the plastic ties that had held Princess.

He would remove all traces of their presence at the scene.

'No one knew what a seriously ill man he was,' he murmured.

When the worm turns, it really turns, thought Berlin.

'What about the Glock?' she asked.

'It was his anyway,' said Kennedy. 'Met issue. Bertie gave it to Mortimer.' He reached for his mobile.

Berlin realised he had stopped trembling. He was calm, in charge. She caught a glimpse of the capable officer.

Kennedy was waiting for his call to be answered.

'There's never a policeman around when you want one,' he said.

He glanced down, startled, as Princess touched his hand in a mute gesture of thanks. Removing his blood-spattered glasses, he cleaned them on his shirt, slipped them back on and smiled at her. To Berlin he said, 'I'm sorry.'

Not as sorry as you will be, she thought.

The air outside seemed sweet after the stench of the charnel house, but Berlin could still detect the odour of death clinging to their clothes.

Doors and windows were open to expel the heat of the day, the lives inside spilling onto the street; screams and cries, shouts and gunshots that could come from the TV. Or not.

Princess's nose had stopped bleeding, but her cotton top was dark with it. The kid was docile, compliant. In shock.

'His mum was wrapped in plastic,' she said.

'Come on,' said Berlin.

Princess took her hand and gripped it.

Berlin gripped back.

Even those who stood in doorways scanning for soft targets turned away from the woman and child as they moved through the night. Menace went with them.

They walked on in silence, each resigned to a solitary fate that would be dogged by violence.

When they finally reached Berlin's flat in Bethnal Green, she circled the block, just in case. It was very unlikely the police would be waiting for her. Kennedy had said his boss hadn't issued a warrant yet. Anyway, she and the kid were both shattered and had nowhere else to go.

She didn't turn on the lights in the flat, just flung open every window and poured herself a very large Scotch with a shaking hand. Gestures to celebrate the fact that they were still alive. It had been a close call for the kid.

The Scotch was also a substitute for something stronger. She had missed yet another appointment with Rolfey. The small voice reminding her she had run out of caps would soon turn into a roar.

She stripped off and wrapped herself in her dressing-gown. She ran a bath for Princess and gave her an old shirt to wear as a nightie. She stuffed all their clothes into a large bin bag and tossed it under the sink. The kid didn't ask why.

When it was Berlin's turn for the bath, she took the bottle of Scotch with her and lay in the tepid water for a long time in a bid to dissolve the anxiety scrambling her brain and the pain plaguing her body. By the time she got out, Princess was asleep on the sofa.

She stood at the open window for a moment and wondered if it would ever rain again. The air itself was parched. Even the weeds that grew between the bricks had withered as the mortar shrank and fell. London sighed and the city's crevices yawned as the moisture evaporated from her foundations.

Berlin lay down and yielded to desolation, slipping into the rifts between her past and her future.

36°C

67

The flat light before dawn barely penetrated the thick glass of the small, square window high in the corner of the interview room.

Kennedy's paper suit was itchy. He'd already been grilled by two blokes from Professional Standards, and now Snowe was sitting on the other side of the table. They were letting him have a go.

Snowe's cold, clipped tone couldn't conceal the anxiety in his eyes. Kennedy knew all the signs.

'Why did DCI Burlington initiate a request for firearms officers to respond to any sighting of Catherine Berlin?' asked Snowe.

'I assume he believed she was armed.'

'It wasn't his case,' said Snowe.

Kennedy shrugged. 'Is this going to take long?' he asked. 'I'm a bit shaken up, you know. My mate blew his head off in front of me only hours ago.'

'Why do you think he did that?'

'What? Involved armed officers, or topped himself?'

'Involved armed officers,' said Snowe.

'I've no idea,' said Kennedy. 'He'd known Jock McGiven a long time.'

'And if his death was suicide, why would he do that?'

'He'd just gone off on stress leave, under the cloud of an inquiry,' said Kennedy. 'I went to check up on him, concerned about his state of mind, and he did it right in front of me, before I could stop him.'

'My understanding was that the raid on the apartment in Whitechapel was triggered by an anonymous call,' said Snowe.

'Anonymous?' echoed Kennedy. 'Then there was the death of his mother,' he added. 'To whom he was very attached. As evidenced by his retention of her remains.'

'And don't forget the difficulty of feeding his habit during the drought,' said Snowe.

Kennedy affected shock.

'Let's talk about the Glock,' said Snowe.

'What about it?' said Kennedy.

'It had been issued to DCI Burlington,' said Snowe.

'So I believe,' said Kennedy.

'A bullet from it was dug out of the wall at the residence of Catherine Berlin's mother,' said Snowe.

'Is that right?' said Kennedy.

'What was his interest in Berlin?' persisted Snowe. 'He wasn't working any case involving her. Your boss Hurley was running the Steyne investigation. Why didn't Bertie tell him about his contact with Commander McGiven?'

'I don't know,' said Kennedy. 'He didn't discuss it with me, or of course I would have informed DCI Hurley.'

Kennedy knew that the direction of the interview depended on whether Snowe trusted Berlin. If he suspected she had warned Kennedy about Snowe's investigation, or that Kennedy had warned her she was a suspect in the Steyne murder, they were both stuffed.

Snowe opened a file and took out a sheaf of photos. They were long-range shots of Bertie and Kennedy leaving Sonja's.

'Who took these?' said Kennedy, feigning surprise.

'Tell me what you were doing,' said Snowe.

'You know what we were doing,' said Kennedy. 'It's no secret. You can check the logs; they're all up to date. We were running a job on Cole Mortimer so we kept an eye on his wife. De facto, I should say. The question is, why were you watching us?'

Attack is the best form of defence.

'Where is Cole Mortimer?' asked Snowe.

'If I knew that I'd have him in custody,' said Kennedy.

'Did you know Burlington had the child?'

Kennedy sensed his tongue swelling in his mouth. He wanted to spit it out. He wondered how the fuck Snowe knew that.

Snowe's next question came hard and fast.

'Did you murder Burlington in order to cut him out of a heroin deal?' he barked.

Kennedy felt the universe wobble.

'Jesus Christ,' he yelled, and stood up. 'What is this?' He paced the room, shouting at Snowe, making sure the camera caught his reaction and every word.

'Am I under caution?' he stormed. 'No! I'm talking to you out of professional courtesy. Now you're telling me I've been under investigation and you're making wild fucking accusations about a dead man who can't defend himself! Fuck off.'

'I'm on to you, Kennedy. So sit down,' said Snowe.

Kennedy hesitated, then sat down. 'This is bollocks,' he said. 'I don't know what you're talking about. I was transferred to the Kylie Steyne murder and Berlin is a suspect. That doesn't have anything to do with Burlington, Cole Mortimer or drugs.'

'What do you think it's to do with then, Kennedy?' asked Snowe. 'The weather? Thank you for your co-operation.'

He stood up and left the room, leaving the door open.

Two uniformed officers walked past. Sonja was between them.

It was so stage-managed that Kennedy could see the funny side.

Sonja saw Kennedy sitting there as they passed the doorway. He was wearing a white paper suit and it looked like he was on the wrong side of the table.

The cops steered her into a room and sat her down, then positioned themselves either side of the door as a black bloke in a suit strode in and shut it behind him.

'My name's Snowe,' he said, flashing his ID at her. He didn't sit down. 'I ordered your arrest on suspicion of concealing a serious offence.'

She didn't ask which one.

He slapped her mobile on the table. The photo of Princess was displayed on the screen. He pointed at it.

'Who sent you that?'

'I don't know,' she said.

'It was Detective Chief Inspector Burlington,' he said.

'Who?' said Sonja.

Snowe produced a photo from a file and put it in front of her: Bertie and Kennedy outside her place.

'Who are these men?' he asked.

'I don't know,' she said.

'Why would a policeman tie up your daughter and send you a photo of her?'

'I don't know,' she said.

'What did he want?'

'I don't know,' she said.

'Where is your daughter?' he asked. 'Where is Catherine Berlin? Where is Cole Mortimer?'

'I don't know,' she said.

'Where is your daughter?' he repeated.

'I don't know,' said Sonja.

'I think Burlington sent you that photo to motivate you to give up Mortimer, or the heroin. Or both,' he said. 'Where are they?'

'I don't know,' said Sonja.

'Where is Princess?'

'I don't know!' shouted Sonja and sprang to her feet.

Snowe walked out.

'I don't know. I don't know!' she screamed after him.

The two officers grabbed her.

Kennedy was in the locker room changing out of the disposable suit. He could hear Sonja shouting. A moment later the door swung open with a bang and Snowe strode in. Kennedy bolted into a toilet stall, slammed the door and locked it.

68

Rita was in a quandary. The cops had picked up Sonja early. But which cops? She didn't know what she was supposed to do now. Being an informant was a tricky business when you were serving more than one master. Should she tell everyone or no one? If she told the wrong party, it could spell disaster.

She had a drink to calm her nerves. The cops had sealed the door and window and told her not to go into Sonja's room. But she didn't like to ask them who gave the orders. It would look a bit funny. It was all getting away from her. She wished the whole fucking business was over and done with and she could get the hell out of this dump.

She thought of her father, caught up in the Silvertown explosion when he was five years old. His brother was a baby in his father's arms when the munitions factory went up; the blast took out the window and the baby was killed by a shard of glass. Decapitated. Her dad was below the height of the window and untouched. He said the place was cursed, but he never left.

She would wind up the same. If she had got out long ago she

wouldn't be in this position. But she'd imbibed villainy with her mother's milk. It was in her blood. She gulped her vodka.

A place could tie you down, against all reason. It was as if the very dirt owned you.

She approached the phone, but hesitated. Better the devil you know.

69

Berlin was vaguely aware of Princess tugging at her.

'I'm hungry,' the kid said.

'Go and watch television,' said Berlin, and rolled over.

The tugging became more insistent.

'I'm starving,' said Princess.

'You're not bloody starving,' mumbled Berlin, still half-asleep. 'The poor children in Africa are starving.' Oh god, she thought, I sound like my mother.

That was enough to wake her up completely.

After a battle involving a screwdriver and hammer, the freezer had finally yielded an old packet of fish fingers. Chipping away the ice had exhausted them both, but it had come in handy wrapped in a tea towel and applied to Princess's bruises. Both her eyes were black.

'You look like a panda,' said Berlin as they sat at the table tucking into baked beans and the thick, golden crust that disguised the white flakes inside.

'What fish has fingers?' asked Princess.

Berlin thought she might be serious, until she grinned.

'Ha bloody ha,' said Berlin.

The windows were still open, to let in the desultory breeze. The noise of kids kicking a ball in the street drifted up to them.

'What's your real name?' asked Princess.

'Berlin,' said Berlin.

'Funny name for a girl,' said Princess. 'It's a place. Ever been there?'

'No. I'm not a great traveller,' said Berlin. That was an understatement. She'd left London once in twenty years, to go to Brighton, and that had been a mistake. 'What about you?'

'No,' said Princess. 'I've never been to Berlin, but I've been to Turkey, Greece, Albania and Italy.'

Berlin stared at her. The Balkan Route.

'With your mum and dad?' she asked.

'Usually just Sonja,' said Princess.

'She speaks a lot of languages, doesn't she?' said Berlin. 'That must be useful.'

'Yeah,' said Princess, intent on squashing the life out of a baked bean with her fork. 'And she lies in all of 'em.'

Berlin took a mouthful of tea and looked at the kid. *Tell me something I don't know*, she thought.

'I'm not going back,' said Princess suddenly, and dropped her fork on her plate with a clatter.

Berlin could see she was making a case.

'I'm not,' said Princess emphatically, shaking her head.

'Because Sonja lies?' said Berlin. 'Everyone lies.'

'Not like this,' said Princess. She hesitated.

'Like what?' asked Berlin. She wasn't sure she wanted to know.

'She told you she killed my dad, didn't she?' said Princess.

'Yes,' said Berlin.

'Well, she didn't.'

A sheen of sweat had broken out on the kid's face. Her respiration had quickened. It wasn't the heat.

Berlin put her fork down.

'I did it,' said Princess. 'I killed him.'

70

The vans rolled in at both ends of the road and cut their motors. Authorised Firearms Officers and their colleagues slid open the well-oiled doors. They moved quickly and silently into position.

Anyone glancing out of the window or opening their front door took a step back, staying well out of range.

Officers were deployed at the base of the block of flats, up the staircase and in strategic positions on nearby rooftops. They waited for the signal, sweating in their helmets and stab vests, visors foggy, mouths dry.

A noise like thunder enveloped Berlin and Princess as the door caved in. Berlin tried to shout as she was taken down to the floor, but nothing came out. She was winded.

The cry she heard was not her own.

'Hands behind your head. Hands behind your head. Hands behind your head!' someone bellowed at her.

'Take the kid,' came a command. Boots thundered to obey.

A helmeted head came close to Berlin. The visor distorted the cold eyes, deep set in a florid face, which peered down at her. A heavy boot pinned her, backed up by the muzzle of a semiautomatic weapon pressed into her forehead.

Princess screamed.

Berlin remembered the only thing she knew about being ten years old. It was the age of criminal responsibility.

From the back of the van, Berlin could see the search team dumping her stuff, sealed in transparent bags, into the boot of a car. Including the bin bag of clothes.

A female officer was leaning on a car, applying a bandage to her bleeding wrist. Berlin suspected that the steady beat of muffled thuds emanating from the vehicle was Princess, kicking the roof in a tattoo of defiance.

Berlin had never wanted kids, but the magnificence of the child's resistance struck her as something that would make any parent proud. Of course pride comes before a fall, as Peggy would say.

She had a bad feeling her own was going to be vertiginous.

71

The cell was cool. Walls a foot thick eliminated light and sound. Cold silence. The small window was constructed of opaque glass bricks. The fluorescent strip on the high ceiling was caged. Everything was fitted flush to the wall: the basin, the toilet, the bed. Moulded steel. No sharp edges and no hanging points.

It reminded Berlin of the hotel room. Minus the toiletries and the minibar.

She recalled the old copper's myth that when a guilty man is nicked, he will sleep soundly in his bunk, relieved of the burden of his crime. Only the innocent pace.

She couldn't sleep and she didn't have the energy to pace. She waited. Patience was going to be essential. Every decision now would be made by someone else, according to their needs and the timetable of the system. The afternoon wore on.

She understood why there were no hanging points.

When the social worker walked in Princess saw her opportunity.

'Bryan-with-a-y, I want to complain about police brutality,' she said.

Bryan looked very concerned. He handed her a packet of sandwiches, sat down and brought out his pen and a file.

Princess leant over and peered at it. 'Where have they taken her?' she asked, tears welling.

'Your mum is just answering a few questions,' he said.

She sat back. That was just what she wanted to hear.

'I don't want to talk to them,' she said.

'You don't have to,' said Bryan.

She held out the packet of sandwiches. 'Could I have cheese and pickle instead?' she said.

Snowe waited, impatient for the constable to let him into Berlin's cell. It was more good luck than good management that he'd let Sonja go before Berlin and Princess were brought in to the station. It had been a completely fruitless interview anyway.

He needed Berlin to deliver Princess to Sonja in order to flush out Mortimer. It was non-negotiable. Bertie was gone, but there was still Kennedy and Mortimer. Kennedy would keep a low profile now, but Mortimer would grass him up in order to do a deal. No doubt he would also name his connection to sweeten the bargain.

The problem was that Berlin had been nicked.

The Steyne murder team had finally caught up with her. Two experts had confirmed that fingerprints on a bottle matched those taken when Berlin was arrested on the stalking matter. Hurley had enough to charge her and had conveniently found her at home. He was pissed off, given recent events, and had sent in the heavy brigade.

Bad luck for her and a disaster for Snowe's operation. He didn't believe Berlin had killed the girl. Not that he was going to tell her that. It could come in handy, particularly as he now needed leverage to implement the strategy agreed by the ad hoc committee. Agreed wasn't quite accurate; demanded was more like it.

Princess was in the care of some social worker who was on the record as having dealt with the mother and child previously; they were all under the impression that Princess was Berlin's daughter. He wasn't about to put them straight, but he didn't know how long it would be before the error came to light.

Finally the constable appeared and opened the cell door.

Snowe carried in two cups of coffee. Berlin was even more drawn than usual. The white disposable suit did nothing for her pallor.

'I asked for a doctor and a lawyer,' she said to the constable. 'Not room service.'

Snowe handed her a coffee. She sniffed at it and grimaced. Snowe nodded at the constable, who backed out somewhat reluctantly.

'Excuse me, Constable,' said Berlin. 'I don't wish to be left alone with this man.'

The constable closed the door behind him.

Berlin glanced at the ceiling. There were no cameras in the cell.

'I thought we had an understanding,' said Snowe.

She sipped the coffee. It was truly disgusting.

'Where's Princess?' she said.

'She's giving some social worker hell,' said Snowe.

That's my girl, thought Berlin.

'I know Burlington had her,' he said. 'Then the next thing we know he's dead and she's at your place.'

She gulped more of the putrid coffee. How did he know Bertie had the kid?

'How do the Met feel about another agency poking around in their cases?' she asked.

'Not another agency, *the* agency,' he said. 'And now there are a whole lot more agencies involved, believe me.'

'And no doubt that's a problem for you,' she said.

'That's a problem for *you*,' snapped Snowe. 'Since an officer died in a shoot-out with suspected terrorists. Why were you at that apartment?'

'Who said I was?'

'Come on, Berlin. You shouldn't have gone anywhere near the Demirs, given the stalking charge. It was Burlington who made the "anonymous" call reporting your presence in Whitechapel, did you know that? Why were you there?'

She looked at him, unmoved.

'You're in deep here,' he said, pacing around the small cell.

He's more of a prisoner than I am, she thought.

He came and stood over her. 'I can walk away and leave you to rot, or you can co-operate and I can do you some good.'

'How?' she said.

'What was so important that you had to approach the Demirs again?'

'I'm not admitting I was at the apartment when the raid went down,' she said. 'But the son, Murat Demir, has information I need. He was there the night Kylie Steyne was murdered,' she said.

'How do you know?' he said.

Berlin sighed. 'A woman's intuition,' she said. 'He can exonerate me.'

It was Snowe's turn to utter a theatrical sigh. 'That's bad luck, then, about Murat,' he said.

Her stomach turned over. She remembered the staccato beat of the automatic weapon in the apartment. 'What do you want, Snowe?' she said. 'Just cut to the chase.'

He sat down close beside her on the bunk. His strange coppery eyes looked into hers, his gaze sincere, almost warm. *Here it comes,* she thought.

'You were registered as a CHIS at the time of the raid on the Demirs.'

Berlin looked at him, waiting. 'So?' she said.

'We can make a case to include the drug-related murder of the Steyne girl in a multi-agency operation. You're the link between her, Burlington and the Demirs.'

'But the only link,' she said.

He shrugged. It didn't matter.

'I've interviewed Kennedy,' he said.

She shook her head. She wasn't buying that. There was no way Kennedy would confirm she was at the apartment; given the circumstances of Bertie's demise he couldn't risk pissing her off.

Snowe folded his arms, completely unfazed.

'There's CCTV footage,' he said. 'We may not know how you got out, but we certainly know you went in.'

Oh fuck, she thought. This song and dance has just been a warm-up. She waited for the kicker.

'So,' said Snowe. 'It's up to you; you can be a hero or a scumbag murderer.'

72

Rita knew the way to a man's heart: cold hard cash and the promise of a big score. She was short of the readies, but promises cost nothing.

Terry sat back in his chair and burped.

'Sorry, Nan,' he said. 'That was cracking.'

Rita smiled, indulgent.

Before him lay the ruins of roast beef, Yorkshire pudding, greens and gravy. Jam roly-poly and custard had left its mark on his T-shirt. How he could eat like that in this heat was beyond Rita. Her lunch had come in a glass with ice cubes.

'Now, Tel,' said Rita. 'I think we've been going about this the wrong way.'

Terry blinked and tried to focus. She could see all he wanted to do was lie down on her sofa and have a lovely kip.

'I've done me best,' he snorted, sullen.

'Well, now you're going to do your worst,' said Rita sharply. The adenoidal little devil didn't know when he was well off.

Terry sat up straight, suddenly interested.

All ears, thought Rita. *He loves a bit of bother. Especially on a full stomach.*

Rita had barely got Terry out the door when Sonja slunk past. She hurried out to see what was going on.

'They let you go then, love?' she said, solicitous.

Sonja nodded. 'Please, Rita, I'm very tired,' she said.

'Oh, I'm sure. Didn't charge you with anything then? Did they knock you around? Let me make you a nice cup of tea.'

'I just want to lie down,' said Sonja as she walked down the hall towards her room.

Rita followed.

'I don't know what sort of a state it's in, in there,' said Rita. Although she did. 'They had those people in here like off the telly, *CSI*, you know.'

Sonja touched her forehead, as if she had a headache. Rita thought they might have given her a smack or two.

'But I don't think they found anything,' said Rita. 'No evidence bags, from what I could see.'

'Thanks Rita, I'll talk to you later,' said Sonja. She went into her room and closed the door.

Rita stood there for a moment and considered the implications of Sonja's release. There were only two possibilities: they had nothing on her, or they were using her in some fiendish copper's plot. They had no *compunctation* about that sort of thing. No morals.

Whichever it was, it was a vindication of Rita's decision to keep it in the family.

Something told her that her ship was coming in any day now.

Sonja slumped back against the closed door and surveyed the damage. Every surface was coated in fingerprint powder. The light that managed to filter in through the grimy window gave it a luminescent quality. Hard edges shimmered.

A ghost room.

The old piece of carpet beside the sink had gone. She peered at the bloodstain on the floorboards that had been hidden beneath it. Small scratches at the edge gave the lie to Rita's opinion that they hadn't found anything.

She was standing at the bottom of a cliff. Above her an avalanche was gathering momentum. She screamed at her legs to run, but they ignored her. It wasn't a dream.

73

Snowe had left Berlin alone for a few minutes to 'consider her options', although you could hardly grace them with that term. She suspected this gesture was more about underlining the stark reality of incarceration, and less about giving her time to think.

The key turned in the lock and she feared it was a sound she might have to live with for many years to come. His gambit had been effective.

Snowe stepped into the cell and dismissed the constable with a gesture. He leant against the wall and waited for her answer.

'Let me see if I understand this,' she said. 'You want me to say I was at the apartment, working for you as a CHIS, when the raid went down.'

The irony was gobsmacking.

'Well, you were,' he said, disingenuous.

His logic was faultless, even if the truth it implied was utterly false. 'So,' she said. 'An unmitigated disaster due to shoddy police work becomes a timely, pre-emptive intelligence-led intervention.'

She looked at him, searching for any sign of embarrassment. 'Spin,' she added.

He was not even remotely discomfited.

'And what's in it for me?' she asked.

'We're the leading outfit, so all the others will abide by our strategic and operational imperatives. Including the disposition of other matters in which you may be involved.'

'In other words, they'll do as they're told,' she said.

'We like to think of it as a partnership,' he said. 'But if I do exercise that influence, you and I need to have a clear understanding of what's required.'

'And what you require is half a kilo of heroin, Mortimer and Kennedy,' she said.

'Correct,' he said.

'It's a whitewash,' she said.

'In the interests of national security,' he responded, smug.

The temptation to deploy the dregs of her coffee in his direction was almost overwhelming.

She perused the scrawl on the cell wall, left by other scumbags, looking for a sign. The comments inscribed there led to the inevitable conclusion that lies, fit-ups and injustice had become unremarkable. And she was right up there with the worst of them.

'Of course, I can't guarantee an outcome if you did kill the girl,' said Snowe. 'Justice will take its course. But it will be tempered by your co-operation.'

'You sanctimonious prick,' she said.

Snowe knocked on the cell door to be let out.

'Who survived the raid?' she asked.

'I can't give you those details,' he said.

She was quiet for a moment, defeated.

'I want to see the doctor,' she said.

'Of course,' he said.

'And I want you to leave Kennedy out of it,' she said.

Snowe frowned.

'Kennedy's finished anyway,' he said. 'Burlington's suicide left a bad smell.'

She had to smile.

'There's still the minor problem of ensuring you make bail,' he said.

'Ah,' she said. 'And that's where your multi-agency operation comes into its own.'

74

Berlin contemplated the suit and shirt they had given her. They had returned her boots. The skirt didn't really work with them, but perhaps the judge would think it was a fashion statement.

She had trekked out to Snaresbrook Crown Court on many occasions to apply for warrants, but never under escort to her own bail hearing on a charge of murder. The sun was blazing but the temperature in the car was frigid. Her sweat dried cold.

Snowe had obviously been busy. He had roped in a stray solicitor to act for her. They met briefly in her cell. The walls were institutional green, the colour of bile. An odour to match hung in the air.

'Well, there's not much to say, is there?' said the solicitor. 'The prosecution isn't opposing bail or anything else, from what I've seen. They've even arranged for the witnesses to appear *in camera*. It's a circus.'

The lawyers acting for the commission, Snowe's outfit, had successfully argued that the court should be closed on grounds of national security. So no one would know what was going on.

Her solicitor intimated that she disapproved of the whole business, although she was hardly going to argue that point, unless Berlin had further instructions.

Berlin shook her hand and thanked her for her time.

When they brought her up from the holding cell it occurred to her that she needn't have worried about her incongruous boots. She was in the box. The judge couldn't see her legs anyway. She was half a person. The defendant.

'All rise,' said the bailiff, as the judge entered.

They all rose.

The matter was to be heard by a judge who had a murder ticket and he didn't look too happy at the disruption to his list caused by this odd application.

Not only that, but the courtroom was sweltering and the cheap fans deployed behind the bench were clearly doing nothing to alleviate his discomfort under his heavy wig and robe.

Berlin gazed around at the assembled throng. There was a number of other organisations represented, apart from the Commission and the Met. They each had their own barrister, who was briefed by a solicitor, and behind them sat their clients. They all seemed to know each other and were nodding and chatting in that friendly way that always confuses defendants.

Snowe stood at the back by the double doors. The ringmaster.

'Call the first witness,' barked the bailiff and the usher left the court. He returned pushing a man in a wheelchair. It was Mr Demir, attached to an oxygen cylinder.

The solicitor was right: it was a circus. Except now it was a three-ring circus.

Berlin slipped into the world that Princess inhabited. A universe where she was insignificant and exploited. A pawn.

The custody sergeant at the station had entrusted the court escort service with the painkillers prescribed by the police doctor. They would only dole them out in strict accordance with the instructions.

Berlin felt her body betraying her. She was trembling. Her neck and jaw were suffused with blood. The white collar of the stranger's shirt couldn't hide the crimson pattern of mutilation. She was ashamed, guilty, fearful. And she hadn't even done anything wrong.

Mr Demir swore an oath on the Koran. He agreed with her solicitor that he was currently assisting a number of law enforcement and intelligence agencies. He gestured with a slight movement of his hand at all those represented in court. There had been recent events involving his family.

He asked for a glass of water.

Berlin knew the hearing really wasn't about her bail. She just had a bit part in a much bigger production. Each player was protecting their own interests. All the principals had been briefed by Snowe on

Berlin's role. The current proceedings were so they could cover their arses if it ever came out that they stood by and let a child-murderer back on the street because she was a snout.

Let the judge decide. That's what judicial discretion was for.

Those present listened, rapt, as Mr Demir described the beginning of his relationship with the defendant, the task she performed for him and the bread, milk and Scotch he provided in lieu of payment.

Berlin felt that dying of humiliation was a real possibility. With his every word she heard another nail hammered into the coffin of her professional life. *How low could you go? Investigator: will work for booze*, thought Berlin.

Then one of the barristers asked Mr Demir if he had any knowledge in relation to the charge against the defendant, that of the murder of Kylie Steyne.

'Yes, sir,' he replied.

The barrister asked him to explain.

'My son, Murat,' he said.

'Yes?' asked the barrister, whom Berlin understood was acting for her, as her solicitor was sitting behind him.

Mr Demir glanced at one of the men sitting behind the lawyers, who held his gaze.

Berlin could see Demir was suffering. His wife and son had betrayed him by their involvement in activities he would never condone, but it was a stretch to ask any man to inform on his son.

She could imagine the sort of leverage that had been used to secure his co-operation: he was in the hands of those implicated in the rendition of terror suspects to countries where they could be tortured with impunity. The Turkish authorities would probably also welcome Murat's speedy return for questioning.

The bailiff handed Mr Demir a box of tissues and he wiped the sweat from his face.

'My son put the evidence there. He went to the place, later. He thought Miss Berlin was a spy. It was to . . .' He reached for the word. 'To neutralise her.' Clearly this was the expression someone had used during his briefing.

The barrister addressed the judge.

'I believe Your Honour has certain documents before him which show the defendant is a registered Covert Human Intelligence Source.'

No one was going to ask her. In fact, it was important she didn't speak. They were creating the impression she was spying for them. After all, they had no doubt Murat and his associates were a threat to the nation, although the nature of that threat couldn't be disclosed because of considerations of national security.

Her presence during the raid would provide them with a ready response when questions were asked about how the cell had managed to function right under their noses, given all the resources that were being thrown at serious crime and counter-terrorism.

They could say, quite accurately, it hadn't. They could say surveillance was ongoing. A CHIS was working on it. In fact, *she was there*. Of course, her identity had to remain a secret.

The terrorists had been taken out before they could do any damage. They'd been about to flee without achieving their objective, although their intentions would remain unknown.

A happy ending, bar the one poor copper who died in the line of duty. The dead terrorists were the happy part.

Who would stand up and say the raid was nothing to do with good policing, and everything to do with a corrupt detective who wanted Berlin out of the way?

Not I, said the fly, thought Berlin, sickened by her own complicity.

The judge waved a sheaf of papers.

'These redacted transcripts,' he said, irritably.

'Yes Your Honour, matters of —'

'Yes, yes, national security,' snapped the Judge. 'But it's all hearsay.'

'This is a matter of bail, Your Honour, if I may be so bold. Not a trial of the substantive charge,' said the barrister.

'I'm aware of that,' said the judge. 'I understand the party who is alleged to have planted the evidence cannot be produced,' he grumbled.

Another barrister stood up. Berlin's sat down.

'No, Your Honour,' he said. 'He cannot. We refer you to the documents submitted and to which the prosecution has no objection.'

He sat down. Another barrister stood up. 'That is correct Your Honour,' he said.

Mr Demir gazed at Berlin with a look of utter confusion as he was wheeled away. The rest of the hearing passed in a blur. The judge was no fool. He questioned each of the barristers acting for the various agencies concerning their agreement to her bail, and gave them the opportunity to raise objections.

They conferred with their clients, there was muttering and grumbling, but no one objected.

Going on the record was a two-edged sword. Silence was consent.

75

Berlin signed for her possessions and walked to the secure door. There was a click. She gave it a shove and stepped outside, never so glad to feel the sun on her face.

She stood there for a moment and contemplated a future behind bars, a terrifying prospect that had receded for the moment. *At least heroin wouldn't be a problem*, she thought. There was plenty on the inside.

A door at the side of the courthouse opened. It led onto a ramp. Disabled access. An usher wheeled Mr Demir out and then left him to it.

Berlin stayed close to the wall as she hurried to the ramp to meet him. She limped up to the landing where he sat, marooned.

'Miss Berlin, how did this happen?' His chest heaved with the effort. 'Were you really working for them?' He reached for her arm and gripped it. 'Is it my fault? My son. My wife?'

She touched his hand. 'You had no idea?'

'None. None whatsoever,' he wheezed.

A black car appeared, tooted, sped up and stopped sharply at the bottom of the ramp. Snowe jumped out.

Berlin bent closer to Mr Demir.

'Did Murat say anything about that night, Mr Demir? The night he planted the bottle?'

A bloke with a shaved head, whom she had seen in court, came running around the corner of the building. Snowe gestured at the ramp. The bloke sprinted towards them. Mr Demir's minder.

'Please. Please, Mr Demir, it's very important,' she said.

'Where are they taking me?' he gasped, and gripped Berlin's hand.

Shaved Head was on them. He elbowed past Berlin and grabbed the handles of the wheelchair.

'Here we go, sir,' he said cheerily. He knocked Berlin out of the way and took off.

Mr Demir tried to look back at her. 'They won't let me see him,' he cried.

He raised a hand. She took it as a sign of mute forgiveness.

Snowe was waiting for her at the bottom of the ramp. He stepped aside to let the wheelchair pass, then stepped back to ensure she couldn't follow.

Mr Demir had said, 'They won't let me see him.' With those words Berlin glimpsed the possibility of a brighter future. Murat was still alive. But if Murat was alive, she had been played by Snowe. She glared at him.

'I want to see Murat,' she said.

He took her arm and steered her towards the car.

'It's out of the question,' said Snowe. 'Anyway, he's on the critical list.'

'If he dies his father's evidence won't be admissible at my trial,' she fumed. 'It's hearsay. Even the judge pointed it out. Mr Demir wasn't actually there when Murat planted that bloody bottle.'

'There you are,' said Snowe, opening the car door. 'Enjoy motherhood while it lasts.'

Princess was in the back, reading a comic.

Berlin tried to shrug Snowe off, but he tightened his grip.

'Kylie Steyne's killer is still out there and you don't give a shit,' she said.

'Leave it to the professionals,' he said.

This was the most insulting thing he could say to her, and he knew it.

'You think I'm going to rely on you to get them to drop the charge? What if it doesn't suit your agenda at the time?' she snarled.

Snowe got in her face. His copper eyes blazed with the intensity of a man who would not be thwarted.

'We have a deal,' he said very quietly so Princess couldn't hear. 'You get her to give up the dope, then you take her and it to Sonja. It's simple. Do that and I'll keep my end of it. Fail, and you go down for murder.'

He shoved her into the back of the car.

'Don't forget. You belong to me,' he said, and slammed the door. The driver took off.

'Are you okay?' asked Princess, who was wearing a new pink shirt and blue jeans.

'Oh yeah, great,' said Berlin. 'You?'

'I hate pink,' said Princess, plucking at the fabric, and added, rolling her eyes, 'Bryan!'

'Where did you get that?' asked Berlin, pointing at a smiley badge pinned to the shirt.

'A policewoman gave it to me,' said Princess.

'Of course she did,' said Berlin.

76

The unmarked vehicle dropped Princess and Berlin at the kerb and the driver waved as he drove off. As if the neighbours would mistake it for a mini-cab.

Berlin saw Bella, who lived across the landing, peeking around her curtain. She raised a hand in greeting and mouthed a question: 'The filth?' Berlin nodded. Bella knew the score. The curtain dropped back into place.

Berlin had no faith in Snowe's good offices once she had served her purpose and his job was done. He had lied to her when it suited him. If the Crown Prosecution Service thought they had a reasonable prospect of a conviction on the murder charge, they would go for it, and she doubted he would have the inclination to stop them.

If Murat survived, he would probably refuse to co-operate, and if he was in the hands of counter-terrorism, they would certainly refuse. Why should they do a deal with him to save her neck? Or even give her lawyer access to him? They might even deny having him. He could be anybody, sought by other governments. He could disappear.

On the other hand, if he didn't survive then the truth, and her best chance of acquittal, died with him. She had to try. First she had to find him.

Her flat had been well and truly tossed. Books had been scattered, clothes flung in a heap, the floor littered with her belongings. The door of the cupboard under the sink hung open.

She changed out of the suit and back into her own summer uniform: black jeans and a long-sleeved black T-shirt. She carefully wound the thin nylon scarf around her neck, inspected her boots and got down to business. She didn't ever bother to put the kettle on.

A week ago she had taken her first tentative steps in pursuit of a missing kid. Now the kid in question was sitting on her bed, but she couldn't say she had ever really found her.

Berlin sat down beside Princess, who looked at her, head cocked, expectant.

'What?' she said.

'Where is it?' asked Berlin.

'Where's what?'

'The smack.'

'I thought you had it,' said Princess.

'Give it a rest,' said Berlin.

'The ogre took it. He came back to the hotel when you were gone.'

'Bullshit,' said Berlin.

'That fat prick took it,' said Princess.

'Bertie's dead. He died belting you to get me to give it up.'

Princess was suddenly animated.

'But you didn't,' she said, accusingly.

'Because I didn't have it. Now for the last fucking time, where is it?'

'It was Bertie, honestly! He was tricking Mr Kennedy. He had it all the time, but he wanted to pretend he didn't so he could keep it all for himself.'

Berlin didn't know what to believe. This wasn't unusual in her line of work. It was policy not to believe anything unless you had checked and double-checked it. She had overlooked these basics lately, and look where it had got her.

'Okay,' she snapped. 'If that's the way you want to play it, I'm going out.'

She got up and strode towards the front door.

Princess sprang off the bed.

'What?' she said. 'You're just going to leave me?'

'If you're not going to co-operate, you're on your own.' said Berlin. 'Be gone by the time I get back.' Berlin could see the kid was crushed.

'I've got no money, nothing,' she cried.

'Tell someone who gives a shit. You've got half a kilo of heroin stashed somewhere,' said Berlin. 'Sell it.'

Berlin made sure the door slammed as she left the flat. She went downstairs quickly, in case Princess followed her. Crossing the courtyard, she noticed that the trees were losing their withered leaves. They were pretending it was autumn so they could endure the searing heat of summer. Lying to themselves to survive.

Bertie didn't have the heroin. Kennedy certainly didn't have it, and Berlin knew that Snowe didn't either. Which left Princess. Snowe said the dope was in the backpack when Princess arrived at Love Motel. His source, whoever that was, had confirmed it.

A couple of kids were riding their bikes down the street. They looked like sisters. Berlin stepped out in front of the one with trainer wheels.

'Hello,' she said.

The kid stared at her. Don't talk to strangers.

Berlin walked over and dropped something into the woven plastic basket on her handlebars. The big sister circled, watchful. They rode off. The big sister glanced back over her shoulder, but Berlin had already gone.

'Fuckin' nutter,' she said, then turned to her little sister. 'You always get everything.'

The little sister glanced in her basket and grinned.

Around the corner, an officer watched the blinking cursor on his GPS. His offsider started the car and they pulled out. 'Target on the move,' he muttered into his radio.

'Copy that,' came Snowe's reply, his voice distorted by static.

The techie said that sunspots were playing havoc with the comms. It was a bloody nuisance and would affect the tracking device, too.

'Stay well back,' Snowe instructed through the crackling. 'We might not be the only ones watching.'

When Berlin walked back into the flat Princess sat up and quickly wiped away her tears.

'You still here?' Berlin said.

The kid pouted, defiant. 'You've only been gone ten minutes,' she said. 'Give us a chance.' She slid off the bed and slung on her backpack.

'Just a minute,' said Berlin.

'What?' said Princess.

'What about what you owe me?'

'For what?'

'All that room service.'

Princess looked blank. 'I haven't got any money,' she said.

'I can't let you go while you owe me,' said Berlin. 'You might do a runner. We're talking about serious cash here.'

'What'll we do then?' said Princess, uncertain.

'We'll have to come to an arrangement,' said Berlin.

77

Kennedy was appalled when he opened his front door to Berlin and Princess.

'What the fuck?' whispered Kennedy. 'You can't be here. This is insane.'

Berlin pushed past him. 'I've missed you too,' she said.

Princess followed her into the house.

Kennedy glanced up and down the street, then shut the door quietly. His mum was having a nap, his wife had taken her medication and was out for the count, and his other two kids were at his sister's to give him a bit of a break.

He was on compassionate leave after his terrible experience with Bertie. It was a polite term for suspension.

He followed Berlin and Princess into the living room, where his little boy was in bed.

Princess stared at the kid, surrounded by medical equipment, an oxygen mask covering his small, pinched face.

'Are you a boy in a bubble?' she asked, advancing on the pulsing machines, fascinated by the flickering LEDs.

'In the kitchen,' said Kennedy to Berlin, indicating a door off the living room. 'Don't touch anything,' he warned Princess.

Kennedy shut the kitchen door behind them.

'There's such a thing as a telephone, you know,' he said.

'Which you might not answer,' said Berlin.

'Jesus Christ,' said Kennedy. 'I could be under surveillance. You're taking a real risk.'

'Snowe knows everything anyway,' she said. She saw him flinch.

'About Bertie?'

'No. Not about Bertie,' she said. 'There's no reason that should ever come out, is there? He doesn't know I was there.' *It's not really a lie*, she thought. *Snowe only knows Bertie had Princess at some point. He might have a well-founded suspicion I was there, but he can't prove it.*

Kennedy looked baleful.

'I'm not going to give you up,' she insisted.

He didn't seem reassured.

'Snowe brought Sonja in while I was at the station,' said Kennedy, miserable. 'Trying to put pressure on me.'

'And?'

'And nothing. I haven't been near her or spoken to her since you told me I was under investigation. He'll turn over her place, but so what? He won't find anything there, will he?'

Berlin hadn't got time to think about that.

'Listen to me, Kennedy. Just listen.'

Snowe stared at the photo of Princess that Burlington had sent Sonja. It bothered him. Something wasn't right here. There had been no sign of Princess when the uniforms had arrived at Burlington's in response to Kennedy's call.

Kennedy had denied she was there and suggested that Burlington could have already let her go, or had her at another location. *Bullshit.*

CCTV from the Limehouse hotel and the surrounding area should place Burlington in the vicinity and confirm he had snatched Princess. But so what? What happened next? Did Kennedy and Burlington fall out over this move?

Perhaps Kennedy took Princess, Burlington saw everything going pear-shaped, and in the grip of a pharmaceutical cocktail offed himself. Or not.

The thing that was nagging at Snowe was that the next confirmed sighting of Princess was at Berlin's flat, when she was brought in by Hurley's team. Berlin refused to fill in the gaps.

How did the kid get there?

He put in a call to the lab.

'If I do this, I want my cut,' said Kennedy, defiant. 'And Bertie's. I have to have that money to keep all this afloat.'

Berlin caught a glimpse of his desperation. A man struggling to keep his head above water in a drought. He'd had more than one reason to knock off Bertie.

'Fifty per cent of nothing is nothing,' said Berlin.

'Don't give me that,' said Kennedy. 'You've got the girl, so you've got the dope.'

She wasn't going to confirm or deny that. Doubt was her best friend in these circumstances.

'You're in a queue that includes Snowe,' she said.

'What Snowe really wants is Cole,' argued Kennedy.

'And you.'

Kennedy shrugged. 'We'll see about that. But when Sonja gets Princess back, Cole will rise to the surface like the scum that he is and Snowe will nick him. We could hang on to the product. You and me. Everyone goes home happy.'

'There's only one problem with that picture, Kennedy,' said Berlin. 'Cole's dead.'

Kennedy's relentless movement was stilled for a moment, then went into overdrive.

'How did he die?' said Kennedy.

'Need to know,' said Berlin. 'You don't need to.'

'Jesus Christ,' said Kennedy.

'I've done a deal with Snowe,' she said. 'He'll drop anything he has on you and put it all on Burlington.'

'Why would he do that?'

'Because I asked him to,' she said. Kennedy was slow, but not that slow. She saw his expression change.

'He doesn't know about Cole,' he said.

'No,' said Berlin. 'And we need to keep it that way, because the moment he finds out, he will renege on the deal. He'll need to pull someone to justify his existence, and you'll be handy.'

'So what's the deal?'

'Snowe needs my co-operation. And I need yours. I want you to find out where they took Murat.'

When they walked back into the living room, Princess was wearing the oxygen mask and Kennedy's son was lying there giggling at her antics, his chest heaving with the effort.

'What the bloody hell do you think you're doing?' shouted Kennedy as he snatched off the mask and slipped it back over his son's head.

'I was just fuckin' playing with him,' said Princess, offended.

Kennedy and Berlin looked at each other.

'Do you think you can look after him without killing him?' said Berlin. 'It's called babysitting. This is the arrangement.'

Princess thought about it for a moment.

'Okay,' she said.

'She's my friend,' wheezed Kennedy's son.

Kennedy looked doubtful.

'Come on, Kennedy,' said Berlin. 'It'll be fine.'

Princess beamed.

Kennedy smoothed the boy's damp hair back from his brow. 'I have to go out for a while,' he said. 'Mum will be up and about soon. Be a good boy.'

He kissed his forehead.

'I won't be long,' he said.

78

'Stop,' commanded Berlin.

Kennedy braked hard.

The blast of a car horn behind them was echoed by each vehicle down the line. A storm of abuse followed.

'Now what?' said Kennedy.

'Pull over,' she said.

They had driven down to Whitechapel in silence. The tension had been building inside Berlin and she couldn't contain it any longer. There was no time for this, but she could think of nothing else.

Kennedy edged the car up onto the narrow pavement, parked and put the 'Police' sign on the dashboard.

The heat smacked Berlin in the face as she got out of the car.

The waiting room was packed, the air sour with desperation. Rolfey's receptionist took one look at Berlin and shook her head.

'You missed your appointment; you have to go to the back of the queue,' she said.

'It's an emergency,' said Berlin.

There was a general restive muttering from the impatient throng. They all had a fucking emergency.

'I'm not arguing with you,' said the receptionist.

Berlin looked at Kennedy.

He took his badge out of his pocket and displayed it around the waiting room. There was a stampede for the door.

Berlin surveyed the empty chairs.

'Looks like I'm next,' she said.

*

Rolfey stood up when Berlin walked into his office with Kennedy.

'What's this?' he said.

'This is Detective Sergeant Kennedy,' she said.

Rolfey took a step back. He took another, until his back was literally to the wall.

Berlin was surprised, but she didn't have the time to string it out and see where it led.

'Kennedy's here to guarantee my personal safety,' she said. 'I need a script.'

Rolfey sat down before he fell.

A small fan on his desk was limply circulating the stale air.

Berlin noticed dark patches in the armpits of Rolfey's denim shirt. The computer mouse slipped in his damp fingers as he clicked through to her file.

The printer whirred and the script emerged. Rolfey snatched it out of the tray, signed it and thrust it at Berlin.

'I don't know what's going on here, but I must say I don't appreciate these standover tactics,' he said, with a vehemence that surprised her.

'Me neither, mate,' said Kennedy, as he followed Berlin out of the clinic.

Kennedy went back to the car and Berlin went into the chemist.

When the pharmacist handed her just one cap Berlin realised that Rolfey had got his own back. It served her right. She downed it on the spot. Just the act of swallowing it dampened the anxiety that threatened to envelop her. She had to keep putting one foot in front of the other.

Kennedy was leaning on the car when she emerged. He gave her a look but kept quiet. He was in no position to judge.

'Okay, let's go,' she said as she walked past him.

He followed her down the road. They didn't have far to go.

*

Berlin hung back among the listless horde waiting in reception at the Royal London Hospital. Half of them seemed to be there just to escape the heat.

The seven men who met in the Feathers Tavern in 1740 to found an infirmary for the poor would have been astonished by the soaring blue towers of medical technology.

But they would have been less surprised by the clutch of elderly Bangladeshi ladies swathed in bright cotton who sat in a row in the lofty foyer, knitting and chatting.

Nor would they have baulked at the rumour that the mortuary in Newark Street was overflowing with pensioners who had failed to follow the advice to stay well hydrated. Corpses were being shipped to Surrey. The sealed, airless homes of the elderly were ovens. Afraid to leave their doors and windows open, they were cooked by fear.

Berlin watched Kennedy at the counter. The clerk checked her computer, spoke without looking up, and Kennedy moved off in the direction of the lifts. Berlin followed.

They didn't speak in the crowded elevator. When Kennedy got out, so did Berlin. He hesitated, looked left and right, then proceeded to the nurses' station.

Berlin sat down on a chair in the small space off the corridor, which was equipped with a water cooler and soft chairs for friends and family enduring an anxious wait. She picked up a magazine.

Kennedy walked past without looking at her. His footsteps receded down the corridor. A few moments later another set of footsteps approached.

Berlin peered intently at the two-page spread on Posh and Becks. A uniformed officer strode past, an automatic weapon slung across his chest. She heard the ping as he pressed the button to call the lift and then his voice addressing the nurse.

'I'm off to the canteen,' he said. 'Do you want anything?'

Berlin reflected that Londoners had become inured to the sight of heavily armed officers hanging around in public buildings having cups of tea. Even in hospitals. It was a cosy look.

As soon as she heard the lift doors close, she dropped the magazine. She looked along the corridor. About halfway down was an empty chair. Kennedy stood beside it, about to push open the door. He looked up, gave her a reassuring nod, then stepped inside. She sat down again.

Kennedy closed the door behind him. It sealed with a gentle sigh. He gazed around the dimly lit room. The only sounds came from a bank of humming monitors and the regular squeal of a ventilator. He approached Murat Demir, struggling to control his nervous tremor. The idea was that the moment the bloke opened his eyes, Kennedy would question him about the night Kylie Steyne was murdered.

In theory Kennedy was still assigned to the case and entitled to interview Murat. He hadn't been formally suspended. If he obtained useful information nobody would be bothered by how he got it. Berlin was convinced that Murat had seen the perpetrator. They needed a description.

Even if Murat couldn't give one – it was dark under the canal bridge – at the very least he might be able to confirm someone else murdered Kylie. Not Berlin. If Murat died, Kennedy would have his contemporaneous notes of the interview, which would save her bacon. In return, she would save his by keeping quiet on the Bertie thing.

On the other hand, if Kennedy got a description then he could go back to work with a win under his belt, and set about finding the real killer.

After talking to Murat he would just let him drift back to the Land of Nod. No one would be any the wiser. The armed officer guarding him would just be grateful for the break. Of course,

Murat could just tell him to go to hell, although Berlin seemed to think that doped up he would be more malleable. She should know.

Sweat trickled down Kennedy's forehead and his glasses slipped down his nose.

'Pssst. Mate, wake up,' he said, giving Murat's arm a squeeze. No response. He shook him and leant closer. 'Murat Demir. Come on, wakey-wakey.'

Intent on his task, he didn't notice the door open until the light from the corridor spilled onto the bed.

He turned around.

'Yes? Can I help you? I'm a police officer,' said Kennedy.

The bloke didn't look like a doctor. He let the door swing shut behind him.

'Is there a problem here, mate?' Kennedy blustered.

Murat murmured.

Kennedy glanced at him.

Murat opened his eyes and blinked, groggy at first. Then his expression changed to one of fear. Kennedy followed his gaze, which was riveted on the man behind him.

The man stepped forwards and Kennedy felt a knife slip between his ribs.

I won't live to see my boy die, he thought.

Berlin heard the lift doors open. Boots squeaked. It was the officer returning from his unscheduled break.

'Who is he then?' she heard the nurse ask.

'A terrorist,' said the officer.

'Yeah, what's he terrorised?' she wheedled.

'Need to know, innit,' came the reply.

There was a pause. The nurse's tone changed to peevish.

'Yeah?' she said. 'Well, I need to know his vitals, so suppose you go and shoo out his visitors, then you can keep an eye on me while I stick a thermometer up his bum. You never know, you might enjoy it.'

The officer's awkward laugh faded to an uncomfortable silence. 'Visitors?' he said. 'There's just the detective . . . '

There was a clatter and he ran past the vestibule, readying his weapon.

Berlin stood up and held her breath.

A raucous alarm broke the moment of silence.

Kennedy lay on the floor, still at last.

The monitors beside Murat's bed were bleating wildly. His discretion was guaranteed.

79

The police cordon was going up around the hospital already. Lorries were unloading barriers, pedestrians were being herded out of the back streets, special operations teams were flooding the area.

Berlin slowed down. Her Achilles tendon was screaming and she knew that running, or trying to, would just attract suspicion. Better to stand and gawk for a moment while she worked out how to get off the street and avoid the cordon.

When she gave them her ID at the barrier, her name and address would be radioed in and she would turn up immediately in cross-matching. If she refused to give them her ID she'd be detained for further checks.

Her vision blurred as she recalled the blood seeping from under the door of Murat's room. She had pushed it open, registered the carnage, and let it swing shut again. Her ability to remain detached from events seemed to have diminished. No dope. No more soft landings.

The officer on guard duty had run to the emergency exit in pursuit of the assassin. She took the same route, following him down, pausing only to vomit in the corner of the concrete stairwell.

Steel grated on concrete as the barriers were dragged into position. The harsh sound brought her back to her senses and she realised where she was standing.

The receptionist wasn't pleased to see her. Again.

'He's not here,' she said.

But as she spoke, Rolfey came out of his office, head down, scanning a letter. 'Let's call it a day,' he said. He looked up, saw Berlin and scowled.

'What?' said the receptionist, astonished. 'Now?'

'Well, I haven't got any bloody patients, have I?' he said, gesturing to the empty waiting room. 'Lock up before they can get back in.' He turned and marched back to his office.

Berlin followed him. She heard the door slam as the receptionist left.

'We're closed,' said Rolfey. 'Thanks to you. You're well aware what effect the presence of the police has on my clients.'

'They'll be back,' she said.

'Fuck off,' said Rolfey. He screwed up the letter and threw it at the bin. He wasn't really talking to her. She'd never seen him like this.

She dropped into a chair to disguise the fact she was shaking.

'I think I've ruptured my tendon again,' she said. 'It's killing me.'

'I suppose you were running away from someone,' he said, giving her a dark look. 'Well, you can keep running. I'll be damned if I'm giving you another script,' he said.

'How's your relationship with the General Medical Council working out?' she said.

Before he could stop her she bent down and snatched up the letter, which lay beside the overflowing bin. He watched as she smoothed out the creases and glanced at the contents. The GMC investigators were coming, ready or not.

Rolfey ran his hand through his hair, close to tears. 'I had you all wrong, Berlin,' he said. 'I thought you were serious about getting clean.'

'I'm deadly serious,' she said.

She didn't know who was more surprised by this dramatic declaration, her or Rolfey. Her gaze was drawn to the iron-barred window that looked out onto a small loading bay. There was just enough room for one vehicle.

'I don't want another script,' she said. 'I want you to give me a lift to Walthamstow.'

The alley was just beyond the perimeter of the cordon. If she had just walked through the clinic and out the back, they might have spotted her even though it was beyond the perimeter. CCTV would certainly have picked her up. She was much safer in Rolfey's car.

'Were you running from them?' asked Rolfey as they pulled out of the alley. The police were inspecting IDs at the barrier at the other end of the street.

Berlin didn't answer.

'This is very kind of you,' she said.

'I haven't got much choice, have I?' snapped Rolfey. She had reminded him of her intel concerning the local mechanic's vice and his clients.

'Needs must,' she muttered.

'What's the cordon all about, then?' he asked.

'I've no idea,' she said. 'Why would I know?'

'You're pretty tight with some law-enforcement types,' he said.

'What's that supposed to mean?'

'Nothing. After your visit with the detective I thought you might know what's going on.'

She stared out at the traffic and contemplated Kennedy's fate. 'I'd just forget about that visit if I were you,' she said.

A heavy silence settled in the car.

'What's so important in Walthamstow?' asked Rolfey finally.

She gave him a look. 'What makes you think it's important?' said Berlin.

'No reason, I just thought, traipsing out there, needing a lift . . .'

'You can drop me here,' she said.

'What? What about Walthamstow?' said Rolfey, surprised.

'I'm going to be sick,' she said.

Rolfey pulled into the kerb sharply.

She got out and limped away.

Fear crept up her spine. She scratched at her arms as if paranoia were a mould on her skin. Deer scuffed their antlers against bark to remove the velvet. The rub left a scent on the tree, a challenge to others to lock horns. Hunters also used it to track their prey.

It was just the heat, she told herself, or lack of food and sleep. Or withdrawal.

She should have stayed in the car with Rolfey. Her reaction to him was ridiculous but she had suddenly felt uneasy. He was asking too many questions and he had seen her with Kennedy. He had also given her away to Sonja; practically provided her with Berlin's resumé. It could even have been his idea to drag Berlin into the search for Princess.

Now she would have to risk the Tube in a bid to retrieve Princess before the police arrived at Kennedy's. She hoped there was enough credit on her travel card.

Sonja's phone vibrated and she picked it up, wary of the blocked ID.

'She's on her way to Walthamstow,' said a familiar voice.

'Walthamstow?' she echoed, confused.

'I'm almost certain that's where she's got her. It won't be long now, I'm sure.'

The transcriber handed Snowe a piece of paper. He read it and frowned.

'The intel suggests Berlin's on her way to Walthamstow,' he said.

'How did she get through the fucking cordon?' exploded Jock. 'The CCTV shows her going into the hospital with Kennedy and leaving twenty minutes later. *After* the alert.'

'Maybe your lads didn't get the cordon up quick enough,' remarked Hurley to Snowe.

DCI Hurley and Commander Jock McGiven sat on the other side of a desk in the middle of the control room. It had been hurriedly set up by the ad hoc committee to co-ordinate the operation. They were there to keep an eye on him and report back to their masters at the Yard and then to Whitehall.

Inter-agency cooperation.

'Implementation of the cordon was down to the locals,' said Snowe through clenched teeth. 'It was nothing to do with me.' Silently he berated himself for running for cover, just like all the other agencies involved in this debacle.

'You better not lose her now,' warned McGiven.

'Why would she go to Walthamstow?' said Snowe. He waved the transcript. 'This intel is inconclusive.'

'She's your CHIS, Snowy,' said Hurley. 'I was against it from the start.'

'It was you who arrested her using planted evidence,' retorted Snowe.

Hurley stood up, flushing.

'What the fuck are you implying?' he screeched. 'I've done everything by the book!'

Snowe stood up too. 'I'm not implying anything. The evidence indicates Berlin was set up by Murat Demir.'

And now she had set him up. She had wanted Kennedy 'left out of it' and like a fool he had agreed, believing he was one step ahead of her. It had never occurred to him that she would use Kennedy to get to Demir.

'So he set her up,' barked Hurley. 'Why won't you face the possibility that Demir saw Berlin kill the girl? He planted the bottle to make damn sure she was caught and permanently out of his hair.'

Snowe had no answer for that. His conviction that Berlin wasn't a killer was taking a battering as the bodies piled up around her.

Among the stuff seized from her flat was a bag of her and the kid's clothes. He had asked the lab to test them against the samples from Bertie. They were spattered with his DNA.

The GPS had her in Bethnal Green. The transcript from Sonja's phone had her on her way to Walthamstow. Jesus.

Snowe's phone rang and he picked up.

'Tracker one here, sir,' announced the officer. 'We're still in Bethnal Green, now at the Weavers Fields playground. The kid with the badge doesn't look like the description we've got. She's on a bike. And there's no sign of the target.'

'Retrieve the device and get back to base,' snapped Snowe.

The officer hung up and gazed out of the window at the playground full of children and their mums.

He turned to his mate.

'He said you're to go and get the badge off the kid.'

80

Berlin saw the police car parked outside Kennedy's. She was too late. She kept to the other side of the road, watching, hoping that Princess would emerge on her own. It wasn't going to happen. She ran her fingers through her hair, gathered herself, and crossed over.

The front door was open and the sound of sobbing drifted to Berlin as she crossed the threshold and took the few steps down the hall to the living room. A dazed-looking woman, Kennedy's wife, was collecting her handbag and distractedly checking its contents.

An older woman, an even more shrivelled version of Kennedy, sat to one side of the boy's bed. Her head lay next to his, her tears staining his pillow.

Princess stood on the other side of the bed, alert as a cat ready to spring. One of the uniforms was speaking to her quietly.

'There's my mum now!' cried Princess.

Everyone turned to look at Berlin.

The two coppers appeared to be from the local nick.

Mrs Kennedy stared at Berlin, her eyes misty with confusion. 'Do I know you?' she said.

'I'm from just down the road,' said Berlin. 'Your husband invited her in to play.'

The little boy in the bed took the deepest breath of which he was capable and removed his oxygen mask. 'She's my friend,' he gasped.

One of the coppers addressed Berlin.

'You better get her home, missus, this family has had some bad news.'

She had to say something.

'I'm so sorry,' said Berlin. 'I really am so very sorry. I can't tell you how . . . if there's anything I can do . . . I only wish —'

The policeman frowned.

She was babbling.

Princess tugged at her hand and dragged her to the front door.

Out in the street, Princess kept a tight grip on Berlin's hand. The kid was the only thing tethering her to reality.

'What's the matter?' asked Princess.

'Nothing,' said Berlin.

They walked on in silence for a while.

'You need a fix, that's all,' said Princess.

It was a chilling remark.

'Yeah. But . . . the drought,' she said.

Princess brought them to a halt. She squinted up at Berlin, shielding her eyes from the light. Or the truth.

'I can help you with that,' she said.

81

Snowe was under siege. He sat at the desk amid the uproar in the control room, a condemned man anticipating his execution.

The ad hoc committee had enthusiastically adopted his strategy of using Berlin's status as a CHIS to deflect criticism of the raid; of course, he hadn't mentioned at the time that it conveniently meant she was still available for his own operation. But now it had come out and the whole thing had backfired.

A detective had been gutted by an assailant who had also killed

Murat Demir. The woman charged with the murder of a fourteen-year-old girl had been allowed to run free and now she was implicated in those murders too.

Hurley was right: it would have suited Berlin to have Murat Demir taken out.

All the agencies involved were hunting his bailed CHIS. They emphasised 'his'.

Snowe's unhappy musings were disrupted by a bloke on the other side of the office addressing him. 'Hurley just called,' he said. 'Walthamstow is Kennedy's home turf. Explains why the target went out there.'

Snowe was more interested in where she was now.

The council CCTV footage caught Berlin in Stepney Way soon after she left the hospital. She was easy to pick out because of the limp. Then she went into a building and never came out. Google Maps showed a small car park at the back of it, leading into an alley. The exit was beyond the cordon.

Furious, Snowe tapped out an email addressed to the counter-terrorism team: he suggested they review the CCTV capturing traffic leaving the alley and run the vehicles through the Automatic Number Plate Recognition System. At their earliest convenience.

Google identified the building as a medical facility, some sort of clinic.

Someone drove Berlin out of that car park. If she had been on foot the cameras would have picked her up. He wasn't going to wait for bloody counter-terrorism.

He'd pay the clinic a visit.

82

Princess and Berlin trudged through arid streets that underwent a change of character as the night closed in. They couldn't risk public transport. The CCTV from the hospital would have been examined by now and her starring role broadcast. The hunt for her would have escalated.

They passed through once busy high streets, now a wasteland of boarded-up businesses, gaps in the smile of the capital. It was evidence of a crisis that had become a banal predicament. London was littered with these toothless ghosts, communities where only the despairing or dangerous emerged at night. Everyone else locked up tight.

Striped plastic awnings hung limp and brittle, cracked by the sun. Deals of another kind dominated trade in the lifeless marketplaces, but because of the drought they were almost deserted. Almost. Eyes glinting with desperation peered at them from doorways.

Princess seemed unconcerned. She'd seen worse.

They walked south for nearly an hour. Finally, dead on her feet, Berlin relented and they got on a bus. Within twenty minutes they were within a quarter of a mile of Sonja's.

Berlin felt as if she were endlessly holding her breath, fearful of breaking the spell. The kid was leading her to half a kilo of heroin. To heaven or hell. Her quick pulse and shortness of breath had nothing to do with exertion, and everything to do with a panting eagerness.

The bus dropped them at Pontoon Dock. Princess crossed the road, steering them away from the manicured gardens of Thames

Barrier Park, which were illuminated by the penetrating beams of floodlights, and avoiding the new apartments that colonised the riverbank, huddled together in gated luxury, defiant.

Instead, she took the dusty track beside the scrap-metal yard and skirted a mountain of aluminium cans that glinted in the last rays of light. Berlin limped along beside her. They tramped through the industrial estate to the bleak stretch of dirt and thistles beside the river. They passed the derelict factory.

It was the route the dog had taken.

'I've got a dog, you know,' said Princess.

The kid had broken into her thoughts.

'Yeah?' said Berlin.

'Do you think Sonja has remembered to feed him?' asked Princess.

This was as close to home as the kid had come since the night she killed Cole.

Berlin could hear the sucking sound made by the mud as the tide went out. Hollow, drained of feeling.

'You know Sonja,' said Berlin, noncommittal.

Princess stopped dead and looked at her.

'I'm sure the dog's fine,' said Berlin. She couldn't risk a tantrum. Now was not the time for brutal honesty.

The timbers of rotten wharves groaned with the changing tide. Iron roofs snapped and popped, contracting after the heat of the day. Each noise made Berlin jump. She kept glancing behind her, peering at the shadows as they guttered into night.

They cut across the wasteland towards the grim outline etched against the sky. It was a moonless night, but Princess picked her way with ease through the abandoned detritus of wire, rubble and old car bodies.

The foxes paused to watch them.

83

On his way to the clinic in Whitechapel, Snowe called the Waltham-stow police station from the car. He was eventually put through to one of the uniforms who had delivered the bad news to Kennedy's family.

'Was a child there?' he asked.

'The detective's little boy. He's very ill,' came the reply.

'No. A fair girl with spiky hair?' said Snowe.

'He was playing with a girl from down the road. I suppose you would say she had sort of spiky hair. Her mum came and collected her.'

Snowe hung up and smacked the steering wheel. He was a bloody fool.

His BlackBerry pinged.

It was the forensic report from Sonja's place. He opened the attachment and scanned the document as he drove. Everything came into focus. He was an even bigger fool than he'd thought.

He did a sharp U-turn and called for backup. There would be no mistakes this time.

Berlin felt the heat of the day radiating from the giant steel boxes. There were myriad possible hiding places among the stacks of ruined containers.

Princess led the way. The stultifying, narrow passage opened onto the smoky space where the drifting, displaced inhabitants lived out of time and place. Everywhere and nowhere.

A drunk paused in his song as they passed.

Berlin hadn't exchanged a word with Princess since they entered the yard. The mute understanding between them frightened and comforted her. The child she was supposed to save was about to rescue her. It was a yearning that Princess was old enough to understand, but too young to judge.

Within the confines of Love Motel, Berlin felt her resolution to get clean evaporate. It belonged outside, to that other world where standards were set and failure was measured in sentences served, fines paid, benefits lost. In here, blame did not attach. Your downfall may have been chosen, or not; it didn't matter.

Disgrace was a great leveller.

Princess squatted in front of the container that had been Snowe's lair, peering at the sheet of purple plastic that protected her own. It seemed untouched.

Berlin stood a few feet off. She watched as Princess shifted her backpack to hang in front of her and unzipped it. She glanced left and right, then darted over to the container and reached underneath it, between the floor and the ground.

Berlin heard the chink of metal on metal as Princess extracted another sharpened tent peg and slipped it into the back of her jeans. Her last line of defence.

When she reached in again she brought out an old cake tin. She put it in her bag, stood up and walked back to Berlin.

'That's it,' she said. 'Let's go.'

Berlin caught a movement, nothing more than a fluctuation of the darkness between the walls of containers. She put a hand on Princess's shoulder.

Diamond stepped out of the shadows.

His pouting ruby lips contorted into a sneer as he addressed Princess.

'Come 'ere,' he demanded with his wide mouth and slack jaw. A slavering beast.

Princess shrank back against Berlin. 'Fuck off, Terry,' said Princess.

Berlin didn't understand. Diamond's acquaintance with Princess was clearly more than just fleeting. And his timing wasn't just good – it was perfect.

She felt a jolt of uncertainty. How long had he been following her? Had he been there from the get-go, when she began her search for Princess? Or even before then?

From the moment Sonja knocked on her door.

The implications made her dizzy.

Diamond moved closer. Berlin could feel Princess tremble. 'Hand it over,' he shouted. He didn't even look at Berlin.

Berlin thought about Kylie that night. She thought about the dog.

One thing was certain. The dog was not the only connection between Princess and Diamond. It had to be Sonja.

'Give me the tin,' said Berlin.

Princess looked up at her. Berlin could see the doubt in her eyes.

'It will be bad for her if you do,' bellowed Diamond, addressing Princess. He shifted his gaze slightly to take in Berlin. His arms hung loose at his sides. There was a soft click. A switchblade glinted in his right hand.

Princess took the tin out of her bag.

'We should give it to him,' she whispered to Berlin. 'He's mental.'

Berlin crouched down beside Princess and put a protective arm around her waist.

Princess offered Diamond the tin.

As he stepped forwards, Berlin snatched it from her and sprang upright, brandishing the spike she had yanked from the kid's waistband.

'Go home,' she shouted at Princess. 'Run!'

Princess bolted.

Snowe was stuck behind a lorry that was trying to negotiate a narrow street built to accommodate a horse and cart. 'For Christ's sake,' he fumed. He had a unit on stand-by in Silvertown ready to go as soon as he arrived.

He snatched his blue light from the floor, smacked it on the roof and switched on the siren. The lorry driver leant out of his cab.

'What do you want me to do, mate, fly over it?' he said.

84

It wasn't a knock or a call; it was a tap at the window.

Sonja took a deep breath, rose from the table and gathered herself to confront her tormentor. But the pale face that gazed at her from beyond the glass displayed a fear greater than her own.

She opened the window and reached out to Princess.

When Snowe's phone rang he thought it would be his backup, wanting to know how much longer they should sit on their thumbs. He was hurtling down the East India Dock Road.

'I'm on my way,' he said.

There was silence. He thought for a moment he'd driven into a black spot. Then there was a noise like a moan.

'It's me.'

It was the last voice he'd expected to hear.

Sonja murmured as she hugged and kissed Princess. 'Jesus Christ, how did you get away? Where's Berlin? I told her not to bring you here.'

Princess didn't like it and she didn't understand. She struggled free and caught sight of the bloodstained floorboards beside the sink.

'You don't want me because of that,' she said, unable to look away.

Sonja followed her gaze to the floor. 'Oh no, don't think about that,' she said, and reached for her again.

But Princess slipped away. 'You're still pissed off with me,' she said.

Sonja shook her head and opened her arms. Princess shuffled about. Her skin felt too tight. She watched as tears ran down her mother's face. She went to her.

Sonja held her close and spoke very quietly. 'I'm sorry, darling,' she said. 'That's not what I meant. It's just that . . . everything will be okay. Just tell me where it is.'

Snowe stood near the gate and watched as men, women and children were dragged kicking and screaming from their containers. The black night, the unrelenting heat, the stench of fear. Some of the dispossessed filed past with quiet resignation. Spirits broken.

The key holder couldn't be found, so they had used bolt cutters to sever the chain. As it hit the ground, the headlights of vehicles positioned around the perimeter were flicked to high beam. No one could get out without scrutiny. The cry had gone up. *Raid!*

The dogs and their handlers went in first, followed by a dozen officers in full riot gear. Panic swept through Love Motel.

The old drunk whose melancholy dirge had been the soundtrack to Snowe's vigil was brought out and shoved in the back of a van. The vans were lined up, ready to transport prisoners to the station.

Snowe strode through the gate and into the midst of the containers. She'd said she would be here and could explain everything. But she had sounded in a bad way.

Two officers carrying powerful flashlights emerged from among the containers. They shook their heads. Nothing.

She could be anywhere, stuffed into the corner of a container, dead or dying.

'Keep looking,' he said. 'For her and the kid.'

He had another call to make.

85

Berlin staggered past desolate yards patrolled by growling, panting rottweilers. She leant against the immense skips of London's rubbish waiting for transport downriver on barges. She felt she might as well crawl into one and take the trip.

Blood oozed through her fingers as she tried to keep the two sides of the gash together. Diamond's knife had sliced through the top of her arm. She had managed to land one blow with the spike then flee. She doubted he was in any condition to follow.

She limped towards the new estate, which offered a shortcut if she could avoid the security guards. Three blasts of the Woolwich ferry's horn sounded a warning from the tarnished silver thread of the river. She squeezed through a fence. A train roared along the concrete ribbon that soared above her head. Engines screamed as the last planes of the night flew into City Airport, giving her enough cover to cry out in agony. Another hundred yards and she'd be there. But what she would do then, she had no idea.

Sonja was trying hard to sound relaxed.

'Where is she?' she pressed Princess again. 'What happened after she took it from you?'

Princess had shut down at the first mention of the smack and Sonja knew that when she got the sulks she was impossible. Sonja reached for the backpack.

Princess ducked away from her. 'Don't you believe me?' she said.

Sonja didn't want to start anything. She knew she was handling it badly, but she was being pushed to the limit.

'Of course I believe you. Just tell me what happened. Why did she take it? Why did you split up?'

'That's all you're fucking interested in,' shouted Princess.

'Did you make some kind of arrangement with Berlin? Please, please talk to me Princess.'

'Yes! But I looked after the boy in the bubble and then we were quits,' shouted Princess. She got on her bed and crawled into the corner, drawing her knees up defensively, cradling her bag.

Sonja felt her last vestige of hope slip away.

Berlin had gone and taken the heroin with her.

Rita heard the crunch of gravel and went out to take a look. There was someone out there all right, but it wasn't who she was expecting. She slunk back inside again, cursing, and reached for her phone. She was run off her feet tonight.

The rapping at the window brought Princess running. She flung it up and Berlin crawled in, wincing. Sonja grabbed a tea towel and wrapped it tightly around Berlin's arm.

'For god's sake, what happened to you?' said Sonja.

'Your boy did it,' mumbled Berlin.

'My boy?' echoed Sonja. She glanced at Princess. She hadn't mentioned any boy.

'Don't even try that, Sonja. I'm talking about that vicious little sod you've had following me.'

'I don't know what you're talking about,' said Sonja, backing away.

Berlin noticed that the room had lost its stale smell.

'He torched the car, didn't he? I said I was taking her somewhere safe and you wanted to stop me.' She stumbled towards Sonja. 'You're a piece of work. He killed that girl.'

Choked with rage, she wrenched Sonja's head back to look

her in the eye. She was struck by the fact that Sonja's hair felt squeaky-clean. The weird observation made her wonder how much blood she'd lost.

Princess had retreated back to her bed.

Berlin shoved Sonja away and staggered through the curtain into the bathroom. She stuck her head under the shower, turned on the cold water and retched.

She was missing something, but the thought darted away each time she approached it.

She turned off the shower and reached for a towel. It was fresh.

Wiping her face, she glanced at herself in the mirrored door of the cabinet. She opened it.

Sonja was sitting at the table, head bowed.

'You set me up,' said Berlin. 'I fell for your distraught-mother routine and all that crap about wanting to get clean.'

'It wasn't a routine,' said Sonja.

'Was it her you missed or the half a kilo of smack?'

'You don't understand. Please.'

'Stop it!' shouted Princess.

The wail of sirens intervened.

They all froze.

'Jesus Christ,' said Sonja. 'Rita must have seen Princess and called Bertie. We have to go.' She leapt up and ran to the double bed.

'They're not coming here,' said Berlin.

But Sonja wasn't listening. She dragged a bag out from under the bed and began to stuff clothes into it, frantic.

'Listen to me,' said Berlin. 'Bertie and Kennedy are no threat to you any more.'

'He sent a photo . . . ' said Sonja.

'He's dead,' screamed Princess. 'He's dead! He's dead! He's fucking dead!'

The line of flashing blue lights approaching down Silvertown Way was not that unusual. But they were slowing down. Which wasn't right, as far as Rita was concerned. It was all wrong. She rushed out of her flat, went to the big front door, slammed it, bolted it and scuttled back down the hall. Until she heard the kid scream: *He's dead.*

Tyres on gravel, the dying wail of the sirens and car doors slamming all contradicted Berlin's claims. Princess had crawled off the bed and now stood close to Sonja. Sonja didn't move. They waited for the inevitable. But when Sonja's door flew open, it was Rita.

'Quick,' she said. She hurried over and tried to take Princess by the hand, but Berlin stopped her. 'Oh, for Christ's sake,' said Rita. 'I'm doing you a favour. Come on. Both of you.'

Rita led Princess out into the hall. Berlin followed. They left Sonja standing there.

The cops were already banging on the front door and they could hear boots running to the back of the building.

'Don't worry,' whispered Rita. 'That door will hold. TNT couldn't take it out in 1917.'

She steered Berlin and Princess through her flat, then shoved them into her bedroom and shut the door.

The banging got louder.

'All right, all right,' shouted Rita. 'I'm coming.'

Snowe pushed inside as soon as Rita opened the front door. She rubbed her eyes sleepily and peered at him. He took off down the hall with three coppers in tow. One stayed with her.

'What's going on?' she asked.

'Perhaps you wouldn't mind stepping back inside, madam,' said the copper, shepherding her towards her flat.

Rita affected to grumble. The copper followed her, but stopped just inside the doorway. His wrinkled nose indicated that eau de old lady wasn't to his taste.

'Come in, darlin',' said Rita. 'What about a nice cuppa?'

The copper shook his head.

'Just go back to bed, madam,' he said.

Rita sat down in her chair. From here she could see everything. She was protecting her investment.

Sonja stood her ground as Snowe strode in. She stared at him, oddly composed, as his backup filed in behind him.

'Have you seen or heard from Catherine Berlin or your daughter?' Snowe asked. 'They could be hurt, in need of medical attention.'

Sonja shook her head.

'Are you sure about that?' asked Snowe.

'I told her not to come here,' said Sonja.

He knew that much was true. He gestured to one of the uniforms, who reached for his handcuffs.

'Sonja Kvist, I am arresting you on suspicion of the murder of Cole Mortimer,' said Snowe.

He paused, but she didn't react.

'You do not have to say anything,' he continued. 'But it may harm your defence if you do not mention when questioned something which you later rely on in court. Anything you do say may be given in evidence.'

The officer handcuffed the unresisting Sonja.

'Take her away,' said Snowe.

Sonja suddenly uttered an eerie yowl.

Snowe couldn't tell if it was denial or despair.

*

In Rita's bedroom, the spell that had held Princess wide-eyed and silent as she listened to Snowe arrest Sonja was broken by Sonja's cry. Berlin saw her shudder, about to scream. She grabbed her and clamped her hand over the child's mouth. Hard.

The kid fought like fury, but Berlin brought her down to the floor and wrapped herself around the flailing arms and legs. She hung on grimly as the sound of Sonja's cry died away to be replaced by the sound of heavy footsteps leaving.

Princess went limp, and for a horrible moment Berlin thought she had passed out. She heard someone speak to Rita. It sounded like Snowe.

Then Rita's front door slammed and the TV volume went up.

Berlin listened, straining to hear the last vehicle drive away. Only then did she release Princess. The kid was like a floppy doll in her arms. Sobbing.

'It's not fair. She didn't do it, she didn't do it,' she kept repeating.

Eventually her sobs subsided and she lay on the floor, her face blotched and puffy, staring at the ceiling.

Berlin watched her, wondering what was going through the kid's head.

'She could have just said it was me,' said Princess finally. 'I have to save her.'

Before Berlin could respond, she heard a noise at the bedroom door.

It was the key in the lock turning.

She leapt to her feet, ran to the door and rattled the handle. Too late. *What was the old bag playing at?*

'Come on, Rita. This won't do you any good; Bertie and Kennedy are both dead. There's nothing in it for you.'

She could hear Rita laughing and the chink of a glass.

The window was boarded up. The door was timber, not just

veneer. There was no way Berlin could break through it, and anyway, she was in no state to try.

Princess realised what was going on, scrambled off the floor and ran at the door.

'Let us out, Rita. I'll kill you,' she shouted. 'I have to save my mum.'

'Leave it, Princess,' said Berlin.

Princess threw herself at the door and Berlin grabbed her.

'For god's sake stop it. She can't keep us in here forever. She's pissed; she hasn't worked it out yet. She won't take my word for it that they're dead.'

Princess pushed Berlin away and started kicking at the door instead.

Berlin took out her phone. It wasn't a call she wanted to make, but she had no other choice.

Princess kept kicking.

86

Sonja shivered. An energy-efficient light bulb, protected by heavy-duty mesh, emitted a cold glow. The iron door, studded with rivets, squealed as it swung open.

The tiny interview room, by contrast, was sweltering. There was barely room for a small table with two wooden chairs jammed either side of it. Snowe sat on one side and she sat on the other.

Another bloke leant against the wall behind Snowe. He didn't introduce himself and he was watching Snowe, not her. Snowe seemed nervous. She guessed the other bloke was in charge. Snowe's boss.

The atmosphere was thick, the silence absolute apart from the occasional squeak of the twin cassettes spinning slowly in the tape recorder.

The boss had removed his jacket. Sonja could see the blue nylon shirt clinging to his hairy chest. She watched, mesmerised, as the shape of the dark curls was revealed through the thin fabric. She thought of Cole.

Snowe's voice reached her from a long way away.

'Sonja Kvist,' said Snowe. 'You have agreed that you are aware of the criminal record of Cole Mortimer.'

'Yes,' said Sonja.

'Cole Mortimer is the father of your child, Princess?'

'Yes,' she said.

'Do you have any knowledge of the whereabouts of your daughter?'

'No,' she said.

'Do you have any knowledge of the whereabouts of Catherine Berlin?'

'Who?' she said.

'Do you have any knowledge of the whereabouts of Cole Mortimer?'

'No,' she said.

'You are still under caution,' said Snowe. 'So for the last time: forensic analysis has confirmed that the blood taken from the floor of your residence matches that of Cole Mortimer. Can you offer any explanation for this?'

'He cut himself shaving,' said Sonja.

'Are you able to offer any explanation as to the apparent disappearance of Cole Mortimer?'

'No,' she said.

'Do you agree you have been offered access to a lawyer?'

'Yes,' she said.

'Do you agree you have been well-treated and provided with adequate nourishment?'

'No,' she said.

'You will be remanded in custody while our enquiries are continuing. Is there anything you wish to say?'

'I want to make a phone call,' she said.

'Speak to the custody sergeant,' said Snowe.

He snapped off the tape recorder with such force one of the switches broke.

Snowe derived a grim satisfaction from arresting Sonja. It was the first sign of progress in the whole bloody mess. At least he had one in the bag.

The search at the container yard had yielded nothing so far but a pool of blood in the dirt. Berlin was still on the run with the kid. All the hospitals in the area had been alerted. She'd said a hoodie had murdered Kylie Steyne, but he could hardly take her word for it. She was still Hurley's number-one suspect.

He walked back down the corridor into the custody suite. The desk sergeant was flat out processing the prisoners from Love Motel, who had outstanding warrants aplenty. Snowe inspected the bunch of miscreants. He could see vans outside, with officers waiting to deliver others.

The door opened to admit another batch. Among them were two officers with a sullen hoodie. One of the officers signalled to Snowe. He quickly snapped on a pair of disposable gloves, strode over and pushed back the hood. A lump on the youth's temple was still swelling.

One of the officers handed Snowe a large evidence bag that contained a cake tin. He opened it. Inside the tin was a package wrapped in plastic and tape.

'Where did you get this?' asked Snowe.

'I found it, you black bastard,' shouted the youth.

'That's him,' Snow said to the officers. 'Well done.'

'You little mouth-breather,' said Snowe. 'Ten years for possession with intent to supply will teach you some manners. You could be in line for murder, too, if what I hear is correct.'

'What the fuck?' screamed Diamond, and kicked off. The other prisoners took this as a signal to have a go, and pandemonium broke out.

Snowe hit the panic bar that ran around the custody suite and officers came running from all over the station, truncheons at the ready.

Two in the bag, and the heroin. Things were looking up.

87

Berlin sat on Rita's bed. It stank, but she was past caring and she probably didn't smell too good herself. Princess was lying on the floor beside the door, kicking it with a relentless rhythm. She was swearing under her breath and seemed feverish. The kid had lost it.

Berlin's arm was throbbing and the tea towel was already soaked through with her blood. She realised that this new injury might help to keep her in Rolfey's pain-management system. *Every cloud*, she thought, then flushed with shame. She might just as well have put her arm in a vice.

She registered that the sound of the television had died away. She slipped off the bed and squatted down beside Princess, gesturing for quiet. Princess got the message. She lay still. Berlin put her ear to the door. She could hear voices.

'The cavalry,' she whispered to Princess.

Princess scrambled to her feet.

There was a shuffling sound, muttering, then the key turning in the lock. Berlin stood and took a step back.

Princess squirmed past her and ran out as the door of Rita's bedroom opened.

Berlin followed her into the living room, which was lit only by the flickering light of the screen.

Rita was retreating, probably expecting Berlin to clobber her.

Princess made a strange noise.

'Hello, Cathy,' said a bald, middle-aged man with a smirk.

Berlin drew a blank. She looked around for their knight in shining armour.

Princess was backing up, her hands raised in a gesture of surrender.

'Long time no see,' said the man.

The air left Berlin's lungs, as if she'd been winded. 'Cole?' she said.

Princess began to shake her head and babble, as if there were an incantation that could expel this vision. Her hands were not raised in capitulation, but to ward off evil.

Berlin drew breath as the shock flooded her system.

'How about a hug for Daddy, my little Princess?' said Cole with a broad grin.

'You're dead,' said Princess.

'Sorry to disappoint,' said Cole. He lifted his T-shirt to reveal a thick bandage taped around his ribs.

'I'm a bleeder,' he said, laughing.

Rita had moved off to the furthest corner of the room.

Berlin put a hand on Princess's shoulder to try to steady her, but she was still reeling herself. She felt the toxic flowers of betrayal bloom inside her, rushing in to fill the vacuum.

The apparition of a tall, handsome young man with thick, black hair decayed into the bald, flabby bloke before her. The two shared a familiar sinister smile.

'Sonja said you were dead,' she managed.

'When a kid runs off with half a key of smack, desperate measures are called for,' said Cole.

'She's in custody,' said Berlin. 'For murdering you.'

'So I hear,' said Cole, with a nod at Rita. He was circling Berlin very slowly, playing peek-a-boo with his terrified daughter, who was cowering behind her.

'Reunited at last,' he said and made a lunge for Princess.

Berlin jumped back, startled, nearly knocking Princess to the floor. She grabbed the kid to break her fall and hung onto her.

Cole kept circling and lunged again.

Berlin kept Princess behind her and braced herself to take Cole on. In her condition it would all be over with one well-placed shove.

Cole smiled, amused. He was toying with them.

Berlin felt as if she were staring at an apparition, a shade that had escaped hell to torment them.

'Does Sonja know?' she asked. As soon as the question was out of her mouth she realised it was ludicrous.

Cole roared with laughter.

'It was her idea,' he said. 'Do you think the little bugger would have come home if she'd known I was still alive and kicking?' He waggled the toe of his boot, the clear implication being that Princess would soon be feeling it. His playfulness evaporated in an instant.

'Come on,' he said to her. 'Game's over. Give us your precious bag.

Berlin didn't want to think how Cole was going to react when he found out the heroin wasn't there. She kept Princess well behind her.

Cole sighed.

'No hard feelings, Cathy. You did a good job finding her. But she's mine,' he said.

'If I give you the bag, will you let me leave with her?' said Berlin. She had to buy some time. This was the moment at which the cavalry was supposed to arrive. Delay could prove fatal for somebody.

Cole frowned, as if considering her request.

'Er . . . no,' he said, and laughed again. A cold, mirthless sound.

The tinny sound of a heavy guitar riff broke the ensuing silence. Cole took a phone out of his pocket and answered it. He listened for a moment.

'Hello, hello,' he said, and smiled. He gestured to Princess and switched to loudspeaker. 'It's your mum.'

'Cole,' came Sonja's voice. It was difficult to tell if it was breaking with emotion or the poor signal.

Berlin watched Cole relish his power. The ultimate vanity: rising from the dead.

'You're calling a bit late, Sonja,' said Cole. 'You were supposed to let me know the minute our darling daughter made an appearance. You junkies are so fucking unreliable.' He winked at Rita. 'Luckily,' he said. 'I had someone on the inside I could trust.'

Rita glanced nervously at Berlin and kept edging towards the door, her hand to her throat so her gold chains and medallions didn't jingle.

'Please, Cole,' said Sonja. 'They've arrested me for murder.'

Cole raised his eyebrows in a gesture of exasperation. 'Who did you kill now?' he said.

'Just tell them you're alive,' came the plea. 'Take the stuff and leave us be.'

'Mum!' wailed Princess.

'I think dead might suit me better,' he said.

Berlin could see where this was going. She had only one card to play: she knew the smack was gone, but he didn't.

'Give it to him,' she said to Princess.

Princess looked up at her.

'What?' she said.

'Give him your bloody bag,' she said and made a grab for it. Princess went ballistic. Cole watched as Berlin wrestled with her and dragged the bag off her back.

Princess went limp. Berlin knew she had snatched away the kid's last remaining shred of security.

She threw the bag at Cole, who caught it with one hand. The phoenix reared up with his flexed tendons. He was still strong. Solid.

In some awful recess of her imagination she heard Kylie Steyne's hyoid bone crack, the echo a soft ripple in the canal. She saw Cole stuffing the tiny body into the crevice.

'You killed Kylie Steyne,' she said.

Cole dropped the phone on the table, among the detritus of Rita's supper, and greedily unzipped the backpack.

'Prove it,' he said.

'And Billy,' said Berlin.

She reached behind her, slipped the spike out of the waistband of her jeans and inched towards him.

'They'll put me away,' cried Sonja's disembodied voice.

'Good,' said Cole, distracted as he peered into the bag. 'You can rot in hell for all I care.'

'I'll save you, Mum!' shouted Princess.

Berlin used the moment to make her move, but she was slow compared to the kid.

Cole, momentarily bemused, looked up as Princess sprang at him. The knife sank deep into his throat.

He didn't stagger, just dropped to the floor.

Berlin's heart slammed against her ribs. The pounding engulfed her in a great roar. Princess pulled out the knife, wiped the handle and put it back on Rita's table.

88

Snowe walked in alone, but Rita could see all the police vehicles pulling into the yard.

'You've got a lot of explaining to do, Rita,' he said. 'You must think I'm —'

Then he saw Cole. The look on his face, you'd think he'd never seen a dead body before.

'Jesus Christ Almighty,' he said. 'Mortimer.'

He bent down to take a closer look, his fingers at Cole's throat, as if to take a pulse. But there was no point. The jugular had collapsed and he had bled out.

'It was the kid,' said Rita.

'Where is she?' he said.

'Dunno. She took off with Limping Woman.'

Snowe stood up.

'Three hundred quid, Mr Snowe,' she said.

Snowe didn't respond.

'Dead or alive?' she added, hopefully.

For a moment she thought he was going to give her a smack.

'Berlin's wanted for murder, Rita, and right now you're in the frame for aiding and abetting,' he said.

'What the fuck?' said Rita. She brought the diary out of her dressing-gown pocket and brandished it. 'I'm registered and everything. It's all in here.'

Snowe made for the door, but Rita grabbed his arm. He tried to shake her off, but she clung on.

'How about this?' she said, smug. 'I can give you the smack. My grandson Terry's got it.'

Snowe shook her off in disgust. 'Not any more he hasn't,' he said.

He strode out and she scuttled after him. The coppers all stopped to watch them.

'You can't get out of it that easily,' she shouted.

Snowe got in his car, slammed the door and took off in a spray of gravel.

'Filth!' she shrieked. 'You're all the fucking same!'

Snowe drove through Silvertown, cursing. His phone rang. It would be the first of many unwanted calls. He was seized by the notion that somehow this was all his fault. No doubt his boss would share that view. He pressed hands-free.

'Snowe,' he said.

'Desk sergeant here,' said an irritated voice. 'What do you want to do with your prisoner? She's not been processed and she just nearly fainted. If I call the doctor he'll take half the night to come, there's a shift change and —'

Snowe cut him off.

'Let her go,' he said.

He could see a false-imprisonment suit looming. He'd arrested Sonja for the murder of a man who wasn't dead. Then.

89

Berlin was slumped on the toilet seat. Princess sat with her back to the door, her knees tucked under her chin, shivering despite the heat. Berlin suspected it might be due more to the loss of her backpack than the death of her father. She had had to drag the kid away from it. It was covered in blood.

She could hear lorries pulling up at the petrol pumps outside. The guy in the shop had seen them go in, and no doubt he would come looking if they didn't emerge soon.

'What are we going to do?' asked Princess.

Berlin's phone rang, saving her the trouble of lying.

'It's me,' said Sonja's tremulous voice. 'I don't know why, but they're letting me go.'

Berlin turned to Princess. 'Go and buy some crisps,' she said, giving her a quid from her pocket.

Princess looked at her as if she were mad.

'I don't want crisps,' she said.

'Chocolate then, I don't care. Go on.'

'Who is it?' asked Princess. She wasn't stupid.

'Just go,' snapped Berlin.

Princess reluctantly got to her feet, unlocked the door and slunk off.

'Cole's gone,' Berlin said. 'And so has the smack.'

Sonja felt strange. Weightless. The air around her suddenly felt soft and balmy, not clammy and oppressive. But almost at the same moment she felt herself drifting into a void. She had been anchored to cruelty for so long, without it she had no will.

'I loved him once,' she said to the young constable who handed her a cup of tea in a plastic beaker.

The constable smiled. 'You can go when you've drunk that,' he said. 'Someone picking you up?'

'Really,' she said. 'I really did love him.'

There was a polite knock on the toilet door. Berlin dragged herself off the toilet seat and unlocked it.

'I owe you a crate of Scotch,' she said.

'Sorry it took me a while,' said Del. 'It was —'

'Don't tell me,' she said. 'The baby.'

He followed her out of the toilet block.

Princess emerged from the shop devouring a Lion bar. Berlin beckoned and they all shuffled to Del's car.

'This is a friend,' she said to Princess, and directed her into the front seat.

'*The* friend,' corrected Del.

Berlin got in the back and stretched out.

'Where are we going?' asked Princess.

'Where's my change?' said Berlin.

'By the way,' said Del. 'I've been meaning to get back to you about Joseph Snowe.'

'What about him?' said Berlin.

'Straight. Single-minded. A dedicated copper with very good prospects.'

Not any more, thought Berlin.

Rolfey opened the door in his boxer shorts. They were decorated with sailing ships.

'You're at half mast,' said Berlin.

'You're bleeding,' he said.

'You must be a doctor,' said Berlin. She limped past him. Del and Princess followed her inside. Rolfey closed the door without a word.

'Would you make us a cup of tea, Del?' she said.

Del took Princess into the kitchen.

Rolfey's living room wasn't flash. He wasn't a man who spent money on furniture or pyjamas.

'I'm here for my quarterly review,' she said.

'I'm not being blackmailed by the likes of you, Berlin,' he said.

'The likes of me,' echoed Berlin. She advanced on him, fists clenched. 'You've got a damn nerve, given the shit you're involved in. I could break you.'

'The GMC will give me a good hearing,' blustered Rolfey. 'I've made mistakes, but I'm a good doctor. I —'

Berlin held up her hand, as much to restrain herself as to stop Rolfey's self-serving tirade.

'Stop,' she said. 'Let's stop this.'

She didn't have time to get into a debate about their relative moral worth. If they didn't get moving she would soon have plenty of spare time for introspection. The kid's future was hanging by a thin thread. Berlin was about to give it a tug.

'No more lies, Rolfey,' she said. 'It's so undignified. I'm going to give you a one-time-only opportunity. Because I like you.' She paused, giving his apprehension time to build. 'And because I'm onto you.'

She watched as he considered belting her, running or denying everything. Instead he said, 'How did you know?'

'I didn't,' she said. 'But I do now.'

Rolfey groaned.

Amateurs, thought Berlin.

'A change came over Sonja,' she said. 'She was focused, the place was tidy. She wasn't just thinking about herself. What does that mean?'

'She could have got clean!' protested Rolfey.

Berlin dismissed the suggestion with a scornful look.

'And she could have given her heart to Jesus,' she said. 'But she didn't. What she did was call on a reliable source. She had no money, there's a drought on and all her connections had been burnt. Bar one.'

Rolfey sat down and wrapped his arms around his bare chest.

'Okay,' said Berlin. 'This is what's going to happen.'

They drove from Rolfey's towards the City Airport, staying on side roads and skirting the river. They passed the Woolwich ferry terminal. The Royal Victoria Gardens loomed on their right. An oasis of darkness.

'You can drop us here, Del,' she said. 'Thanks very much. You've gone above and beyond the call.'

Del pulled over. He looked worried.

'Are you going to be okay?' he said. 'I can take you all the way there, you know, if you want me to.'

Berlin got out of the back seat and opened the front door for Princess. She slid out.

'It's too risky, Del,' she said. 'Too many cameras. We'll be fine, don't worry. I'll be round with that Scotch to wet the baby's head.'

She shut the door.

The car window rolled down. Del peered out at her, frowning.

'Are you sure?' he said, looking up and down the road, as if expecting blues and twos to appear on the horizon any moment. 'They'll have your description on every alert list in every CCTV control room in London.'

'Del,' she said. 'I can't take chances with the friend, can I? Especially now he's a dad.'

Berlin shut the door.

'By the way, what is it?' she said.

'A girl,' said Del.

Snowe clicked through his emails. It was a dispiriting exercise, just endless requests for briefings and de-briefings at which he would be required to recount his failure.

Counter-terrorism had finally responded to his urgent request for an ID on the vehicle that had driven Berlin through the cordon. They had put together a profile on the owner. At first glance, it seemed unlikely to yield any further leads. Then something caught his eye.

90

Parallel lines of yellow light marked a stairway to heaven, but the skies were silent. City Airport was still closed. The two fingers of water that cradled the runway, once busy docks, were empty.

The night air was muggy. Berlin could see the sheen of sweat on the kid's pale face. She was flagging. Berlin tugged at her hand, urging her on.

'This is going to be great,' she said, without enthusiasm. 'A fresh start, just like we talked about.'

Princess said nothing.

Berlin looked down at the kid, shuffling along beside her. She had been betrayed in the worst possible way; her mother had let her believe she had killed her father, knowing she would be too scared to come home if she thought he was still alive.

Was it Princess that Sonja had wanted back, or the heroin? Berlin couldn't tell, so how could a child? Lies and deception were all the kid knew. Berlin wouldn't blame her if she never spoke again. On the other hand, she wasn't just a naughty child. She was a cold-blooded killer.

Berlin looked away.

The area around the airport bristled with CCTV. Del was right, even without their description any operator would notice a woman and a kid tramping through – there was nothing else moving. They would send out a security patrol to take a closer look. Just being here was a risk.

She tried to limp faster. They followed Albert Road down a finger of once marshy land that poked out into the river. A short bridge over a lock became an overpass, which straddled the channel between the Royal Albert Basin and the dock proper. A yellow haze hung over the water, sodium streetlights refracted in the vapour of the steamy night.

'Nearly there,' said Berlin, trying to sound encouraging as they turned onto a dirt track. At the end of it, she could see the tall gates of their destination. They were barred. 'Oh, Christ,' she muttered.

As they got closer an electronic eye blinked, waiting for Berlin to scan a pass she didn't have. Princess came to a halt. She looked at the gates and then up at Berlin.

Berlin could see the reproach in her eyes; this was just another kick in the teeth.

'Fuck it,' said Berlin. 'Come on.' She turned Princess around and steered her back up the track and onto the overpass. 'Okay. Over you go,' she said. They had no option but to clamber over the parapet and negotiate the steep embankment.

Princess did as she was told and slithered down the steep, dusty incline without a problem. But Berlin's arm was almost useless. It seemed to take forever. She could practically feel the cameras focussing. In the distance a siren wailed. She was almost sure it was on the other side of the river. Almost.

The kid waited for her at the bottom, scuffing her feet in the dirt, seemingly indifferent to the prospect of capture. When Berlin finally arrived she grabbed Princess's hand and hurried her through the yard. An alarm caterwauled, triggered by a motion detector.

They half-ran along the dock, towards a light swaying gently at the top of a mast.

Berlin could hear the yacht's engine rattling in neutral as they approached the pontoon.

From the stern, Rolfey nodded a perfunctory greeting.

'Go,' said Berlin, pushing the kid towards the gangway. Princess tightened her grip on Berlin's hand, forcing her to go first.

Berlin stepped onto the narrow, unsteady plank that bridged the airy nothingness between the deck and the pontoon.

'Come on,' she said.

Princess stepped up onto the plank.

The dark, oily water six feet below them slapped against the rocking boat as they crossed. Halfway, Princess hesitated. Berlin could feel her small, sweaty hand slipping out of her own. The plank wobbled, threatening to tip them both into the river between the shifting pontoon and the crushing weight of the yacht. Princess glanced down.

'Don't,' said Berlin. 'Look at me.' For a second she couldn't tell who was hanging on to whom.

How do you know the difference between a grip and an embrace? She knew then that she couldn't let go.

The kid fixed her eyes on Berlin and took the last few steps.

As her feet struck the deck Sonja emerged from the cabin.

Princess gave an exclamation of joy, dropped Berlin's hand and ran into Sonja's open arms. Sonja kissed her and clasped her tight. When she looked up, she spoke to Berlin.

'Thank you,' said Sonja.

'I'm doing it for her, not you,' said Berlin.

'Please, let me explain,' said Sonja.

'It's not me you have to convince,' said Berlin, glancing at Princess. But Princess seemed happy just to see her mum. She didn't want any explanations.

Rolfey hovered, awkward. 'We haven't got much time,' he said. 'The tide will turn.'

'I didn't know what else to do,' said Sonja to Berlin. 'Cole made me.'

Berlin felt her anger flare. It was the rage that she had visited on Derek Parr in the alley, the fury that consumed Kennedy when he blew off Bertie's face, the wrath Murat Demir turned on anyone who got in his way. But most of all, it was the frenzy that had possessed Princess when she sunk a knife into her father's jugular. Berlin looked at Princess and reined in her temper.

She should follow the kid's example. Princess was putting everything, including Berlin, behind her. The kid clung to her mother's hand and gazed out at the river and beyond; at a future that Berlin couldn't see. She tried not to feel spurned. She thought about Peggy.

Rolfey was casting off the ropes that tethered them to the pontoon.

A siren wailed.

Berlin stepped back up onto the plank and took two quick strides.

When she turned, the plank had gone and the yacht was already moving.

Rolfey was at the wheel. Sonja was standing close beside him.

There it was. The connection.

Berlin crawled up the embankment on all fours and dragged herself back over the parapet. Dizzy, she leant against it for support, the river below swimming with her own shadow, a grotesque shape captured in the stippled light.

A security patrol was parked on the other side of the road. The guard watched her. A moment later a vehicle came over the bridge slowly, staying close to the kerb, as if the driver were lost. Its blue light revolved in silence. The headlights flicked to high beam and it accelerated onto the overpass towards her, skidding to a halt.

Snowe jumped out, gazing in all directions, frowning.

'What are you doing here?' he demanded.

The patrol car drove off.

Snowe looked beyond her and saw the locked marina gates. He swore under his breath. He was looking for something.

Berlin realised that boats on the Thames had to be registered. She felt sorry for him, but not much.

'I asked you why you were here,' he said, scanning the river.

'I was thinking of chucking myself in,' she replied.

Snowe turned to stare at her.

'Too late,' he said. 'You're nicked.'

Before she got into the car she glanced back.

The tide was so swift that the river seemed to boil up out of its depths.

The yacht was just a streak of white in a listing bank of mist.

12°C

91

The lawyer who had appeared for her at Snaresbrook seemed unsurprised when Berlin called from the station. 'I knew this would come back to the bite them,' she said, smug.

Now Berlin sat in the interview room and listened to her in the corridor haranguing three men in suits, who seemed to have very little to say.

The gist of the lawyer's argument was that Rita's account of Cole's admission was hearsay, but given that and Murat Demir's involvement, the case against Berlin for the murder of Kylie Steyne was dead in the water.

Surely the Met wanted this woman off their hands? She had more on them than they did on her: corrupt officers, a disastrous raid, the murder of a valuable intelligence asset while in police custody. At all material times she was a registered Covert Human Intelligence Source and working for one of their officers, who had apparently failed to log all the relevant policy decisions.

Her lawyer invited the men to imagine details of these events in the press. What were the implications for their agencies and national security?

When the lawyer returned to the interview room she put a sheaf of paper on the table in front of Berlin.

'Sign this,' she said.

It was the Official Secrets Act.

Berlin obliged.

'You can go,' said the lawyer. Berlin blessed British justice.

'I'm going back undercover,' Snowe said to her as she walked out. 'I'd rather be someone else.'

92

The brass knocker gleamed in the weak light of a cold, grey dawn. Berlin knocked carefully, wary of tarnishing it. There was no response. She tried again.

The peephole below the knocker went dark. There was the sound of a bolt being slid across, then the door opened a chink. The chain was still on.

'What do you want?' asked Peggy.

'How are you?' said Berlin. 'I just wanted to see if you were okay.'

'You could have rung,' said Peggy. 'Have you been drinking?'

'I'm sorry, Mum,' said Berlin.

'You're always sorry,' said Peggy. 'Just like your father.' She closed her eyes and uttered a deep, juddering sigh.

'Cup of tea?' said Berlin.

'I'm sorry,' said Peggy. 'I just can't do this any more.'

The door closed softly.

Berlin went to see what the arrangements were now that Rolfey was gone. Maybe there would be a locum. Maybe. But there wasn't a queue outside. The despair of those who had been shut out was already inscribed in graffiti on the front of the building. Bad news travels fast. The receptionist was inside, surrounded by archive boxes. Berlin tapped on the glass.

The place was even tattier without occupants. 'What about

them?' Berlin asked the receptionist, gesturing to the queue of ghosts in the waiting room.

The receptionist shrugged.

So that was it then. Berlin hadn't just shot herself in the foot – there were hundreds of people out there now looking for an alternative. In all the wrong places.

'What about you?' asked Berlin. The receptionist had always been a stern, disapproving presence in the place, but Berlin realised she was as worn out as the furniture. The receptionist gave her a weak smile.

Berlin followed her into Rolfey's office. 'Dr Rolfe sent me an email,' said the receptionist. 'He wanted to explain.'

'And did he?'

'Not really,' said the receptionist. 'But he thanked me for my good work.' Her voice caught. 'And he wanted you to have this.'

Berlin's heart leapt, hoping for a prescription.

The receptionist picked up a painting that was leaning against the wall and handed it to Berlin. It was the one Rolfey had gazed at so often. His yacht, moored in the idyllic harbour.

Berlin laughed. Her ship had come in. She noticed the particular curve of the land, the distinctive skyline.

'Where is it?' she asked.

'I don't really know,' said the receptionist. 'Somewhere in Turkey.'

Granite clouds studded the sky.

A hooded boy slipped a ten-quid deal into Berlin's hand.

'Don't be a stranger,' he said.

Dust and litter swirled about her feet as thunder rolled across London.

Her scars stung. When she touched them, they were wet.

She put her fingers to her lips.

Could rain be salty?

ACKNOWLEDGEMENTS

Thanks to the gentleman at the Red Lion in High Barnet whom I overheard tell the story of his father's lucky escape, and his uncle's sad fate, in the Silvertown explosion. I owe you a pint.

ACKNOWLEDGMENTS

ALSO BY ANNIE HAUXWELL

A Morbid Habit

The third instalment in the Catherine Berlin series

The hands were warm. Soft fingers, but flesh inflected with iron. Squeezing. The tongue lolled and protruded from the mouth. Vertebrae fragmented, one, two, three, until finally the hands relaxed and the limp body slid from their embrace.

Blood turned to ice and sealed the nostrils.

It's the week before Christmas. Catherine Berlin's scars have faded, but she still walks with a limp. Broke, she's working nights as a relief CCTV operator, and looking for something more substantial. Her heroin habit is under control – only just.

The night shifts end, but now Berlin herself is being watched. When an old friend offers her a job in Russia, she quickly agrees. The details are vague: an oligarch with a shady past, a UK company offering a high fee for Berlin to investigate. Easy enough.

But Berlin arrives in Moscow to find that her problems are only just beginning. A body is found at the airport: a man clutching a sign reading 'Catherine Berlin'. There are figures following her, and her guide, a Brit named Charlie, has secrets to hide. When Berlin's oligarch goes missing, she finds that she cannot trust anyone or anything, even her past, if she is to survive.

WILLIAM HEINEMANN: LONDON

ALSO BY ANNIE HAUXWELL

In Her Blood

The first instalment in the Catherine Berlin series

'A stylishly written and assuredly paced debut that heralds a promising new series.'
Financial Times

When heroin addict and investigator Catherine Berlin finds the almost-headless body of her informant, 'Juliet Bravo', she is unsurprised to discover the death is linked to a local loan shark. But when Berlin's own unorthodox methods are blamed for the murder, she realises bigger predators are circling.

Then, after stumbling upon the body of her GP (an unconventional doctor who would still supply prescription heroin), Berlin begins to fear for more than her job...

Suspended, incriminated, and then blackmailed into cooperation by the detective leading the investigation, Catherine Berlin has seven stolen days of clarity in which to solve the crime – and find a new supplier.

'I'm hooked on Annie Hauxwell and hanging out for my next fix.'
Radio National Books and Arts Daily

arrow books

The Golden Egg

Donna Leon

The eagerly anticipated twenty-second instalment in the bestselling Brunetti series.

While making routine enquiries into a possible bribery case, Commissario Brunetti receives a call from his wife, Paola. The deaf-mute man who worked at the Brunetti's dry cleaners has been found dead. An empty bottle of pills points to suicide, but Paola is unconvinced.

It is a surprise to Brunetti just how little was known about this man-child. His mother is angry and contradictory when questioned about his death, and Brunetti can find no official records to prove he even existed. With the help of Inspector Vianello and the ever-resourceful Signorina Elettra, the Commissario sets out to discover the truth in what rapidly becomes a dark and troubling case.

PRAISE FOR DONNA LEON

'Leon's books are a joy.'
Guardian

'She is a truly fine novelist, period, and should be acclaimed as such.'
Times Literary Supplement

'[Leon's] portrait of Venice and modern Italy is, as always, captivating.'
Evening Standard

arrow books

Good Bait

John Harvey

'Brilliantly constructed, coolly written,
chillingly sharp and utterly contemporary'
Daily Mirror

When a seventeen-year-old Moldovan boy is found dead on
Hampstead Heath, the case falls to DCI Karen Shields and her
overstretched Homicide & Serious Crime team.

Karen knows she needs a result. What she doesn't know is that her
new case is tied to a much larger web of gang warfare and organised
crime which infiltrates almost every aspect of London society.

Several hundred miles away in Cornwall, DI Trevor Cordon is
stirred from his day-to-day duties by another tragic London fatality.

Travelling to the capital, Cordon becomes entangled in a lethally
complex situation of his own. A situation much closer to Karen's
case than either of them can imagine.

'I devoured *Good Bait* in a day, and defy any reader to do otherwise'
John Connelly

'Terrific plot and, in Karen Shields, a splendid new heroine'
The Times

arrow books

Flesh and Blood

John Harvey

Fifteen years ago Susan Blacklock disappeared. Although Detective Inspector Frank Elder has taken early retirement, the case still plagues his mind. Prime suspects, Shane Donald and Alan McKeirnan, were convicted a year later of the brutal rape and murder of a young girl, and now that Shane has been granted parole, Elder feels compelled to revisit the past.

Then Shane disappears and another young girl is murdered. Elder's involvement is now crucial. Taunted by postcards from the killer, an increasingly desperate Elder battles to keep his estranged family from being drawn into the very heart of the crime.

'John Harvey is lights out one of the best and with this book the word is going to spread far and wide'
Michael Connelly

'A gripping and powerful thriller'
Mark Billingham

'A sinister thriller . . . one of Britain's leading masters of atmosphere'
Guardian

arrow books

Cold in Hand

John Harvey

Two teenage girls are victims of a bloody Valentine's Day shooting; one survives, the other is less fortunate . . .

It's one of a rising number of violent incidents in the city, and DI Charlie Resnick, nearing retirement, is hauled back to the front line to help deal with the fallout.

But when the dead girl's father seeks to lay the blame on DI Lynn Kellogg, Resnick's colleague and lover, the line between personal and professional becomes dangerously blurred.

As Lynn, shaken by this very public accusation, is forced to question her part in the teenager's death, Resnick struggles against those in the force who disapprove of his maverick ways. But when the unimaginable occurs, an emotional Resnick takes matters into his own hands. No one could have foreseen where this case would lead, and this time Resnick will need all his strength to see justice done . . .

'Reveals modern England in all its most depressing messiness while engaging the reader with characters whose warmth and humanity give real pleasure'
Times Literary Supplement

arrow books

Gone to Ground

John Harvey

Will's first thought when he saw the man's face: it was like a glove that had been pulled inside out . . .

Stephen Bryan, a gay academic, is found brutally murdered in his bathroom. Will Grayson and Helen Walker, police detectives investigating the case, at first assume that his death is the result of an ill-judged sexual encounter: rough trade gone wrong.

But doubts are soon raised. Bryan's laptop has gone missing – could the murder be connected to a biography he was writing on the life and mysterious death of fifties screen legend, Stella Leonard?

Convinced there's a link, Bryan's sister Lesley sets out to prove that Bryan had uncovered a dangerous truth, and that – desperate to keep it hidden – Stella Leonard's rich and influential family have silenced him.

But soon both Lesley and Helen Walker find themselves victims of the violence that swirls around them, as gradually the investigation uncovers the secrets of a family corrupted by lust, wealth and power . . .

'Harvey is a master craftsman.'
Guardian

arrow books

dead good

*For all of you who find
a crime story irresistible.*

Discover the very best crime and thriller books on our
dedicated website – hand-picked by our editorial team
so you have tailored recommendations to help you
choose what to read next.

We'll introduce you to our favourite authors and the
brightest new talent. Read exclusive interviews and
specially commissioned features on everything from the
best classic crime to our top ten TV detectives, join live
webchats and speak to authors directly.

Plus our monthly book competition offers you the
chance to win the latest crime fiction, and there are
DVD box sets and digital devices to be won too.

Sign up for our newsletter at
www.deadgoodbooks.co.uk/signup

Join the conversation on: